In The Pockets of Dreams

—ƞ—

Wendy Schultz

ISBN: 1505395771
ISBN 13: 9781505395778
Library of Congress Control Number: 2014918356
CreateSpace Independent Publishing Platform
North Charleston, South Carolina

Thanks and appreciation to Tarn Wilson, Madelon Phillips, Michael Karpa and Jan Stites, authors all, who read every page and helped nudge this book along; to Denise Siino and Noel Stack who read every page and fixed the things that needed fixing; to Sadie the dog who kept me company during the process and brought me her Frisbee when she thought I needed a break and to my husband Bob, who didn't read a single page, but who liked the book anyway.

Chapter One

The door opens

I could have sworn the old woman inside the curio shop was dead. Her head
was propped on her hands, but the jangling bell on the door hadn't moved
her. I peered into the gloom of the shop at the woman's silent and rigid form,
thinking maybe I should step back outside into the overcast October day and
find a different store to visit. Curiosity, the ever-present force that always guaranteed trouble in my life, propelled my size twelve, time-killing feet over the
threshold and changed my life forever.

Astrella's Antiques & Curios was squashed between two renovated buildings in a street full of pretentiously renovated buildings. Amid stores and res-
taurants newly painted in fashionable shades of taupe, terra cotta, periwinkle,
biscotti, and ivy, the dark, unpainted storefront looked like a missing tooth
in a sparkling smile. Somehow, the recent revitalization of historic downtown
Bedlington had missed the curio shop.

The two small storefront windows were dusty and shed little light. I could
barely see the shelves, much less any curios that might be on them. I let the
door close behind me, hearing the bell once again. The woman behind the high
wooden counter turned her head in my direction. I felt air whoosh out of me
in relief; at least my first visit to Bedlington, Oregon wouldn't be ending in a
coroner's office.

A bronze gooseneck lamp, with a curved snake encircling the base, illumi-
nated the right side of the woman's wrinkled face, leaving her left side and most
of the store in shadow. Shelves of dark wood lined the walls to the left and
right of the room and the wall behind the counter as well. Each shelf held only

one or two objects. Unlike the usual antique store clutter—shelves bulging with dishes, doilies and figurines—this curio shop was curiously empty.

There was an unframed painting propped inside one shelf on the left wall, the head from a statue on another. A red leather playing card case glowed dimly on a third shelf. Behind the old woman at the counter, a long shelf held an alligator skull, a large silver jar with a chain attached to its metal cap, and another skull I couldn't identify. A double hand drum, a blue vase, a hood ornament in the shape of an Indian head and a glass ashtray occupied the shelves to my right. No teapots, Teddy bears or jars of vintage buttons here.

The wide-planked wooden floor was bare. I walked over to the counter and nodded to the old woman who hadn't moved or spoken during my survey.

"Good morning, ma'am," I said.

She nodded at me; at least I think she did. It was too dark to tell for sure. Outside the store, I could hear the wind rattle leaves and debris down the street.

The shop smelled faintly sweet and spicy, like a dried bouquet of flowers. Maybe the scent came from the old woman, although she didn't look like the perfume type, with her dark, stern eyebrows and tucked-in mouth. Her white hair was swept back into a bun. A red and black checked turtleneck peeked out of the maroon shawl that swathed her, its modern fashion looking out of place next to all the wrinkles.

I waved a hand at the shelves. "Are you…going out of business?"

"Eventually."

Unsure what to do with that response, I walked over to the painting propped inside the top shelf on the left. In the picture, a woman was wading into a pool of water up to her waist. Light from an opening between the huge boulders that ringed the pool shone down on her hair and naked back. The water behind her was rippled and green; the water in front of her was dark, with a spot of light. It looked as if she were entering a cave. The artist's signature in the lower left hand corner was impossible to read, but there appeared to be a date of '77.

Thirty years old, hardly an antique. A piece of masking tape stuck a red tag with a handwritten price of five dollars to the side of the painting.

I know nothing about art and had no idea if the painting was particularly good or if the artist was well known since I couldn't read the signature. But I am the type of guy who will buy a painting of a naked woman just because I have a lot of blank walls in my house and it seemed like the right thing to do. For five bucks I couldn't go wrong. A frame would cost extra, but the artist had thoughtfully continued the painting around the sides of the canvas, so I wouldn't need one.

"What's the story behind the painting?" I asked the old woman.

She looked at me blankly. "What do you mean?"

It was a curio shop. There had to be a story.

"Where did the painting come from?" I persisted. "Is there a history about the artist?"

"My husband acquired it and he's dead. I don't know anything about it." The reply wasn't hostile but it didn't give me anything to go on.

GPop, my grandfather, taught me there was always a story—even if he had to make it up himself. I spent a lot of time with my mother's parents until they died in an eight-car pile-up on Highway 120 when I was fifteen. They knew every back road and antique shop within a two hundred mile radius of San Mateo and their favorite pastime was to go antiquing in their dark green 1965 Corvair convertible. I loved flying down the road in that car, scrunched in the back, the wind whipping my face as I sang Beatles songs with my grandparents.

Wandering around inside crowded little shops, trying not to touch anything was torture for a seven year-old boy, until GPop appealed to my imagination.

"Every object has a story, Davy," he said. "Let me tell you about this one…" He would launch into a story about an old telephone or a cut-glass bowl—whatever happened to catch his eye. I would be hooked and GMa would have time to look around.

Some of my grandfather's stories were funny and crazy and some were a little scary and crazy. Once, he pointed out a hole in the wooden siding of a slot machine and told me all about a wild gunfight in the Cal-Neva Lodge where a bunch of people and some slot machines got shot up. That one gave me nightmares for a week.

Eventually, GPop began to ask me what I thought the story might be, or he might start a story and challenge me to add to it. Soon we were trying to cap each other in creating wild and improbable biographies and uses for the things my grandmother was fondling in the shop. We'd get louder and more ridiculous until GMa shushed us or a disapproving look from the proprietor sent us outside.

Sometimes the shop owner would volunteer the history of an item, supposedly true, or GPop would ask about its background. There was always a story—just not this time.

In spite of the old woman's lack of friendliness, I bought the painting, more as a gesture of goodwill in a town where I had business than because I liked it. Besides, there were all those blank walls in my condo. And it was cheap.

The shopkeeper wrapped the painting up in brown paper and tied some twine around it. She put my five-dollar bill in the cash register without any display of excitement. I took my painting and left.

The old woman watched him walk out the door with the painting tucked under his arm. He was tall and dark-haired with a good smile. It wasn't quite true that she didn't know anything about the painting. There used to be a newspaper clipping attached to it; maybe it was upstairs. She'd look for it and give it to him if he came back. There was something about the boy, something Padgett would probably have recognized at once.

Chapter Two

A goddess appears

Bedlington and Astrella's were new finds for me. For the past two years I had been working for a company specializing in providing computer systems for small businesses in Oregon. Most of the time, I worked from home in Portland providing sales and technical support, but since our clients liked to know that the David Peltier they talked to on the phone was an actual human being, I obliged them by making the rounds throughout the state every few weeks.

The few hours before a meeting with my newest client, O'Donigal's Myrtle Wood Creations, had given me time to check out the town and step into the first antique store I'd been inside since my grandparents died, eleven years earlier. Having dispatched the shopping, it was time to eat.

I skipped the rest of Main Street to search for a hole-in-the-wall place to have lunch. It's my theory that hole-in-the-wall places, usually bypassed by the tourist crowd, have the best food. Two streets behind Main, I found a real gift.

Sandwiched between a pharmacy and a shoe repair shop was Betsy's, a genuine, dyed-in-the wool, scruffy, greasy diner. I walked in and surveyed the place, my burger-loving heart beating wildly. A counter with green vinyl and chrome stools, six green vinyl booths, three tiny tables, a fake brick linoleum floor and a pie case. Oh yeah, this was the place.

The waitress behind the counter noted my arrival with a nod. It was just 11:30, but the place was already busy. All the counter seats were filled, so I slid into one of the booths.

Another rapidly moving waitress dropped off a menu on her way to the kitchen. I was checking out the burger offerings when she reappeared with a plastic glass of water and a straw and set them in front of me. I peered over the menu at the vision before me and my appetite took a sudden detour south of my stomach.

"Are you ready to order?" the vision asked. She looked a few years younger than me, maybe in her early twenties, with long, curly hair the color of aging copper, wide brown eyes and a freckle spattered face. The nametag on her form-fitting white t-shirt said "Melanie." My new favorite name.

"What's the best thing served here?" I asked when I could breathe again. She eyed me, considering. "Entrée or dessert?"

"Entrée."

"I'd get the Pirate Burger."

I looked at the menu. "There is no Pirate Burger on this menu."

"That's correct. Do you want one anyway?" Her eyes danced.

"Yes, absolutely." Those dancing eyes captured me. Whatever she was serving, I would eat, even cardboard.

Ten minutes later, Melanie set an oval plate with a hamburger the size of a pick-up truck before me; crisp shoestring fries dusted with something red cuddled against one massive side. I took a bite of fry while she waited on another table. The slightly crunchy, greaseless outside dissolved into soft chewy potato with a heavenly flavor.

If the fries were that good, I might die of joy with the burger. I hefted the thing up to my mouth and dove in. A mound of perfectly cooked hamburger, egg, Cheddar cheese, bacon, red onion and tomato made magic in my mouth. Melanie reappeared at my booth, eyebrows raised in question.

Unable to speak, I simply moaned. She grinned and whirled away. I gave myself up to the burger.

When she stopped by to refill my water glass, I surfaced long enough to ask, "Why is it called a Pirate Burger and what's that amazing red stuff on the fries?"

"It's a Pirate Burger because I stole a little bit of everything in the kitchen to make it. We always sprinkle our fries with a little smoky Spanish paprika."

"You made this piece of heaven?"

"With my own two hands." She whisked away again.

While she and the other waitress whirled around the diner, I savored my lunch and checked out the pictures on the walls. Most of them were black and white or sepia-toned photographs of the past glories of Bedlington. Several were of buildings. One showed a guy on a tractor in the fields, another one an old lady wearing an enormous hat standing next to a mule. Apparently the town had some association with agriculture.

I washed the last bite of burger and fry down with water. Melanie appeared from nowhere and asked if I wanted dessert.

"Today, we have ollalaberry pie, pumpkin pie and apple pie—they're all homemade."

I goggled at her. Who could possibly have room for pie?

"They all sound good, but I'm full of Pirate Burger. Did you make the pie too?" If she baked, I would have to marry her immediately.

"No," she laughed, preserving my bachelorhood for another few minutes. "Ross, the owner, bakes the pies."

She tore off the check, laid it on the table and left again. I lingered for a moment, hoping to catch her eye, but the diner was packed and I took my check up to the cash register after leaving a tip. Just before the counter waitress came over to ring me up, I took back the check and wrote underneath the order, "best Pirate Burger in the world—I'll be back—Dave Peltier." The counter waitress glanced at it when I handed it back and grinned. Maybe Melanie got a lot of those notes.

The meeting with the new clients went well despite my strong desire for a nap, and after a couple of hours of negotiation, I took an order for a good computer system that met most of their needs and didn't completely demolish their budget.

At five o'clock, I was in my Saturn making the two-hour drive back to Portland, perked up from a burger-induced slump by a cup of Anneke O'Donigal's coffee. By the time I pulled into the driveway of my condo at eight o'clock, I was Jonesing to see how the new painting would look on the wall.

The painting was my second attempt to alleviate the bareness of the condo after Jennifer, my last girlfriend, moved out. The first was a home theater system that I bought about thirty seconds after she left. I'd lived in the condo for a year, alone except for Jennifer's four-month reign. Having no one to discuss proper picture placement with was good with me.

While I was in the bathroom, releasing Anneke's coffee, it occurred to me that the off white walls could use something of interest. A woman bathing in a pool would probably work on a bathroom wall. I fetched the painting.

Peering at the back of the canvas, I looked for any information about the artist or the subject of the painting, but there was nothing but the staples that held the canvas to the frame. There wasn't even a hanger. I tapped a nail into the wall above the towel rack and perched the painting on it. It looked good there, even without a frame, and the gray of the painted boulders were a match to the tiles around the tub and sink.

For the next few days, I worked from home and got used to the painting. I caught myself glancing at its reflection in the mirror when I shaved or brushed my teeth, checking it out when I was occupied on the commode. And I wondered who she was, the woman in the painting, wading nakedly out of the light into the dark water. The boulders at her back looked ominous, as if they might close ranks behind her if she went any further into the cave.

Friday night was poker at my place. My friends Nate, Steve and Patrick showed up at seven with two extra-large pizzas. I supplied the beer.

"Who's the naked chick in the bathroom?" asked Steve after returning from the john during a break in the game. The phrase "naked chick" was enough to mobilize Patrick who promptly left the table.

"There's a naked chick in the bathroom?" asked Nate, his brown eyes lighting up.

"Yeah, it freaked me out when I saw her in the mirror."

Nate looked at me reproachfully.

"It's just a painting, Nate." I glared at Steve who gave me a blank expression in return.

Patrick reappeared, the corners of his mouth drooping as he added, "And you only see her backside."

Nate stood up. "That's my favorite part."

"That part," said Patrick "is under water. No joy, dude."

"So…who is she?" asked Steve again.

I told them about buying the painting at the curio shop.

"It was only five bucks and I wanted to fill in some of the empty walls around here."

Nate looked at me, horror-stricken. "You mean you...decorated? Like that TV show, *Queer Eye for a Straight Guy?* Dude," he shook his head.

Patrick said, "Couldn't you have found a frontally naked woman?"

Steve had another piece of pizza.

To salvage my reputation, I told them about Betsy's, my diner find, but left out the part about the red-haired waitress. Our discussion about what constituted the perfect burger lasted for an hour.

The game broke up around one in the morning and I fell into bed, pulling the comforter over my head. With a six-pack inside me, I was asleep in seconds.

I woke up a couple of hours later, the room spinning lazily around me. I squinched my eyes up tight, hoping that the nausea and dizziness would disappear or I'd fall back asleep—it didn't matter which one happened first. Somewhere in the middle of pretending to sleep, I dozed off and fell into a dream.

In the dream, I was both an observer and the woman in my painting, wading into the water. I felt the cool water against my thighs and belly and heard the woman's thoughts even as I watched her glide further and further into the cave:

The sun scorches my shoulders and breasts. Water like liquid diamonds pulls against my belly, thighs and legs in delicious contrast. I enter the grotto, feet gliding across the silky bottom. The sunlight falls away behind me and I am enfolded in darkness.

Ahead, there is a tiny pool of light. I can't see its source yet, but I bob slowly forward on the tips of my toes as the water creeps up to my shoulders. The waters of light and voices of the angels are my quest. Señora Delgado, the woman who owns the guest cottage I rented for two weeks in Diablo Gordo told me about this place—a magic grotto, a healing place where all that is not right and harmonious in one's being is soothed away by the waters of light and the voices of the angels.

I move cautiously, toes feeling the way, hoping the grotto doesn't house creepy swimming things along with angels. Slipping off the panties that are my only article of clothing, I toss them onto the sun-warmed boulders behind me. It seems wrong to enter the Grotto of the Angels with wet underwear. No one but angels will see me; the beach is remote and the grotto known only to the local folk.

The pool of light on the water draws me, but I hesitate, feeling vulnerable in my nakedness. There's an inky, mysterious stretch of water I must traverse to the light. I can hear the sound of water lapping gently against rock.

I continue moving toward the light, the lapping sound becoming a musical, splashing flow. It must be the waterfall that Señora Delgado told me I should drink from to clear my mind of all falseness, my heart of all hate, and my spirit of all fear.

Shivering with anticipation, I slide into the black stretch of water. The water is cold and swirls around me as if alive. The sand beneath my feet is coarse and my toes find miniscule pebbles. Goose pimples rise on my arms, my nipples harden and the skin on my thighs tingles. The sound of splashing water is louder now, with a vibration that I feel in my bones.

I stand still, trying to identify the source of the vibration. It's on my forehead, my back, on the right side of my torso and along my left arm. I feel it through the soles of my feet and the fillings in my teeth, as though I am being hummed.

The vibration fills me, controls me, and I can't take another step. My internal organs shift, ordered into position by the hum. It's a very odd feeling—not painful at all, but as if my organs had been chaotically tossed into a room and now they are being neatly put away in their correct places. Space blooms inside me.

I straighten up—I can't help it. My bones feel pulled and straightened into alignment. Newly created room opens between them.

I breathe in the hum and let it out, feeling it inside my head, in my brain. Every cell is tingling and my hair is standing on end, with each follicle trying to pull out of my ponytail and reach for the vaulted ceiling of the grotto. I am tempted to pull the band off and let my hair go where it will, but I am not here to play. The vibration lessens and I can move once more.

Reaching the pool of light, I plant myself in it, just as Señora Delgado told me to do. No matter where I stand, the light covers me equally but I can see no opening in the roof of the grotto overhead or in the walls to provide it. The rest of the grotto is dark. The vibration feels muted in the light, but the peculiar feeling of being put into order intensifies. From the soles of my feet right into my eyeballs it feels as if every cell has been shifted, placed and given a pat.

Just as the ordering reaches my brain and the intensity and speed make me feel like a rocket about to explode, it stops. A face with terrified eyes, wide with incredulity, flashes against the screen of my mind—I remember that face. Thankfully, it disappears and I am left alone in the light.

Weightlessness replaces the feeling of impending explosion. There is no earthbound heaviness in my bones, my skin, or my thoughts. Light fills me and then I become the light.

After a few seconds, hours, days—time has no more meaning than does weight or mass—I find myself back in the grotto and out of the pool of light. Droplets of water bounce against the left side of my face. The waterfall's musical movement fills my ears and I reach out with my left hand. A cascade of water flows between my fingers and across my palm. Reaching further, the backs of my fingers brush against the rough permutations of volcanic rock.

After the light, I can see nothing. As I turn to face the unseen waterfall, the rushing noise of water against rock blocks out all other sound, filling my ears and growing louder and louder although I can feel the flow of water remaining constant.

Señora Delgado said I needed to drink the water, but I hesitate. After coming all this way, to this place, do I want to change? We're rare, we women who kill, and I am unique—a brilliant huntress, unsuspected and unknown.

If I drink the water, who will I be? Another unmarried secretary working for the state, missing the excitement of the kill and the fun of outwitting the pedantic police force? Women who kill aren't caught by men who ticket.

But my dreams are troubled and my unease is apparent to all, even strangers like Señora Delgado. The vacation to this foreign country that I thought would stop the dreams and the faces flashing before my eyes has not. Every night, I thrash in my sleep trying to get away from...I don't know. Even during the brightest and warmest of days, the world becomes a dark place and I catch glimpses of a shape following me out of the corners of my eyes. I'm not afraid of ghosts, but this is not a ghost.

Murder is supposed to be wrong. Maybe it is. For me, it's a puzzle, fitting each piece so seamlessly to the next that nothing can be detected. I have been successful beyond belief, easily outwitting the male investigators who can't seem to imagine anyone but a man committing such heinous crimes. Still, perhaps the time has come to stop. I long to hear the music of the angels.

Enough. I reach forward, my hands cupped together. The joyous water roils into them and I bring it to my lips.

I woke up, my heart pounding. I hardly ever remember my dreams. Sometimes when I wake in the morning, there's a dream in my head, but it vanishes like a cobweb as soon as I try to recall it. Out of thousands of dreams over the twenty-six years of my life, I could remember only four. Now, there were five.

Chapter Three

I get the heebie-jeebies and develop a need to clean

The digital clock read 4:57, but I was wide-awake. My right hand searched out the hair on my flat chest while my left found Big Jake and the Twins, right where they were supposed to be. I was still Dave, but every part of me was buzzing and vibrating as if the dream had invaded my body. Even my hair was quivering.

It had to have been the beer, I thought, but I'd had plenty of practice with beer drinking and it had never affected me like this. If a six-pack of Newcastle could make me feel like I'd grown breasts and murdered people, then beer was no longer on my beverage cart.

I got out of bed and vibrated my way to the bathroom without turning on the light. I didn't want to see that painting. Something bad had happened to that woman and apparently she deserved it. The thought of her, at my back, in the dark, was enough to freeze the beer inside me and I couldn't pee. For a second, I thought of taking a whiz in the kitchen sink instead, but that grossed even me out. An image of how horrified my ex, Jennifer, would have been to find me peeing in the kitchen sink flitted into my mind. The chuckle that picture induced was enough to release the beer and let me escape from the bathroom.

I pulled on jeans and a t-shirt and then turned on the television in the living room. My head was pounding, and despite the pictures flashing by as I channel surfed, I couldn't shake the dream. My body twitched and tingled and my mind kept replaying the woman's thoughts. I cleared out the pizza boxes and beer bottles, cleaned up the kitchen, made coffee and took out the garbage just to keep moving. Two hours later, as the sun came up, I was still vibrating.

Gradually, the buzzing stopped and by 8 a.m. I had fresh coffee, the remnants of a headache, and some lady's thoughts still inside me. The phone rang. It was my mother. At eight o'clock on a Saturday morning.

"Hi honey. I didn't wake you up, did I?"

"No, Mom, I've been up for a while."

"Oh me too. Cynthia and I just got back from taking pictures of the sunrise on Shasta for our photography class. It was fabulous."

My mother lived in Mt. Shasta, California where she moved after divorcing my father and changing the spelling of her name from Susan to Sioux-San. Cynthia, one of her many New Age friends, was her business partner in the Alchemy Rock Shop. Sioux-san's path is taking her to some strange places, but she's still my mom, and she's a lot of fun.

"I just had the feeling I needed to call you," she chirped. "Is everything okay?".

"Yeah, Mom. Things are fine. We played poker last night and I didn't get a lot of sleep."

It was on the tip of my tongue to tell her about my dream, but I wasn't in the mood for a discussion of my yin and yang or to hear about mugwort dream pillows to make my dreams sweeter.

We talked for a few minutes about my work, her shop, and the classes she was taking at the community college and then hung up. Mom divorced my father five years ago and it was still hard to see one parent without the other. Holidays were a crapshoot, especially since Dad had remarried and my little brother, Jeremy, was in Greece on an international fellowship program.

Off the phone, I considered the painting. My first impulse was to take it off the bathroom wall and hide it in a closet, but this solution was too bizarre for my rational mind that blamed the dream on beer and pizza. Instead, I threw a towel over the thing, thinking that I'd take it off later when the dream was out of my head.

During the next few days, a feeling of other worldliness persisted as if I were still partly in a dream state. My mind circled the dream, fragments of thought, and wisps of my own memories like a dog chasing his tail, trying to grab hold of something elusive. It didn't leave much room in my brain for productive activity. I called a moratorium on alcohol—just in case—but I didn't really think beer was the cause of the dream that had taken over my mind. In any event, the moratorium lasted only three days until pool league night and the dream didn't reoccur.

My mind snapped back into action and out of the dream state after a couple of days, except for that niggling feeling of memory that I couldn't pin down.

The towel continued to cover the painting in my bathroom. I didn't bother to take it off even after our poker games rotated to Nate's basement apartment and Steve's house in turn. Despite the lack of visual cue, the dream of the woman in the grotto remained crystal clear in my memory and it surfaced at unexpected times.

Twice, while inputting a bunch of figures into a report, the grotto from the painting had flashed into my mind and I'd felt that vibration beginning to tingle through my hands again. I stopped, completely focused on the woman in my dream. She'd seemed so real. Did she ever hear the angels sing or did she just pick up her panties and go back to working for the state and killing people? To think of her, out there, thirty years after the picture was painted, maybe looking like someone's grandmother, gave me the creeps.

Once, driving into the condo parking lot, I caught sight of my next-door neighbor going into her condo.

Mrs. Browning was a perky lady in her forties. I had fed her cat a few times when she and her husband went away for the weekend. She'd waited at my place for the cable guy when I had been out on a call. We had an informal, come-over-for-Christmas-drinks kind of relationship, but this particular afternoon, as she headed into her doorway with her back to me, I felt the grotto close around me and a buzzing started in the top of my head. She disappeared inside and, after a minute or two, the vibration stopped and I was back in Portland sitting in my parked car.

Chapter Four

Another encounter with the woman behind the counter and

the Pirate Burger Babe

In early November, I headed back to Bedlington with supplies and technical support for O'Donigal's Myrtle Wood Creations' new computer system. Peter and Anneke O'Donigal were fearfully excited about computerizing their business, but I was thinking about Pirate Burgers and paintings.

Astrella's Antiques & Curios hadn't changed in the month since my first visit. The old woman behind the counter wore the same maroon shawl and red checked turtleneck, the shelves carried the same few items, and the place was still dark.

From her station behind the counter, the woman looked up from her perusal of *Elvis, Jesus and Coca-Cola* by Kinky Friedman, as I entered the shop. Kinky has always been a favorite of mine. I introduced myself.

"Hi, my name's Dave. I bought a painting here about a month ago."

The woman put the paperback down and opened the cash register. She lifted up the drawer and pulled out a newspaper clipping, which she handed to me.

"I found this after you left. My husband had it attached to the back of the painting, but it fell off."

Her voice was rusty sounding, as if she didn't use it much. I took the faded and fragile clipping from her wrinkled hand. The clipping was from the May 1977 issue of *The ExPat Herald* and in the dimness of the gooseneck lamp, I skimmed the story:

NUDE WOMAN FOUND ON BEACH

Quetzalcoatl, Mexico—The body of a naked woman was found Friday morning on a remote beach 40 miles west of Quetzalcoatl by an early morning swimmer.

According to the police report from the nearby town of Diablo Gordo, the woman was found washed up on the sand at Playa Del Angeles at 5:30 a.m. Friday morning by local resident, Juan Mirada, 27.

"I have never seen her before," said Mirada. The championship swimmer said he was completing a training swim at Playa Del Angeles when he discovered the body. "She was just lying on the sand, half in and half out of the sea," said Mirada.

The cause of death has yet to be determined. Women's clothing and a canvas knapsack were found on the rocks above the beach.

"She does not appear to be a local resident," said Rogelio Ortiz, chief of the Diablo Gordo Police Department, "and we would appreciate anyone who knows of a missing tourist or visitor to come forth to help us identify her."

Playa Del Angeles is a little-used beach far from tourist activities, near a grotto where the waters are known locally for their healing properties.

The hairs on the back of my neck were standing upright. "So, it's true?" I asked the woman who had returned to her book.

"What's true?" She stared at me. Either she was acting or she had no idea what I was talking about. To cover my confusion, I pretended to look at the statue head on one of the shelves.

It had to be a coincidence. Maybe her husband had found the clipping and attached it to the painting as a joke; maybe he knew someone who had painted the picture after reading the article—there could be a lot of explanations for the clipping and the painting. My dream might have been the result of seeing the painting every day or of too much beer and imagination. But the name of the beach with the grotto? Even my high school Spanish was good enough to decipher Playa Del Angeles to Angel Beach.

"That statue came from England."

The old woman was holding Kinky in one hand and apparently addressing me. I pulled my mind back from its swirl of questions and looked over at her.

"My husband brought it back from London in '65 and there aren't any other parts." She went back to her book. Maybe the speech was her idea of a sales pitch.

I glanced back at the statue head. It lay on one side and had been severed from the body of the statue with a diagonal blow. Faint orange and greenish stains discolored the gray and white surface of the marble as if lichen had once grown across the hair and face of the thing. A piece of masking tape held a five-dollar price tag to one stone ear. I picked the head up with both hands. It must have weighed fifteen pounds.

The statue's face with its far-seeing blank eyes was grave, but there was a hint of a smile around her mouth and the cluster of leaves and fruit around her hair looked festive. Perched on the miniature mantel above my gas fireplace, the head would be bizarre, but interesting. Nate would probably speculate about her other parts. I bought it.

Standing at the entrance to Betsy's a few minutes later, I peered around for Melanie, the burger-making vixen with the copper tresses. I saw her whisking around the diner as I settled into a booth and thumped the box with my purchase down on the green vinyl seat.

"Hey, you're back!" Melanie pulled up in front of my booth with a smile and a menu.

"Told you I would be," I said in a nonchalant tone as I picked up the menu. She raised her eyebrows.

"What's in the box?"

"My Thanksgiving turkey…and a Pirate Burger."

I popped the flaps to show her the statue. She peeked inside the box while I snuck a glance at her. Snug black shirt, a pair of Lucky jeans showing off her assets and that glorious shiny hair pulled back into a ponytail.

"Oh, you've been to Astrella's," she said, looking over at me as I pretended to study the menu.

"How'd you know?"

"That stuff has been in her store for the whole year I've worked at Betsy's. Ross, the owner here, said she's been going out of business for nine years—ever since her husband died. He says she's planning to travel the world once all the stuff is sold. Nice of you to help her out."

"I'm helping her even more than you think. This is the second thing I've bought in that store." I sat back in the booth and stretched my arms along the back of the booth, feeling expansive.

"Wow, you must have decimated the place," she grinned. "By the way, would you like something to eat? Another Pirate Burger or maybe something from off the menu?"

I like women who use big words and cook. "How about some pie? Last time I was too full of Pirate Burger to try it. Which one is the best?"

"We have pumpkin, apple, lemon and ollalaberry—all baked by Ross and all good. It depends on what you like, but you seem like an ollalaberry man to me." She tilted her head toward me and waited.

"Is that good? Being an ollalaberry man, I mean?" I sat up straight and tall in the booth. Berry pie is my favorite, but I would be willing to swear that I loved kidney pie if she recommended it.

"Some people think so," she shot back over her shoulder as she headed for the pie case.

Melanie dropped off my pie, along with a cup of coffee before whirling away to another booth. The place began to fill with the early lunch crowd as I took a bite of pie. The berry filling burst in my mouth with a knee-smacking blend of tart and sweet, rich as a glass of port. The crust wrapped it in loving flakes with a chewy underside. Yes, I was definitely an ollalaberry man, a Betsy's ollalaberry man, anyway.

I rolled appreciative eyes as Melanie sped by laden with dishes of food. She grinned and nodded. In a few minutes I had demolished the pie and coffee. Melanie stopped by with my check.

"You look like you have places to go and people to see," she said.

"And you're psychic too," I marveled. "Can you guess what I'm thinking now?"

For answer, she pulled a little notebook out of her apron pocket and wrote something on one of the pages. She tore it off and put it upside down on top of the check. She looked into my eyes, gave a big smile and left.

I slid out of the booth and picked up my box and the check, stuffing the notepaper in my back pocket on the way to the cash register. A tall man with a graying ponytail stood behind it. I handed him my check and pulled out the note. Melanie's phone number and email address were written there. I grinned—couldn't help it—and looked up to find Ponytail's brown eyes leveled knowingly at me. He rang me up and told me to have a nice day. With Melanie's note in my pocket, it looked like a slam-dunk.

Chapter Five

Paperweights take on a new significance

I emailed Melanie as soon as I returned home from Bedlington and the O'Donigals. On the drive, I'd rehearsed my approach. It had been months since my last date and my groove felt rusty, so email seemed easier than a phone call in case of rejection.

> *To: legallyred@comcast.net*
> *From: dcompute@peltier.net*
> *Subject: Pirate Burgers*
> *Hey Pirate Burger Babe,*
> *How do you feel about reggae? I have tickets to see Fine Wine in Eugene on Nov.13. Would you like to go with me?—Dave Peltier*

I didn't have tickets yet, but I could get them. Hopefully. I pressed, "Send," and the phone rang.

"Hi Honey."

"Hey Mom."

"Have you made any plans for Thanksgiving yet?" she asked, going right for her target.

Thanksgiving was far from my thoughts and my answer was vague. "Uh, no. I haven't even given it a thought."

"Oh good, because I was thinking…with Jeremy still in Greece, maybe I could come to Portland and we could have Thanksgiving together. I still haven't seen your place."

My mind reeled as I thought about my options. It wasn't quite true that I hadn't thought about Thanksgiving at all—it was more that I was avoiding making a decision. Last year, I'd spent the holiday in Mt. Shasta eating tofu turkey and organic cranberry sauce and participating in a smudge stick cleansing with Mom's friends. This year Dad and his new wife were going to her parents' house for Thanksgiving in Santa Rosa. I was invited, but it felt too weird to have acquired a new set of grandparents at age twenty-six.

Nate and Patrick would each be spending Turkey Day with their parents and Steve would be with his wife's parents. I knew all their families and the thought of spending Thanksgiving with them was more juju than I could handle, even with a smudge stick.

Mom said she could close the rock shop and drive up. She could only stay for three days. I could show her Portland; we could go exploring. Despite the three day stay, it was by far my best option. After a little tussling because I would not let her drive over the Siskiyou at night after she closed the shop, and her insistence upon a vegetarian restaurant for Thanksgiving dinner, we agreed that she would drive up Thanksgiving morning. I had two weeks to find a vegan restaurant and do my laundry. The restaurant would be the easy part.

There was an email waiting for me when I hung up:

> **To: dcompute@peltier.net**
> **From: legallyred@comcast.net**
> **Subject: Jammin'**
> **Hola Travelin' Man,**
> **Fine Wine is the bomb. I'd love to go. It's a long drive back to Portland after the concert. Do you need a place to stay—you can sleep on our couch —PBB**

Our couch? Email was too slow. I broke out the cell phone and made an immediate call.

Melanie and I talked for an hour and a half about our lives and her three roommates before finalizing plans for the concert. When we hung up, I was buoyant with her laughter and full of energy. I ran back outside and brought in the box with the statue and a snarl of computer hardware off the floor of my car. Inside, I cranked up the stereo system and repacked the hardware, accompanied by surround-sound reggae.

With Bob Marley impelling me at full volume, I pulled the statue out of the box and placed it on the mantel above the fireplace. The severed stump of its neck prevented it from setting in an upright position so it looked ridiculous, lolling on one ear as if overcome by too much ganja. I tried it in a few other places before plopping it down like a giant paperweight on top of a stack of files in my corner home office. If a hurricane suddenly struck downtown Portland, at least my papers would be safe.

I went to bed full of plans for the concert and ideas about Thanksgiving. When my mental hamster finally climbed off its wheel, I fell into a sound sleep.

Edmund threw himself down on the swath of thick green grass at the center of the maze, watched only by the blank eyes of a marble statue.

She wasn't coming; she wouldn't be coming to him ever again. The marriage banns had been announced and in little over a month, his Katharine would be leaving a cathedral in London with her businessman husband for his estates in the North.

She'd been sold like a slave to pay off debt and salvage family pride. He'd seen the prospective husband a few times, strutting in and out of the manor house. The man had not seen him—the wealthy and important did not see the servants who held bridles, clipped hedges or emptied their nightjars.

The grass tickled Edmund's face, making him think of all the times he and Katharine had played in the maze as children and, later, how it had become their trysting spot for love. The statue of Lady Victory in the center of the maze had been a conspirator to their growing passion, seeming to beam down upon them in mute acceptance as they nestled in the grass at her feet.

Katharine named the statue Maude, a name she said suited its solemn demeanor and the carved ribbons draped over its stone breast. Maude became their code word for assignation, a private joke all the richer because Maude was also the name of one of Edmund's aunts who lived in the village and was subject to fits.

"How is your Aunt Maude?" Katharine would ask as she passed him on her way to the stables or to the gardens.

Edmund would look up from his rake or hoe and say, "She is well, mistress. I thank you for asking."

Katharine would nod brightly and continue on her way while Edmund smiled to himself, knowing that they would meet near Lady Victory later that day.

Even during their most passionate moments, they had known they would be separated. Edmund had tried never to think of it. Katharine, born in a castle, would not be allowed to build a future with a gardener's assistant.

Tomorrow, the men hired from the village would be here to dig up the yew hedges and haul away the statues. After a winter in Italy, Katharine's mother wanted Italian-style gardens with sweetly scented flowers, fountains and marble benches—not a dark old-fashioned maze. And she wanted it before the wedding so that the stream of visitors coming to congratulate the young couple could enjoy her creation.

Edmund sat up, his back propped against Lady Victory's marble feet. His uncle, Brookings, the head gardener, would be in rare form overseeing and bullying the villagers, decrying their slothful ways and sloppy workmanship with relish. Edmund would be working alongside them tearing out the hedges along with his heart.

When they pulled the Lady of Victory from her home in the heart of the maze, they would find it, the only thing he had left of Katharine, except for a ring made of her hair that he kept in a wooden box with a comb and his few shillings.

The day he and Katharine had recorded their love was sunny and warm for mid-May. A few alabaster clouds sailed the bright blue sky and Katharine brought her paint box and easel out to the maze—her excuse for spending a few hours there. Edmund had been clipping back the outside hedges and slowly worked his way inside the maze, trundling his cart and tools further and further into the labyrinth until he could no longer be seen by anyone passing by. He raced the last few turns, arriving breathless and laughing at Katharine's side. She stood before the easel, smiling at him in the noon sunshine. On her paper she had already painted Maude and the bench next to the statue.

"I want a picture of us," Katharine said.

She made him sit on the bench while she painted him into her picture. Edmund fidgeted, making up silly stories to make her giggle until Katharine shook her head at him in mock wrath saying, "I can't paint when you make me laugh."

He sat still, enjoying the opportunity for uninterrupted observation—watching her frown in concentration; noticing a springy golden curl slide out from under her hat to be tucked behind her ear. At last, Katharine put down the brush.

Edmund bounded up at once and she moved into his arms, planting tiny kisses on his face. Then, reaching behind her, Katharine picked up the paint brush and handed it to him.

"Now, you paint me."

She seated herself on the bench, leaving the space where Edmund had been sitting empty. While she fussed with her skirts, Edmund looked at the painting. Katharine's strokes had caught his bright brown hair and the glint in his brown eyes as he laughed at her. She had even captured Maude's stiff face and squared shoulders. Edmund could do no less. He set furiously to work.

As the sun slid down the sky and the lengthening shadows of the yew darkened the heart of the maze, Edmund painted in Katharine's seated figure wearing her favorite blue dress. Using his natural artistic ability and years of drawing the animals and plants of the estate, he painted her honey colored hair with loving strokes. It was with her periwinkle blue eyes and laughing mouth that he took the most care—taking so long that Katharine grew tired of sitting in the shaded maze and came to peek around his shoulder. When her chin brushed against his bicep, he jumped.

"It's beautiful," Katharine breathed. He kissed her, pleased with her reaction. "Can you paint us touching hands?"

With another kiss for inspiration, Edmund extended the arm Katharine had given his painted figure and added a hand. He completed the portrait of Katharine with one of her arms extended toward the Edmund figure; her fingers nestled inside its upturned palm. After adding a few lines and some green to suggest the yew hedges, Edmund set the brush in the tray and stepped back.

They looked at their creation together, arms wrapped around each other. Katharine's slim white fingers sketched an imaginary frame around the painting. Now, with his back against Lady Victory, Edmund remembered the golden warmth and love he had felt at that moment; the feeling of utter content that swelled his heart.

A sudden coolness in the air had broken into their warmth as a cloud passed the sun. Lady Hastings' voice could be heard calling for her daughter.

They exchanged another kiss as he helped Katharine pack up her paint box. She scurried toward the voice, reluctantly leaving the still wet painting with Edmund. He tucked it under the marble bench to dry, weighted with one of his tools, and went back to clipping the hedges.

A few days later, after wrapping the painting in a piece of oiled silk, Edmund and Katharine had put it in a metal box and buried it at the base of the statue.

"I want to know where it is," was all that Katharine said, but he knew what she meant. Such a portrait of their love could only bring disaster if found, but Edmund too, had wanted to capture those golden days.

"We'll dig it up one day and laugh at how young we looked," said Katharine. A look of pain crossed her pretty features before she turned away and patted soil around the box in its hole. She kissed him then and left the maze. Edmund had silently shoveled clods of dirt into the hole and packed down the turf, as heavy-hearted as if he were burying a child.

How could he live without her? Katharine brought light into his life and emblazoned his days with joy and his nights with expectation. Every part of his world was better with her in it.

Tomorrow night he would come out and dig up the box. With all the digging going on, no one would notice one more hole. He would move it to a new hiding place, one that he could protect.

I opened my eyes. Edmund, his anguished thoughts and the maze were gone, replaced by the digital numbers on my bedside clock. I listened for a moment, wondering what had woken me up. Another crazy dream—at least this time I wasn't a female serial killer. I turned my pillow over and went back to sleep.

The worker stared at me when I pointed. "Dig here," I told him.

It was two paces from the base of where the statue had stood—a little stretch of carefully clipped grass, unblemished and anonymous in a garden that was full of such stretches of grass. The other workers had removed the Lady Victory statue at my instructions and were trundling her toward the waiting wagon. None of them questioned my right to this; they were accustomed to doing whatever the wife of the master wished.

The worker frowned, but placed the point of his shovel on the ground below my finger.

"Here, mum?" he asked.

I nodded. He gave a tiny shrug of his shoulders, obviously humoring me; perhaps thinking I was mad with grief. Possibly I was mad—mad to have run away from my husband; mad to have stolen a statue from what was now his property; mad to be digging a hole in a garden that was not my own, but I was not mad from grief. Eight months of nursing my parents through the illnesses that took their lives left me weary to the bone, but it wasn't grief I was feeling. It was hope.

Watching the worker turn up the turf, I remembered when hope first flickered into being.

My father was ill and Mother needed my help. I packed up my three children, too young to be left to their nursemaids, and moved to our London house to be near them. Burton stayed behind in Scotland to manage his businesses. The freedom of being without him after ten years strengthened the flicker to a tiny flame.

Months of traveling the three miles between sick parents at the family estate outside London and lively children at our townhouse bolstered my determination to live a life of joy with my children instead of a life of fear and misery with my husband. When my parents died within months of one another, hope was a banked fire, waiting only for a catalyst to fan it into a conflagration.

The catalyst appeared in the place I had avoided for a decade, since the awful morning they found Edmund's broken body.

It had become my habit to take a break from the fetid air of the sickrooms to walk about the gardens. Daily, my walks took me closer and closer to the statue and the marble bench by her side until one day, I finally allowed myself to sit upon the bench. Against my will, my gaze drifted toward the rose bush planted over the hole where Edmund was found, impaled on a mattock left there by the village workers hired to remove the yew hedges. The rose bush was fat with emerald green leaves and beginning to bud.

Next the rose bush, and almost as difficult for me to look at, was the statue of Lady Victory. Maude, I'd named her years ago when Edmund was alive and had all my love.

Her gray face, mottled with patches of rust and white lichen stared out over the gardens as it had the night he died. Edmund's footprints, still visible in the dew-drenched turf the next morning, showed that he had tripped over a mound of earth and fallen into the hole. It was an accident, they said. What he was doing alone in the maze in the middle of the night was a mystery, they said. Maybe he had come to retrieve the forgotten shovel and mattock. It was just like Edmund to be so conscientious, they said. Servants whispered that blood must be spilled with new construction. Maude was left in her place and a rose bush planted in remembrance.

I sat on the sun-warmed bench, remembering things that could not be spoken. As I gazed into Maude's marble face, a feeling of gentle encouragement seemed to flow from the statue into my heart. Edmund's voice whispered "All will be well," and I burst into the tears I'd been holding back for ten long years.

After, it was as if a stone had been lifted from my heart, making space for hope. Maude and Edmund became my confidants. To them I could whisper my thoughts for the future and make my prayers for help or weep at the death of my parents without restraint. And I always left the bench with hope renewed.

Two months ago, I was sitting on the marble bench under Maude's watchful gaze, going through the pile of tradesmen's bills and sympathy cards that had built up since my mother's death. In the pile were three letters addressed to my husband in the same feminine scrawl. Burton was in Scotland. Possibly they were sympathy notes.

They were not. The letters were from Lady Kingston and expressed a passion for my husband in a manner that both shocked and bewildered me. Lady Kingston was not Burton's usual class of companion—she was a member of Society and Lord Kingston was one of Burton's most powerful and influential patrons.

Though Lady Kingston's language shocked me, the evidence of my husband's infidelity did not. I was about to throw the letters away, when I realized what a powerful weapon they could be.

Did I have the courage to change my future and that of my children by using them? To face down a man who held all the weapons of money, property, power and the potent right of being a male in his ever-ready fist? Was I willing to die if I were wrong, because die I surely would, either hidden in Scotland where no one could hear my screams, or of anguish that I could not spare my children from the monster I had married.

I closed my eyes, trying to think my way to a decision. The scent of roses, strong and sweet, permeated the air. I opened my eyes and looked over at Edmund's rosebush. It was covered with deep crimson blooms, the color of blood...and passion. Where was my passion now?

Maude stood stalwartly next to the bush. Her face was grave as though her victory was a costly one, but the indentations around her carved mouth indicated a smile not far behind the solemnity. A victory wreath of oak leaves and grapes—symbols of strength, endurance and peace crowned her forehead. All the power of youth and hope was in that slim figure.

Edmund had tried to protect me. Could I do less for my children? Love hadn't made me brave enough to defy my parents, but its example gave me courage now. I looked at Maude and hope burst into flame within me.

That fire carried me through the first terrible confrontation with Burton. With my family's longtime solicitor, Mr. Peasley, by my side, I told Burton that I could and would provide proof to Lord Kingston's solicitors of his wife's adultery with my husband if he did not allow me to live apart from him with our children. My voice did not shake although my body felt like a clenched fist.

Burton rose from his seat with such rage on his face that my heart shook inside my chest and Peasley, that ancient soul, reached for his stick. His face purple with fury, my husband informed me that nothing I could do would cause him to release me to live like a whore with our children.

I closed my eyes and pictured Maude and her ribbons of victory. Then I opened my eyes and unfolded the first letter to read aloud: "Burton, my heart, I cannot wait until I feel you inside me again. We need not wait. Kingston is off to France.

Come to me now. I will meet you anywhere to feel your hands on me, your mouth on my…"

Burton's roar could be heard for blocks. Poor Peasley's wrinkled visage was red and his eyes averted, but I was unmoved as I handed the letter to him and said, "There is more and you can confirm the signature, I'm sure."

Through his incoherent frothing, I assured my husband that Lord Kingston would not only succeed in his bid for a divorce with my help, but he would sever all his support of Burton's businesses and make sure that his influential friends did as well. Ranks would close. Burton would be ruined.

Burton owned everything, including my parents' home. I had three letters and hope. With that hope, I found the courage to set the terms for my future.

In front of my husband, I directed Peasley to send the second, more inflammatory, letter to Lord Kingston in a week's time if a satisfactory agreement had not been reached. As I rose to leave the office, Burton grasped my arm with rage, but Peasley and his intrepid clerks proved their mettle and, three days later, my husband's solicitor accepted my terms on his behalf.

Now, in my home, my own home where I live with my children, I open the rusted box that Edmund died for. Under the silk covering, a watercolor of two lovers touching hands is revealed. There is a spot or two of mildew along the edges, but the colors transport me back to glorious May sunshine, the feel of Edmund's arms tight about me as we gaze at our picture. I feel the sweetness of his lips on mine and know that I am safe. There is nothing I cannot do with him at my side. I am Lady Victory.

This time when I woke, the clock read 4:22. I got up and went into the bathroom to take a leak, the towel-covered painting at my back causing me to shiver. How was it possible to experience two parts of the same dream with the thoughts of two different people? I sat on the edge of my bed wanting to grab a few more hours of sleep, but worried that the dream would continue. My warm bed called to me and finally, I gave in. Wrapped in the comfort of the covers, sleep came for me in seconds.

Giggling, Ellie clambered over the snarls of iron fencing. The three-quarter moon provided more shadows than illumination, as she skirted hummocks of unidentified foliage and debris, waving the bottle of champagne at Jamie following behind her.

"I believe I'm stuck," he said, trying to pull his suit jacket free of a jagged piece of iron.

"Sssh," Ellie whispered as she stood still, peering into the night. Finally, she circled a particularly bumpy patch like a dog before sleeping and plopped down in a nest of weeds. Jamie freed himself from the fencing and joined her.

"Something tells me this would have been easier with a torch," he said, lowering himself down beside her. From his coat pocket, Jamie produced two glasses pilfered from the restaurant where he had proposed marriage to Ellie earlier in the evening.

"I thought you said you wanted to tell your grandmother about our engagement," he said as the champagne fizzed into the glasses.

"And so I do. Before the war, this was my grandmother's house," said Ellie waving her arm at a barely visible pile of bricks and wood behind them.

"This," she patted the ground beside her, "was Gran's favorite spot in the garden. She was sitting here when a bomb fell and killed her."

Jamie looked around. "She's not buried here, is she?"

"No, silly. But this is where I feel closest to her. Uncle Thomas has sold the property and next week, it will all be cleared out to build smart flats for the society crowd."

"Well, then let's drink a toast to your gran," said Jamie, touching his glass to Ellie's. "How can you tell that this is the spot? All I can see are lumps and bumps."

Ellie indicated a large chunk of lichen-covered marble buried in the grass. "This used to be a statue. Gran called her Maude. She came out here to sit with Maude every day because she said it helped get her head and heart straight."

Jamie took her moonlit fingers in his. Ellie cuddled into his side.

"The garden was lovely," she sighed. "Gran used to read to me out here and when my cousins and I got into fights or had troubles, she brought us out here to talk them away. She told us that hope was a fire you should keep banked in your heart."

Jamie poured more champagne into Ellie's glass.

"Gran was amazing, really," said Ellie as she sipped. "She left her wealthy husband in the 1890's and raised three children by herself. It caused a scandal, but she didn't care. Gran was the happiest person I've ever known.

"When her husband died in a boating accident, she took over the running of his businesses until Uncle Thomas was of age. The society matrons called her a suffragette and shunned her, but she was so good at business that Uncle Thomas and my dad relied on her for advice right up until she died."

"She sounds like a strong woman." Jamie settled himself more comfortably, stretching his long legs out in front. His foot bumped into something rounded and hard, which rolled slightly when he pushed at it. It didn't feel like a rock. He reached down for it.

"Even during the worst of the war, she was always sure that things would be better one day soon," said Ellie. "When the bombs came during the Blitz, she sent all of us with our mothers and the cook and gardener to the Tube, but she wouldn't go. Uncle Thomas and Dad weren't here and none of us could make her leave." Ellie shook her head sadly, moonlight silvering her profile.

"We found her, later. The garden and house were just rubble, but Gran didn't even look dead. She just looked peaceful. There was an old watercolor painting from her bedroom under her body. She must have brought it outside with her, which doesn't make any sense, but then neither does Gran's death." Ellie shrugged. "It's been fifteen years, but I still miss her."

Jamie squeezed Ellie with one arm and then hefted up the object he'd kicked. Ellie craned a look at it. "I think I feel a nose," said Jamie. "Or perhaps it's a tail."

"It's Maude," Ellie's smile glowed white in the moonlight. She put down her glass and took the heavy marble head into her lap. "You can feel the grapes and leaves around her head and here are her eyes. Just think, she's been here all this time."

"Should we take her with us?"

"Let's. I don't like to think of her being thrown in a rubbish bin or ground into dust by machinery. It's like a piece of Gran."

"We'll clean her up and put her on the mantel, shall we?" Jamie laughed, "And when I forget to pick up my socks and you can't stand another of my horrible jokes, you can look at Maude and remember to have hope that you'll survive."

"No, I'll look at Maude and remember this night and all the hope we have together," said Ellie. "… and then I'll pick up your socks."

Chapter Six

Mud and sweat as therapy

I came awake slowly, the dream curving inside my head like a Hallmark movie, gentle and sweet. As I lay there, questions began to filter through my mind. I was thinking of my experiences as dreams, but no dream had ever placed me inside someone's head and allowed me to see what they saw or feel what they felt. No dream had ever let me get up, walk around and then come back to it as a different person. It wasn't frightening, but it was disturbing.

The dream of Edmund and Katharine had been an improvement over the female serial killer dream, but twice now, I'd been inside a woman's head and maybe that was the most disturbing thing of all.

It wasn't possible to lie calmly in bed while pondering why I was having transgender dreams. I rolled out of bed, pulled on some jeans and paced into the living room. Two dreams, two objects and no beer to blame it on this time. My steps carried me into the kitchen and my need for action carried me through the steps of making coffee, but all I could think about was the dreams. That feeling of a memory tapping at my brain, looking for an open door came back to me. The dreams were like memories—not mine, but someone else's. And yet, it felt as if they were tied to something I couldn't quite remember. I don't like things I don't understand or can't control. People always act as if I'm a go-with-the-flow kind of guy. Maybe that's the way it looks from the outside, but I always have my finger on the control button.

Maybe I was spending too much time in front of a computer playing video games. I left the coffee maker to do its thing while I paced around the living room.

Was I so suggestible as to invent stories about curios in my sleep, like the stories my grandfather and I had made up about antiques? None of our goofy stories ever came close to the scope and detail of these dreams. Or was there something about the objects themselves? Not for the first time, I wished GPop was still around. For my mother's father, the weird and strange was part of his daily fare—perfectly normal and nothing to fret about. He and GMa had invited Beat poets to their coffee house, lived in a commune and hung out with hippies before I was born. It was all cool with GPop and he was always in easy control. I didn't want to be like my father whose idea of control was browbeating people into submission.

I circled the living room again, accompanied by the smell of brewing coffee and stopped in front of the statue head weighing down a huge stack of papers and file folders. I reached down and picked up the head, running my fingers over it to feel the rough edge of the severed neck and the silky smoothness of one carved cheek. She did look sort of like a Maude, and when I touched her I could still feel Katharine's triumph and Edmund's despair. I could see the moonlight on Ellie's face. It was as if I was part of a family I didn't know.

The phone rang, startling me from my thoughts. It was Nate, telling me to get my act in gear as he was on his way over. We'd made plans to go mountain biking and Nate, whose punctuality was otherwise a joke, was not to be denied. I told him I was ready, then hung up and sprinted through the condo rounding up my gear. Gratefully, I shoved the dream and my thoughts to the back of my mind.

Nate roared up in his old pickup, with Patrick riding shotgun. I put my bike in the back. Patrick squeezed into the middle as I slid in and we took off for the hills above Portland. There's nothing like flying over rocks, pelting down narrow trails or lugging up hills to focus your mind and clear your head. Portland was between rains so the sky was blue and the ground was muddy, but it kept my mind on the trail and away from exploring the dream.

We came off the trail around one o'clock, threw the bikes in the back of Nate's pickup and went to Ralph's Diner for breakfast. It didn't matter that it was afternoon: Ralph's served a huge breakfast all day long.

"What's up?" asked Patrick, turning his inquiring mind upon us all. Nate reported the possibility of a new job as a graphics designer at a real company— a grown-up job. When our *huevos rancheros* arrived in all their massive beauty,

Patrick and I schooled him in the art of acing the interview—not that we had vast experience in interviewing for grown-up jobs, but we had more than Nate, who was still working for the same entertainment newspaper where he'd been working since high school.

We got him squared away just before the second cup of coffee and Patrick turned questioning eyes in my direction. I reported much new decorating and described in detail the fluffy pillows and potted plants fictionally scattered throughout my condo before he chucked a package of grape jelly at me.

By the time I got home and scraped some of the mud off my bike, it was after three o'clock. The dream, while still clear in my mind, was no longer at the forefront of my thoughts—Melanie was. I knew she got off work at four, so I planted myself on the couch and waited until 4:15 before calling her cell. She answered at once and we talked as she did her weekly grocery shopping and a load of laundry.

Like me, Melanie was a transplanted Californian from the Bay Area, but while I come from a tribe of laborers, Beatniks, New Age goddesses and financial consultants, Melanie came from an entire family of doctors and nurses. Both parents were doctors; an older brother was completing his residency in pediatric medicine and her younger sister was in pre-med at Stanford. Even her grandparents were in medicine.

"My mom's parents are a cardiologist and an OB-GYN and Granny Trish, my dad's mother, was a surgical nurse until she retired," she said. "I'm the only one who doesn't want to be a doctor. I'm the black sheep, especially since I'll be going to law school starting next fall. In Oregon." She said the last two words firmly.

The fierceness in her voice told me not only that it had been a hard won fight to buck the family occupational trend and to seek education in another state, but that she was proud of the battle.

I wondered why it was so important to her to be a lawyer and why she had chosen to go to law school in Oregon, but decided that was something for a later conversation. I liked the determination I heard in her and I liked her—a lot.

Chapter Seven

Melanie gets a piece of my heart and I start singing

I kept my mind focused on work, pool tournaments and Melanie for the next week. Maude lay atop my filing system and the painting remained under the towel, but I had no dreams I could remember. I tried not to think of the two that were still so clear. Thinking about the dreams took me off into an endless loop of questions and I didn't know where to find the answers.

The day of the Fine Wine concert was a Tuesday—one of Melanie's days off. I set the GPS for her address, planning to arrive early. A few minutes after three o'clock, I pulled up into the side yard driveway of an old, white two-story outside Eugene.

Melanie met me at the door as I came up the steps of the screened-in porch. I'd dressed to impress—a button-down shirt, with sleeves rolled and tail out, jacket, jeans and a splash of Sean John along my jawline. Melanie was wearing jeans too, but they looked a lot better on her. A tiny white lace see-through shirt with a tank top peeking from underneath and a mane of wavy, shiny hair completed the picture. I tried not to drool.

"Right on time," she said as I came on to the porch. "And you smell good too."

Standing next to Melanie for the first time, I felt taller than my six feet, two inches. The top of her head came to just above my shoulder. Just the right height to rest an arm around her shoulders without having to scrunch. She also smelled good, but I wanted to say something original.

"I'm always punctual with pretty ladies," I offered, sounding like my own grandfather. She rolled her eyes. Score one for punctuality and cologne, penalty points for conversation, I thought. I shifted my attention to the jungle of house-plants filling every inch of the porch. "Wow, someone has a green thumb."

"Yeah, Karen can grow anything and does it everywhere. We'll have to beat a path to the door. Got your machete?"

We laughed, but the greenery was dense. I remembered Melanie telling me about Karen, one of her roommates who worked for a nursery in Eugene and was getting her master's in environmental sciences.

I followed Melanie into the living room. The walls were a brownish-orange with cream-colored trim. It could have been awful, but it wasn't. I'm a white wall man myself, but the combination of warmth on the walls and pillows and the cool cream tones of molding and couches worked. There were abstract paintings in bold colors on the walls and some sort of wall hanging with rusted iron implements woven through it over the couch. I hoped the weave was strong because some of the implements looked heavy and I was going to be sleeping on that couch. Another roommate, Gillian, was an artist. The woven thing and paintings were her work.

All three of Melanie's roomies were at work until five, so she gave me a quick tour of the four bedroom house and the back yard, with the winter garden already sprouting cabbage and chard in the last of the November sunshine.

We'd been comfortable and easy with each other on the phone, but it was taking longer to get comfortable in person. I brought in my duffle and we had a beer. Another pleasant surprise. Melanie liked beer and there was a little stash of great Oregon microbrews in the refrigerator. We started talking about the merits of hops vs. malt and the last bit of awkwardness melted away.

We had reservations for dinner in Eugene, so at five, we got into my car and left for the restaurant. Over dinner, we talked about life, divorced parents, computers, music, food and everything else we could cram into two and a half hours. I asked her why law school and why in Oregon.

"I want to provide a service," Melanie said. "There are two things that scare most people—when they get sick and have to go to a doctor and when they have trouble and need a lawyer.

"My family has the medical bases covered, so I want to make the process of law less frightening for families going through divorce and custody battles. I want to make it as understandable and helpful as possible, diffuse some of the fear and make sure the kids are taken care of."

I nodded, thinking that my computer job was pretty small potatoes in comparison with Melanie's goals. "But why Oregon? Does it have the best family law program?"

"There are great programs in California," she said. "But my dad wasn't happy that I had putzed around in college trying to figure out what I wanted to do. He and my mom threw a fit when I decided on law because they think lawyers are the scum of the earth. I decided not to ask for their help in paying for law school so I wouldn't have to answer to them. Once you establish residency, Oregon is less expensive than California, so I took time off to earn some money and to make sure that this is definitely what I want to do. And it is." She smiled gloriously.

Amazing woman. I was in so deep that only a tractor could pull me out.

The concert was loud and wild. Melanie proved to be a stander-upper, jumping up and dancing at her seat when favorite songs came up. She didn't press me to join her, but I shucked off my usual concern about annoying the people who sit behind and stood next to her, rocking with the beat. I actually found myself singing along, even if it was under my breath.

I put in a Bob Marley CD on the way back to Melanie's house and we sang all the way home—an activity completely alien to my personality. Some people don't have sex on a first date. I don't sing. Not even on a fifth date.

Four cars filled the driveway and street in front of the house. Melanie directed me to park next door, saying the neighbors wouldn't mind. She was out of the car before I could get around to her side, but I swung the yard gate open for her as gallantly as Edmund might have done for Katharine in my dream.

Melanie stood on the top step turning the key in the front door lock as I waited below. She said something and turned her head toward me, our eyes almost level with each other. Everything stopped.

The sound of the lock popping open started my heart beating again, bringing us back to the porch steps of a white Victorian house with roommates sleeping inside it. Melanie ducked her head with a little smile and went inside. Following her, I could feel my grin.

A lamp glowed in the living room and a pile of pillows and blankets had been placed on one end of the couch.

"Bethany," nodded Melanie. "She's like a mother hen." Bethany was the roommate who worked for a title company and liked to cook.

We stood awkwardly by the couch. The goodnight part is always full of decisions. Make a move or wait for her lead? Brush a politely dry Shredded Wheat kiss on her lips or plant a juicier kiss full of promise? Hands or no hands?

Melanie took charge before I could lean in. "I had a really good time, Dave, but I have to get up early to go to work," she said, throwing cold water on my hot thoughts.

As she picked up the sheet and began tucking it into the couch she said, "I'm flying home for Thanksgiving out of Portland next Monday—driving up on Sunday and staying with a friend. Do you want to go to the Baghdad Cafe for beers and a movie Sunday night?"

I laid out the blanket on the couch wondering if this was a polite way of telling me that she had another guy on hold. "With you and your friend?"

My darkening night brightened as Melanie socked the pillow into my arms and said, grinning, "Just you and me."

I held the pillow and nodded, grinning back at her. She swooped in and planted a kiss on my cheek before disappearing up the stairs. It burned like a star, lighting my way to sleep.

Around five-thirty in the morning, the roommates began appearing. First, a sturdy blonde who identified herself as Karen after she tripped over the last stair, followed by Melanie and then a girl with long brown hair who apologetically told me her name was Bethany as I sat up on the couch, the blankets wrapped around my waist. Gillian, the artist, hadn't yet appeared.

The roomies finished quick breakfasts as I slipped into the downstairs bathroom to brush my teeth and change out of the flannel pajama bottoms and tee shirt I had worn for the occasion. Melanie was waiting for me when I emerged and offered me a yogurt and an apple.

"I've got to go, Dave," she said, "but I'll see you next weekend?" I nodded. "Call me later, okay?"

I nodded again. She reached up and kissed me quickly. This time I made sure it was on the lips. Then she went out the door smiling, her leather jacket almost matching her red-brown hair.

Karen had already left and Bethany wavered by the door. She picked a gym bag off the seat of a kitchen chair and looked at me as if trying to decide whether she should stay until I left, or take off. I stood there holding a container of banana yogurt and the apple, feeling the awkwardness between us.

I said, "I'll be going too. Lots of work today."

She nodded and I sprinted over to the couch and began folding up the sheets and blankets. Then, I slipped on my shoes and threw my clothes into the duffle bag. Bethany held up my jacket and I put it on.

"Nice to meet you. Thanks for letting me spend the night," I said.

She said, "It was nice to meet you too," and shifted the gym bag on her arm.

I looked at my watch while I warmed up the car. It was 6:15. I thought about dropping by Astrella's in Bedlington to talk to the old woman about the objects in her shop, but it was too early for anything to be open and I didn't want to hang out.

If things with Melanie continued on this path, I thought on the way home, nursing an extra-large coffee and a sausage McMuffin, I'd have plenty of opportunity to visit the curio shop.

Chapter Eight

In which Mom tries dreams on for size and I learn sun salutations.

Thoughts of Melanie crowded out my questions about the dreams. No weird experiences marred my regular sleep patterns and my worries about being a woman in the ones that were still so clear in my mind were dispelled by very male thoughts regarding the red-haired waitress.

The beer and pizza movie night at the Baghdad Café with Melanie was a huge success. We laughed and whispered through two movies and walked back to her friend's apartment through downtown Portland. Our goodnight kiss at the door was promising. Neither of us was rushing into this, whatever it might be.

Wanting to spend as much time with Melanie as possible, I asked her out for breakfast before her flight. To my delight, she agreed at once, making me feel as if she wanted to spend as much time with me as I did with her.

More discoveries at breakfast—both of us preferred pancakes to waffles and bacon to sausage—and we were both morning people. Our goodbyes at the airport were light-hearted and lingering. Instead of my usual casual approach, I decided to call or email her at least once a day, wanting to keep the spark alive. The mileage between us was a challenge, but figuring out ways to get together would add something purposeful and fun to our conversations.

On Thanksgiving morning, the piles of dirty clothes from my bedroom had been transformed into clean and folded laundry through dogged determination and the entire stash of quarters I'd earmarked for the slot machines at the Indian casino. I checked the Weather Channel hourly for reassurance that Mom would have clear skies for her journey.

My worry-wart tendencies were something of a joke in my circle of family and friends, earning me the nickname "HP"—short for Henny Penny. I was the one who made sure we had a designated driver, usually me, enough money to pay the burger bill, or stepped in to block a punch or an insult thrown at one of us. To me it just made sense, covering the bases to avoid future problems that would be harder to take care of. I'd always looked out for Jeremy and my friends, but in high school I started looking out for my mom as well, making sure she was okay when Dad spent more and more time at work, helping to do the things around the house he should have done. The self-imposed responsibility put more distance between Dad and me and I ended up choosing sides. It was something that Mom had tried to avoid for us, but that I couldn't help.

At two o'clock in the afternoon, after I'd made a flurry of anxious calls to Mom's cell phone, tracking her progress, her Toyota RAV appeared in the parking lot. I bounded down the steps as soon as she pulled into a visitor parking space. A few bone shattering hugs later I was hauling Mom's bags, one of which was heavy enough to be full of rocks, into the condo. Mom toted a plant in a red pot.

"It's a Good Luck bamboo plant," she explained when we got inside. She looked around for a place to put the thing. "It needs warmth and filtered light and has to be watered twice a month."

A dependent. It didn't sound like good luck to me and the directions for its care were suspiciously like those for the cat Jennifer had tried to leave with me when she moved out.

"You need something green and alive in this room," said Mom, finally depositing my good luck on the coffee table, the only piece of furniture in the living room besides the couch, desk and office chair. "Something that will get the *qi* circulating in your life."

She was dressed in her usual uniform: long black knit vest over a long-sleeved pink tunic, black leggings and a pair of low topped black Converse. In winter she varied the color of the tunic and the color of her Converse and, on snowy days, she swapped the Converse for a pair of Uggs. In the summer, the uniform was khaki shorts, tank top, long tan knit vest and Teva river sandals.

Today, as usual, she wore her long honey colored hair in a single braid and her power crystals—a clear quartz crystal with the ghost of another crystal forming inside and a translucent pink rose quartz crystal—around her neck on a silver chain. Polished stone bracelets that she'd made herself and silver and gemstone earrings completed the picture. No rings, no dresses and no makeup for Mom.

"I gotta move and I gotta be comfortable," she always said. It was a radical change from the sophisticated style she'd affected when she and Dad were married, but it suited her better. With her trim figure, unlined skin and the long-lashed hazel eyes that she'd passed down to me, Sioux-san looked about fifteen instead of her chronological forty-eight.

She whipped open a shiny red faux crocodile duffle bag and pulled out a large piece of quartz with ten clear crystals spiking it. This she put into my hands.

"I knew you would need a crystal, but not one of the little ones you hang around your neck. This is sort of manly, don't you think? I found it in the desert."

Leaving me holding a piece of red-stained, white quartz the size of a fat Chihuahua, she took off for the bathroom. I looked around for a proper resting place for the rock. I already had a paperweight. I placed the rock on the hearth in front of the fireplace, afraid it might collapse the coffee table nursing the plant.

Mom returned with a funny look on her face. "Why is there a towel over that painting in the bathroom? Were you afraid I'd be offended by a naked woman's back?"

Crap. I'd gotten so used to the towel, I'd forgotten to remove it. Now I'd have to tell her about my curios and the dreams that came with them so she wouldn't think that I considered her a prude. The dreams might make me sound wacko, but at least Mom's interpretation would be interesting.

"We have reservations at the restaurant at three," I said. "How about if we finish putting your stuff away and I'll tell you all about it there?"

To my relief, Mom did not believe that I had become delusional once I filled her in about my dreams. She did take exception to the restaurant I had chosen for our Thanksgiving feast as it was not strictly vegan, having both vegetarian and barbarian meals on the menu. I stood my ground.

"Mom, I have to feel thankful too, and I'm a lot more thankful when I'm not eating tofu."

She laughed and ordered the tofu turkey with pecan, raisin and herb stuffing, garlic mashed potatoes, sautéed carrots and green beans. The meat lovers side of the menu had almost the same offering except the turkey was a Tom and the stuffing had sausage instead of raisins. I pointed out the similarities as Mom dissected my dreams.

"You say, in one dream, you were a woman and the other dream was like a movie that you watched, but you were a woman in part of it too," she puzzled. "How did you feel when you woke up?"

"Well, being a female serial killer scared the crap out of me and the other dream was just kind of…nice."

"Which was the scary part—being a woman or being a serial killer?" Mom teased. For answer, I fished out my wallet and handed her the folded newspaper clipping.

"When I went to the shop the second time, the old woman gave me this."

Mom read the short article while the waitress cleared away our plates. When she looked up, her face was white.

"This is some weird stuff, Davy."

She hadn't called me Davy since I went away to college. "I know it's weird, Mom, but it's no big deal."

"Davy, what if something is trying to use you to come through? I have friends who have been possessed and it's a very serious problem."

I'd met her friends. Some of them might have been possessed. "C'mon, Mom, you don't really believe in that stuff, do you?"

"Well, not exactly, but there are a lot of things in the universe that aren't easily comprehended."

The waitress brought the dessert menu and we studied it carefully, although I knew that we'd both order something with chocolate. Pumpkin pie may be tradition, but chocolate is the way my family rolls.

"Have you talked to the woman in the curio shop about the dreams?" Mom persisted. "Maybe she'd know if other people have had dreams about the things they bought."

I shook my head. That thought had been in my mind too; I might not be the only person having dreams and the shop owner might know something about what caused them.

Our cell phones rang at the same time. Mom's call was from Jeremy and mine was from Dad, on his way to Thanksgiving dinner. Dad kept cutting in and out as he wound his way from Burlingame to Sandra's parents' house in Santa Rosa, so we kept the conversation short. But then, our conversations were generally brief and had been since I was in high school. Usually adversarial as well.

Mom was still talking to Jeremy when I hung up. She handed her phone to me.

"Hey man," my younger brother's deep voice boomed, sounding surprisingly awake for three o'clock in the morning.

"Hey yourself," I said. "Did you already celebrate the holiday, Pilgrim?"

Jeremy affirmed that he had indeed celebrated Thanksgiving ten hours earlier with a lamb, a block of feta cheese shaped into a turkey, ouzo and a lot of student friends. Most of his studies seemed to involve ouzo, women and fishing. He was planning to come home for Christmas. I hoped he wouldn't be deported before then. We hung up, after promising to email more regularly.

That evening, Mom slept in the bedroom, after insisting that I prop the painting at the foot of the bed and put the statue on the nightstand to encourage dreams. She wanted to experience them for herself. I slept dreamlessly on the couch.

In the morning, she was up at the crack of dawn doing sun salutations on the living room floor. I hunkered deeper into the blankets and turned my back to her in a vain effort to sleep.

"I didn't have any dreams about either of the objects." Her disappointed voice floated over my back. "Maybe, tonight, I'll just put one of them in the bedroom and see what happens."

Ten seconds of relative silence in which all I could hear was her cleansing breath going slowly in and then out in a deep exhalation, a little like the sound Darth Vader makes before he speaks. It wasn't conducive to sleep.

Then she said, "I brought my mountain bike. Where are we going to ride?" It was time to get up.

Sunday morning, I waved good-bye to my mother who drove off with bags of books from Powell's Bookstore, CDs of photos she'd taken all over Portland and disappointment at three dreamless nights. As we loaded the bags into her car she said, "Davy, those dreams of yours really worry me. I'm going to talk to Winona—she's a numerologist who's also certified to do dream interpretations."

While I was puzzling over how and where a person could become certified in dream interpretation, Mom continued, "But, I really think you should talk to the woman who sold you those things. She'd be the most likely person to know about any affects they might have on people."

She gave me a hug and climbed into her car. An hour after her RAV rolled out of the parking lot, the usual after-holiday let down set in. I found myself wondering what I was doing with my life and where I was going. I bitterly imagined the carefree and financially irresponsible life my brother was living in a foreign country. I spent some moments missing my grandparents the way I always did during the holidays, worried about what my dreams might mean and finally, debated with myself over Melanie's feelings for me. It was a bad seven minutes.

Melanie would be back at work the next day and the old woman at Astrella's never seemed to leave the shop. A quick trip to Bedlington might give me some of the answers I needed.

Chapter Nine

Crotchety crones and life after Pirate Burgers

I arrived in Bedlington just before noon on Monday and went directly to the curio shop. It was forty-five degrees outside so I wasted no time in ducking inside the dark little building. The bell jangled and the old woman, Mrs. Astrella, according to Melanie, looked up.

"Hi," I said, nodding at her as though we were old friends.

She was reading *A Hitchhiker's Guide to the Galaxy*, and she glanced at me over the top of it while her finger kept place. The same combination of red and black checked turtleneck and maroon shawl I'd noticed the previous two times I'd been in the store covered the woman up to her bony chin. Either she really liked the outfit or she didn't give a rat's patootie how she looked. I leaned toward the latter explanation.

Stepping toward the counter, I noted that the Indian head hood ornament was no longer on the third shelf. The red leather card case was missing too. A quick look around didn't turn them up, so maybe there were other customers besides me. It was hard to believe.

I picked up an old-fashioned glass ashtray and a blue vase. Each of them bore the same type of red tag, with the price of five dollars printed on it in black felt pen. I peered at the alligator skull and silver jar behind the counter and tried to figure out how to ask about any unusual affects the objects might have on purchasers without sounding like a crazy man.

"Is everything in the store the same price?" I finally asked. Mrs. Astrella narrowed her dark brown eyes and stared at me as if I had suddenly lifted my leg on the shelves.

"Yes," she said, turning her eyes back to the book.

"Do you ever get new inventory?"

"Not any more. What you see is what there is," was the surprisingly long-winded response made into her book.

I circled the shelves. "There are less than ten objects in here. What if someone came in and gave you fifty dollars for all of them?" I could feel her eyes on me, but I kept my eyes on the shelves.

"It doesn't work that way."

I was procrastinating, but her answer took me by surprise. Nothing about this store was comprehensible, least of all, the proprietor. Now, she was being cryptic. I hate cryptic. I felt like leaving, but I didn't.

I stopped circling and stood directly in front of the counter, challenging her to look at me. I noticed that the curving line of the gooseneck lamp wasn't a snake as I had first thought. It was two separate but intertwined figures, but it was hard to tell what they were.

"What do you mean, it doesn't work that way?" I persisted. "I have fifty dollars; couldn't I buy everything in the shop?"

The Hitchhiker's Guide captured her attention once more.

"No."

God knows, I didn't want to buy everything in the shop. What the hell would I do with an alligator skull? But, *why* couldn't I buy it? I dug my MasterCard out of my wallet and put it on the counter. "I'd like to buy everything in the store, please."

"No," came from the book.

"Is it because I'm using a credit card? I can get cash."

"No."

This woman was nuts and she was making me that way too.

I selected the blue vase from the second shelf and put it on the counter. "I want to buy this vase."

"That will be five dollars." She emerged from her book and reached under the counter.

I put five dollars on the counter and then picked up the Moroccan hand drum.

"I'd like to buy this too." I put the drum on the counter along with a ten dollar bill and took back my five.

Mrs. Astrella, now holding a gray cardboard box, met my eyes at last. She spoke clearly and slowly, as if I were very deaf or not very smart. "You can't buy that."

I think my eyes bugged out at this point. I know I stopped breathing.

"Why can't I?"

"It's not for you."

"What do you mean, it's not for me? Are you holding it for someone else?" I could feel my views on the sanctity of the elderly undergoing a slight shift.

"The drum is not for you; if I sold it to you, you would bring it back," she said with certainty as though she knew all about me and could see my future as a drum-returning deadbeat.

"No, I wouldn't bring it back," I said gently mimicking her deliberate tone.

"Yes, you would." The crone peered at me over the box. "That's what always happens when someone buys an object that isn't right for them. It comes back." She glanced towards her book as if bored with the conversation.

My mind was awhirl with questions, sarcastic rejoinders and confusion. I picked up the vase again.

"But I can buy this?"

She nodded. I held the vase uncertainly until she reached over the counter and took it from me. I slid the ten off the counter and replaced it with a five-dollar bill as she pulled some newspaper from under the counter and wadded it in the box. She wrapped more newspaper around the vase, placed the vase in the box, folded the flaps closed, and handed the box to me. Then she slid the five dollar bill into the cash register and picked up the *Hitchhiker's Guide to the Galaxy*, continuing to read as if I weren't standing right in front of her. She was completely silent during the entire process.

I needed a Pirate Burger badly.

It had been all she could do to keep from laughing. The boy had been so insistent that she'd had to focus her eyes on the pages of the book so she wouldn't snicker. He'd had other questions when he first came in; questions she didn't want to answer. She had felt them poking out of him like pins in a pincushion. Then he'd gotten sidetracked wondering about buying everything in the store and she had seen a way to keep him from asking questions she didn't want to answer.

The vase was the third object he'd purchased. She knew he was the one. The question was: how long would it take him to realize it?

Chapter Ten

The Right Person

I strode down to Betsy's, carrying my cardboard box and a load of confusion. I arrived at the door before I'd had an opportunity to walk off my angst. Melanie was taking an order from a couple at a table near the door. She smiled at me as I looked around for a booth. There were counter seats available today, but Melanie didn't work the counter. She didn't work Mondays either, as a rule, but from our phone calls I knew she was making up for the time she'd taken off at Thanksgiving.

I nodded at the waitress behind the counter and took myself over to a booth towards the back. Melanie came by with a menu and a glass of water.

She greeted me with, "You look like your hair's on fire."

I indicated the cardboard box on the table. "I've been to Astrella's. That old woman is crazy. I tried to buy her whole store and she said I couldn't. I need a Pirate Burger."

Melanie raised her eyebrows and pressed her lips together as if she were trying not to laugh.

"It sounds like you might need something more substantial than a Pirate Burger. I'll be back in a few minutes." She whirled away while I tried to imagine anything more substantial than a Pirate Burger.

In five minutes, she placed a microbrew and a frosty glass in front of me, and my angst at the crone began to recede. Ten minutes later, Melanie arrived bearing an enormous concoction on an oval platter and the slight confusion about the old lady's business practices became a fading blip on my radar. After a few bites of the toasted hoagie roll filled with spicy marinara sauce, peppers, hamburger, pepperoni, and covered with melted mozzarella and cheddar cheese, I was willing to concede that Mrs. Astrella might just be an amusing eccentric.

Melanie checked my hair on her next pass. "Looks like the fire's out."

I nodded, mouth and heart too full to speak. This was the girl of my dreams.

A tall thin man wearing a blue plaid flannel shirt and jeans loomed up behind her. Ponytail Man from my last visit to Betsy's. He tapped Melanie on the shoulder. She turned towards him slightly and said, "Dave, this is Ross, my boss."

Ross smiled as if he'd heard that rhyme a zillion times before, but didn't mind it. He said, "Heard you've been patronizing Astrella's. Mind if I sit down?"

What could I say? Melanie winked and gave me a little nod. I waved my hand at the seat opposite me and swallowed mightily.

He glanced briefly at the hoagie and grinned, showing good teeth and a dimple. "Not from the menu—she must like you."

"I hope so."

The grin again. "Mel told me that you've bought a couple of things from Astrella's. I've known Daria Astrella a long time and she can be ... interesting."

"That was exactly the word I was thinking of."

He nodded at the box on the seat next to me. "Is that your latest acquisition?" I nodded, wondering about his curiosity. "May I see it?"

I opened the flaps on the box and handed it over to him. He gently pulled back the newspaper and the cobalt blue of the vase peeked out. He nodded as if he recognized it and wrapped it up again, tucking the flaps down.

As he handed the box back to me, Ross the Boss said, "I know that vase. I tried to buy it from Daria a few years ago, but she wouldn't sell it to me."

"Did she tell you that it wasn't right for you?"

"Yep...and I'm a friend of hers and was trying to do her a favor, so it really pissed me off." He shrugged.

"Well...do you want it?" I wasn't sure of his purpose in talking to me.

"No, thanks," Ross laughed. "Daria told me that it would just come back into the shop if the wrong person bought it, and I've seen that happen a few times, so I believe her."

"How does she know if you're the right person?"

"I don't know," said Ross, sliding out of the booth and standing up, "but she does, and it's more important to her that the right person have the right

object than it is for her to make a sale. Her husband, Padgett, was that way too."
He looked at me appraisingly. "It's illuminating to meet the right guy at last."

There seemed to be more to his words than their sound, but I didn't know
what to say. I wanted to ask how the objects came back to the shop and what
happened to the people who had those objects, but Ross was already smiling at
a new customer so I just nodded. Ross returned the nod and walked back into
the kitchen.

I finished my hoagie monstrosity thoughtfully. Melanie dropped by with
the check and the smile I had driven one hundred and fifty three miles to see.

"I know it's a long drive for you, but do you want to come up next Monday
or Tuesday when I'm off and we can go on a hike?" she said. "There are some
great trails around here and you can stay at our house if you want."

We'd be into December by next Monday—not the best time of year for
hiking in Oregon. I was about to say this but realized in time that if it rained
and we couldn't hike we'd just have to think of something else to do. Even
though I hadn't gotten any answers from Daria Astrella and I had a long
drive back to Portland, I had a vase that was going to make a great Christmas
present for Mom and another date with Melanie. It had been a productive
visit all in all.

"See you on Monday," I grinned.

Chapter Eleven

Another dream invasion

After leaving the diner, I checked in with the O'Donigals at the myrtle wood factory. They welcomed me with a spate of questions that kept me hopping for a couple of hours. Finally, around four o'clock, I was able to fend off being showered with myrtle wood gifts and head back to Portland.

I sped down the highway, wondering if I would have a dream about my newest acquisition from Astrella's. A few miles before Portland, traffic slowed to tortoise speed. Twenty-eight minutes and one mile later, it stopped altogether. The traffic station on the radio announced a jackknifed big rig carrying hazardous material on the interstate and three hours later I pulled up in front of my condo, hungry, tired and grumpy. I brought my laptop and the box with the vase inside, ate some Top Ramen and went to bed. There was no dream that night.

I worked long hours the rest of the week. Spending time with Melanie on her days off was going to cause a few changes in my work schedule, so I set up a round of client visits in southern Oregon to start after our Monday hike. The vase sat in its box on the coffee table and I had no dreams—making me think the other dreams had been the result of too much beer and an overactive mind, after all. It was a relief, but also vaguely disappointing. Instead of a mystery, I had only a Christmas present for my mother.

On Saturday morning I woke with a hangover from the previous night's pool tournament celebration with Nate, Steve and Patrick. It was raining hard and the grayness outside mirrored my sour disposition.

I washed down three ibuprophen with a bucket of water and answered emails for an hour. When I finally got up from the computer, my headache had improved but my mood had not.

I slid onto the couch and gazed blearily around the living room. In my present state of mind, nothing looked right. The bare walls looked stupid, indicative of the lack of purpose in my life; the office in one corner of the room was just a pile of folders and computer disks and the giant piece of quartz on the fireplace hearth looked especially silly and out of place. I picked it up and carried it into the bedroom where I couldn't see it anymore.

Back in the living room, I pulled the vase out of the box and set it on the coffee table across from the Good Luck plant. The vase was a rich deep cobalt; round and full in shape with an inward taper toward the bottom, a fluted rim, and two S-curved handles at the widest part of the vase. There were a few spots where the smooth glaze had cracked; making me think the vase might be old. I turned it over. On the bottom, there was a stamp, but it was so worn that I couldn't make it out.

I thought how much Mom would like the vase and congratulated myself on having completed one-fourth of my Christmas shopping even though Daria Astrella had shanghaied me into the purchase. Christmas was going to be at Dad's this year which guaranteed tension, but Jeremy would be home, according to his latest email, and that was worth the awkwardness of trying to relate to my emotionally distant father and a stepmother who was only nine years older than me.

Rain pounded away outside, matching the throbbing in my head. I didn't feel like doing anything that required movement, but I managed to get a can of Dr. Pepper out of the refrigerator before settling into the couch with the newest Clive Cussler novel.

Dirk Pitt, Cussler's erstwhile hero, was starting off on another adventure, but I didn't get too deeply into the story before my eyes closed.

The July sun sent rivulets of sweat trickling down Derry's sides as he and the mule plodded down the dusty road. It had been four months since he and Moho set out on their seasonal circuit. They would be in Bedlington today, more than halfway through their figure-eight circuit.

The two left the small monastic community in Flat Rock Valley where they wintered, and traveled up to the towns of Willamette and Rainbow, down along the McKenzie River and through Nimrod to Bedlington. From there they would continue to Emmittsville, around to Leaburg and then back through Nimrod once more before returning to Flat Rock Valley, stopping at every town, farm, hand-hewn log house and shack along the way carrying tools and sundries for sale.

Derry offered services such as knife sharpening, pot repair and horseshoeing. He ferried messages, letters and a few small objects from customers at one end of the loop to customers at the other end and sometimes stopped to lend a hand with harvesting or haying along the way. It was both a solitary and gregarious life—the only one that Derry the tinker had known for all of his twenty years, first with his father and now with Moho the mule.

"It seems strange that your dad would take off wandering to California and you wouldn't go, Derry," one of his farmer customers once said, "It's a young man's life, exploring the world. I wish I could do it."

But Derry couldn't explain to this farmer with the itchy foot or to his other customers that he felt no need to see other places, except maybe the stars. There was something satisfying in completing the circuit each year—seeing the same faces; bringing them the news; seeing how much had been accomplished since the last visit; noting who looked prosperous; who looked despairing; who had added to their families; who had lost family members. Sometimes he turned up at a farm and the owners had trekked away into the wilderness, looking for better land and more opportunities. There would be new owners. Derry liked to see the changes they made and his knowledge of every farm, deer trail, creek and ridge along his circuit was invaluable to them.

From November to March, Derry and Moho lived in the tiny Benedictine community at Flat Rock. While Moho spent his time getting fat and consorting with the few monastery animals, Derry paid for their keep by doing construction and odd jobs for the brothers. It was an arrangement his father had started when Derry was a newborn and now the monks regarded him almost as one of their own who went out into the world for them. This year, it had been especially hard to pull the love-struck mule away from a cranky gray goose.

Derry's father used a stick to guide his mules along, tapping gently along a flank in the direction he wanted the mule to go. Early in their acquaintance, Moho trained Derry that flank tapping was unacceptable. Derry preferred to walk next to the mule's head anyway, sometimes talking, sometimes trudging along in companionable silence as he was now.

As they approached Bedlington, Derry tugged the mule's halter to the right, making the decision to go to the Pedersen ranch first instead of directly into the town. All he needed was a chance to sluice off the road dust and he could get that in the creek.

A thump startled me out of the dream, if that's what it could be called. The Cussler I'd been reading lay on the carpet beneath the couch. Another story, like Edmund and Katharine's, was unfolding. Curious, I wanted to see what would happen if I tried to go back to sleep and into the dream. I lay on the couch with my eyes closed, willing myself to sleep.

Derry turned off the track toward a meadow ringed by blueberry bushes. Moho followed, hastening his pace, ears pricked forward. Cutting through the meadow, Derry stopped to pick some fat blueberries, hoping Mrs. Pedersen would have time to make a cobbler. If not, he could always eat them out of hand. It didn't really matter to him; picking blueberries when you saw them was one of the rules of the road he'd learned from his father.

Moho took advantage of the blueberry picking to fill up on the grasses growing in the meadow. Derry filled a tin saucepan with the berries, moving between bushes and taking a few from each.

"Pick some and leave some," Brother Anselm taught him. "Other creatures need food too and the plant must not be discouraged."

Derry's father, Phineas, had shaken his head at the monk's philosophy.

"Pick everything you can. Who knows when the next food will come along?" he told Derry, adding with exasperation, "Plants don't get discouraged."

Phineas was often at odds with the brothers, but Derry loved the hours he spent with Brother Anselm learning about plants and the stars.

When the pot was filled with berries, Derry followed the creek bordering the meadow to a massive oak tree. Under its shade, he pulled off his boots and socks, and then his flannel shirt and brown wool trousers which he hung over a branch. He waded into the cool, dark water of the creek. The water bubbled and churned around his legs and Derry dug his tired feet through smooth pebbles to the softness of the sand beneath them. He crouched in the water feeling its tickling rush against his backside and sluiced the wetness down his arms and into his face. Moho followed the sound of his splashing, giving Derry a reproachful look as he dropped his nose into the creek for a drink. Derry laughed and splashed in the mule's direction, but Moho snorted and moved further downstream.

Derry stood up and shook himself all over, feeling refreshed and alive. He climbed out of the creek and lay back in the meadow grass, drying off in the warm summer air. He looked forward to the evening at the Pedersens'. Last summer, Olaf Pedersen had asked him if he could fashion a special kind of latch for a pen Olaf planned to use for wiener pigs and Derry was eager to show him what he had come up with.

He jumped up and threw on his sun-warmed clothes. Carrying his boots in one hand, Derry whistled to Moho. They splashed across the creek and up the bank into the woods. Derry put on his socks and boots and the two followed a deer track through the shadowed forest. From time to time Derry pushed away low hanging branches that caught on the mule's packs. When they came out of the woods to the edge of the Pedersen property, Moho nosed his back with impatience. The mule was fond of the white mare and an ancient yellow hound belonging to the Pedersens.

Below the bluff where Derry and Moho stood, the land fell away to the Pedersen fields, glowing green in the late afternoon sun. The house squatted in the middle of the fields, sunlight bleaching the grayish wood almost white. There was a barn, twice the size of the house, on the left. Derry looked for Olaf or his son, Tark, in the fields but saw no one. The pastures were empty of cattle and Derry didn't see Freya, the mare, in the yard. The ranch looked forlorn. Derry felt a shiver across his shoulders.

Another nudge from Moho started him down toward the nearest field. Derry had helped the Pedersens with field work in years past, depending on the time of year when he reached the place. Now he looked approvingly at the neatly planted fields of oats and barley as he and Moho walked the path between the fields. The rows were clear of weeds and the plants sturdy, but small. To Derry it looked as if the farmers had planted late.

The place remained silent as the pair drew closer to the house. Derry missed the excited barking of the hound that usually came out to greet them. Remembering the dog's difficulty in moving around last summer, Derry thought it likely that their old friend hadn't made it through the winter.

He began calling out as he and Moho came into the yard in front of the house. People didn't like to be startled by a sudden appearance.

"Hello? Hello, Mrs. Pedersen?" he called. "It's Derry the tinker."

He clumped up the lopsided porch, making as much noise as possible. As with many farms, the house was less sturdy and attractive than the barn which housed the valuable livestock. Even so, it seemed to Derry that Olaf and Tark could have made time to shore up the sagging porch and clear away the collection of old tools that littered it.

"Hello, helloo," he called again. "It's Derry, Mrs. Pedersen."

He knocked on the weathered gray door and waited. He clumped around the porch some more, keeping away from the low side, and dodging the tools. Derry listened, but heard no sound from within.

Moho glanced at him inquisitively from out in the yard. None of the mule's animal acquaintances were to be seen. The only sound breaking the silence of the farm was the soft clucking of Mrs. Pedersen's chickens under the porch.

Derry couldn't imagine where the Pedersens could have got to on a Wednesday afternoon. It was too early to leave off the field work and not the right day for church. He turned to come down the porch steps and heard a series of crashing sounds from inside the house.

He sprang back to the door and peeked in the lone window on the low side of the porch but the blue flowered curtains were drawn against the sun. Then he heard a voice calling his name.

"Deh...ree, Deh...ree." The slow, drawn out syllables didn't sound like Mrs. Pedersen's voice, but Derry gently pushed open the unlatched door and peered inside.

It took a moment for his eyes to adjust to the darkness. Then he recognized the huddle of cloth lying at the foot of a wooden rocking chair amid shards of broken glass as being Rachel Pedersen.

Derry bounded over the wooden floor and carefully turned the woman over on her back. Her face was an unrecognizable mask of swollen and discolored flesh. Blackened eyes, drying blood on her forehead and cheeks, her nose and mouth bleeding and twice their normal sizes. A groan came from her misshaped mouth, followed by a rasping breath.

"Mrs. Pedersen, what happened?" Derry asked, pushing aside the still moving rocking chair. She gave a low whimper. He gently straightened her out on the floor, clearing away glass from a broken lamp with his foot.

There was a bed against the wall nearest them. Tark's, he supposed. A set of stairs led upward to the loft where Olaf and Rachel Pedersen slept, but Derry doubted if he could carry the woman up the stairs without hurting her or himself.

"Let me get you off the floor, Mrs. Pedersen."

Derry saw that she was unconscious, or almost so. He took two steps to the bed and pulled back the bedclothes. Then he scooped her into his arms, stumbling as he got up. Rachel Pedersen wasn't a large woman, but her apple-shaped frame and dead weight threw him off balance. Derry stood for a moment with the injured woman in his arms, catching his breath and readying himself to place her in the bed with as little jostling as possible.

He lowered her hips and legs into the bed, letting it take her weight as he slid his hands up her back, supporting her torso, and then he guided her head onto the cotton covered pillow. She moaned once.

Derry looked around the room for water or a bucket. Finding a tin pail of water on a table against the far wall near the woodstove, he plunged his neckerchief into it. On his knees, Derry sponged off the woman's face with care, dipping the cloth in the pail again and again. Her labored breathing evened and she turned her head slightly toward Derry, eyes swollen shut. Blood oozed slowly out of the hair just above her left temple.

Derry sponged that off as well. The water in the pail became a deep crimson. He got up to fetch fresh water from the well in the yard, but the woman reached out her hand and touched his leg.

"Stay," she said on a breath.

"I need clean water, Mrs. Pedersen. I won't be but be a minute."

The woman's fingers closed on the cloth of his trouser leg and Derry had no heart to pry them away, however much he needed fresh water.

After a moment, the clutching fingers relaxed as the woman lapsed into semi-consciousness. Derry tucked the bedclothes around her, grabbed the pail and sprinted for the doorway.

Out in the yard, he poured the bloody water out on a thatch of daisies growing near the door and dashed to the well halfway between the house and the barn. As he pumped water into the pail, he looked over at Moho, still alone in the yard. Where were Olaf and Tark?

Derry left the pail at the well and ran to the barn. The doors were open slightly. He ducked inside the hot, dark barn and pushed the door open wider to let in the light.

"Olaf? Tark?" he hollered, but the barn was empty. The hard packed dirt floor was littered with old straw and he could see dried cow droppings, surprising because Olaf's barn had always been immaculate and his prized cattle well bedded in straw that was mucked out daily. Derry returned to the well and grabbed the pail, still looking around for the farmers.

He considered taking off Moho's heavy packs, but disregarded the notion because it would take more time than he wanted to spare.

Still, he took a few seconds to pour a pail of water for the mule in the wooden trough in the yard before refilling the pail with fresh water and running back into the house.

Rachel Pedersen's blackened eyes were open to swollen slits. She called his name in a barely audible voice as Derry pulled up a stool by the side of the bed and dipped out a cup of water for her to drink.

"It will be all right, Mrs. Pedersen. Here, try some water."

Derry kept up a patter of soothing sounds and words as the woman's tongue licked at the water on her lips. She choked when he tried to give her more and he laid her head back down on the pillow. She vomited immediately. Derry cleaned her up as best he could and rolled the pillow under her neck, propping her head up. Her murmured apologies hurt his heart to hear.

As he placed the dampened neckerchief across her forehead, Rachel gave a little sigh and fastened her eyes on his face.

"Derry..."

"Don't try to talk, Mrs. Pedersen. Just lie there and rest." He hoped that one of the farmers had saddled up the horse and gone for the doctor.

Rachel Pedersen couldn't rest. "Olaf died...winter." she breathed. Derry could barely understand her and he leaned closer. "Tark...hurt me."

He sat up in shock. Her eyes glimmered and two tears spilled slowly down her battered face. Derry's heart hammered in his chest.

"Olaf is dead and Tark did this?" he repeated, unbelievingly.

"Yes" came out on a gasp. More tears coursed down her cheeks, but Rachel Pedersen had more to say. "Leave... not safe."

Derry shook his head. "I'll not leave you, Mrs. Pedersen, unless it's to get a doctor. Where is Tark?"

"Courting...Margaret."

Derry stared at her, unable to imagine the farmer beating his mother much less leaving her to die while he was off courting the wealthy mill owner's daughter.

The nearest farm was more than two miles away and it was almost four miles to Bedlington. He couldn't leave the injured woman alone long enough to fetch a doctor or a neighbor. His own medical skills were limited to salving over Moho's occasional pack sores or picking stones out of the mule's shoes and massaging away lameness.

As Rachel Pedersen lapsed back into unconsciousness, Derry finished sponging off her head and face. There were smears and drops of blood on the bodice of her calico dress and on one sleeve as if she had tried to wipe her face. A trail of blood led back from the rocker to the woodstove. His flesh crawled at the sight of a hank of hair and skin clinging to one corner of the stove. If Rachel Pedersen's head had hit the corner of the woodstove after she was struck by Tark, the injury could be very serious.

He remembered one of the monks who had neglected to duck the low ceiling when coming up out of the monastery's root cellar. Brother Nicholas had taken a smart blow to the forehead that knocked him senseless for a few seconds. Then he opened his eyes, sheepishly rubbed his head, and went on about his business. A few hours later, he fell asleep during vespers and never woke up again.

This on again-off again consciousness couldn't be a good sign. The next few hours would probably tell him whether she would live or die. He could do nothing but make her comfortable and wait.

Derry made another trip to the well for fresh water. No telling when Tark would return and what would happen when he did. He led Moho into the barn, took off the heavy packs and scrounged up a little hay for him from the hayrick. Derry wished he had time to rub the sweaty animal down, but he had to get back to his patient.

Rachel Pedersen was still unconscious when he returned to the house. Derry lit the lantern he found on the table even though it was still light outside. He built a fire in the wood stove to boil water for tea or soup, whichever he found the makings of first. After tidying up the broken glass from the lamp on the floor, he brought in his pot of blueberries and opened the curtains and the window, letting in the late afternoon light and the sweet summer air.

Between the housekeeping tasks, Derry darted back to the bed to dampen the handkerchief on her forehead or the piece of cloth torn from the pillowcase he placed across her poor broken nose or to peer into her face and chafe her hands, keeping up a verbal report of all that he was doing as if she were wide awake and vitally interested.

Finally, unable to think of anything else to do, Derry sat down on the stool next to the bed and watched the woman breathe. He hoped she would wake and he would be able to tell if she were getting better. From time to time, she moaned, but her eyes remained closed.

It grew dark outside and Derry began to feel sleepy. Unused to sitting for any length of time, he shifted his weight on the stool and looked out at the night sky. When he looked back, Rachel Pedersen's eyes were open.

He took her hand and smiled at her reassuringly. One of her eyes seemed larger than the other, the pupil fixed and dilated. She spoke softly and Derry leaned down to hear better, but her words were slurred and distorted and he was unable to make sense of them. She repeated herself and although he heard her words this time, they confused him.

"Blue vase," Derry heard. Her index finger pointed to the ceiling. "Blue vase" came again, stronger this time and again, the finger pointed.

Derry looked up at the ceiling of the cabin. There was a loft and a set of stairs leading up to it. He didn't understand what a blue vase could have to do with anything at all, but he had to do what he could to keep her from being agitated.

He sprinted up the stairs. The loft contained a single bed, neatly made up, with a cedar wood chest at its foot. There were a few dresses hanging from pegs on the wall, a small round table with a pitcher and basin on it, a rocking chair and a footstool. No blue vase.

He opened the chest. The smell of lavender and wormwood filled his nose. A man's cotton shirt and woolen trousers lay folded atop a heavy quilt. Another man's shirt was wrapped around something. Derry unwrapped the shirt enough to reveal the deep blue color of a porcelain vase. He closed the chest and bounded back down the stairs, carrying the vase.

Derry sat on the stool next to the bed and pulled the shirt off the vase. Rachel turned her head toward him and opened her eyes. Her hand reached up. Derry held the vase so that she could touch it. He didn't think she was strong enough to hold it on her own, but she didn't seem to want to hold it. One finger drifted down the rounded smoothness of the vase, stroking it, and the woman appeared to take strength from this touch.

She said in a clear voice, "Take it to my sister."

Seeing that something was expected of him, Derry said, "Yes, ma'am. I'll surely do that. Who's your sister?"

Instead of answering his question, the woman said, "My mother's vase. Her mother's before her. Grandmother brought it when she came to this country. It was supposed to go to the eldest daughter."

She turned her face away from Derry. Tears rolled down her cheeks. Her broken nose distorted her words and there were gasps of breath between sentences, but Derry understood her.

"Kept it when my mother died. Told Susan that Mother gave it to me because I took care of her." Rachel's tears soaked the sheet Derry had drawn up to her chin. "She knows I lied. Haven't seen her for ten years."

Her voice cracked and she tried to sit up. Derry soothed her and got her to settle back down, but she grasped his hand as it smoothed the pillow under her head, holding on with surprising strength.

"Take it to her." Her eyes glittered with intensity through the bruised and swollen flesh surrounding them. "Promise. Take it. Tell her I'm sorry. I'm so sorry and I love her. Promise me." She raised her head off the pillow towards him, "Please."

"I'll make sure she gets it safely, Mrs.

Pedersen," said Derry patting her hand. He would have done almost anything to alleviate the agitation he feared would sap her strength. "Tell me her name and where she lives. I'll get it to her."

Rachel Pedersen sank back against the pillow, closing her eyes. Her grip on Derry's hand softened. "Susan Fox…. Emmittsville." Then her eyes flew open again, "Don't tell Tark."

Derry nodded.

"Promise," she gasped out.

Derry nodded again. "I promise."

The woman closed her eyes and released his hand.

Through the long night, Derry kept watch over Rachel Pedersen. Her breathing became shallow and she appeared to sleep, but shortly before dawn Derry saw that her breathing had stopped altogether. He felt for her pulse, but there was nothing. Rachel Pedersen was dead.

A vast sorrow and anger overwhelmed him. Derry had little experience with mothers, having lost his to milk fever when he was a week old, but they were precious in his eyes. He had seen Tark angry before, but would never have thought him capable of such violence. The realization that he, Derry, would have to inform the sheriff of the circumstances of Rachel Pedersen's death weighted his sorrow like a rock on his chest.

He straightened the bedclothes around Rachel Pedersen, folded her hands on her chest and smoothed the silvering strands of her brown hair. In death, her bruises were even more appalling, but Derry tidied her as best he could.

He banked the fire in the wood stove and blew out the lantern. He picked up the vase and wrapped it in Olaf's shirt once again. At the door Derry stopped to look back at the woman on the bed. From the doorway, she looked at peace, free of the violence he had walked into. Silently he thanked Rachel Pedersen for her blueberry cobblers and quiet friendship and prayed for her soul. Then he headed for the barn.

It was like swimming up to the surface of a vast lake but, at last, my eyes opened. I was curled on my side on the couch. The gloom that filled the living room was disorienting after the dawn sunshine where I had just seen a woman die. A confusing whirl of sorrow and dread filled me. I rolled off the couch and went into the bathroom, trying to let the dream go. Was it just a dream? Could it have really happened?

It felt as if it was still happening. I'd seen the blue vase, the object from Astrella's, but there was more to this—I could feel it. Derry's mixture of sorrow and worry wasn't leaving me. I walked back into the kitchen and got a glass of water. Did I want to know more? Could I stand it? I'd already seen a person die in this dream and it didn't seem likely to have a happy ending. I sat on the couch with the remote and turned on the television, turning it off again in seconds. I had to know what happened to Derry. I had to know how this dream stuff worked.

I picked up the blue vase and ran my fingers over it. Set it back down. I had to know. I lay down on the couch taking a last look at the vase before closing my eyes. The dream enveloped me.

It took Derry more than an hour to find Sheriff Ripley who had been eating breakfast at the Grand Saloon. He was standing out on Bedlington's

Main Street, telling the sheriff about Rachel Pedersen's death and Tark's part in it, when there was an altercation at the north end of the street. A knot of people gathered around a horseman who was shouting something and the sheriff excused himself, telling Derry to wait for him.

At Moho's sudden snicker of interest, Derry looked more carefully at the horse and rider. The horse was white. Freya. The rider, then, must be Tark Pedersen.

A boy detached from the crowd around the horse and rider and ran down the street toward Derry crying delightedly to one and all, "Tark says there's been a murder! Someone broke into his house and killed his ma and busted everything up!"

Derry's heart stood still. It seemed that Tark had returned to his home after all. When he found his mother laid out in the cabin, he would have understood that someone likely knew what he had done. To protect himself, he must have tried to make it look like a robbery happened before he set off pell-mell for town to spread his story.

Aside from Rachel's words, Derry had no proof that Tark had beaten her and he could give no reason for the attack. It would be his word against Tark's and who would believe a man could murder his own mother? If they searched him, the sheriff would find Rachel Pedersen's blue vase. They would think he'd stolen it.

Derry turned on his heel and led Moho down a side street without haste. They looped around toward the outskirts of town, heading for the old Simpkin place, abandoned after Reg Simpkin died two years ago.

Traveling with a loaded pack mule would slow Derry down and force him to stick to the roads. He could ditch Moho's packs in the cave on the Simpkin place and go cross-country to Emmittsville over Sleeping Elephant Ridge, avoiding the road around it. The sheriff would likely ride out to the Pedersen place to verify Tark's story. He might have sent someone out to round up Derry already. If Derry could get back to the monastery, the prior, Brother Anselm, would be able to help him, but first, he had to make good his promise to Rachel.

He and Moho cut across the Simpkin farm to look for the cave Reg had shown Derry years before. The entrance was obscured by manzanita and rabbit brush. Derry passed it twice before catching sight of the blackness behind the brush. The entrance was only half a man's height, but, immediately inside, the cave opened to vast space. Derry pulled his lantern off Moho's pack and lit the wick. Flashing it at the entrance, he waited. When he didn't hear anything, he walked inside the damp coolness of the cave.

He moved the lantern around to check for rattlers and animals. A freshet of water flowed toward the entrance from somewhere within the cave. The floor was littered with old animal bones and smelled of wet earth and rock, but Derry found no recent scat nor animal scent.

Following the convolutions of the cave, Derry came upon the antechamber he remembered from Reg Simpkin's tour. In the lantern light, the stalagmites ringing the floor looked like the milky teeth of giants. At the back of the chamber a massive stalactite, marbled yellow and white, reached for the floor. Behind it, there was plenty of space for Moho's packs.

On the way back to the cave entrance, Derry discovered another, larger opening to the cave, one that Moho could easily enter, if Derry could talk him into it. They could rest until the moon was up and then head for Sleeping Elephant Ridge.

Once again, I could feel myself, the dreamer and observer, take a mental step back from the dream. Another crossroad—wake up now and it was just a dream, or allow myself to go deeper to whatever lay ahead. I chose to go.

Branches clawed at his face and grabbed at his shirt as Derry burst through the screen of manzanita bushes at the top of the ridge. If a posse were following, he'd left them a swath of broken branches and trampled brush clear enough for a blind man to track. Can't be helped, he thought. It would have been easier to head out alone, but he couldn't leave Moho behind. The mule was Derry's livelihood and, right now, his only friend.

Derry peered down the slope toward the little valley. He'd come up out on the ridge almost exactly where he planned, and now he and the mule had to drop down the other side and get across the public road without being seen.

Moho snorted behind him and Derry turned, ruefully noticing scratches along the mule's hide that hadn't been there two days ago. Two days of following deer trails through manzanita, forests of pine, and fallen snags up the steep slope of Sleeping Elephant Ridge. Going down the other side would be faster but just as difficult.

It wouldn't get easier standing around where someone might look up and see them. Derry rubbed the mule's nose, settled the pack on his own back more securely and started down the slope.

He was trying to get a grip on his panic and formulate a plan, but his thoughts kept skittering around, focusing on only two things—getting to Brother Anselm at Flat Rock and leaving the vase with Susan Fox. A part of him nagged that taking the vase to the widow was a foolish risk, but he'd made a promise to a woman to ease her dying and that was a sacred responsibility.

Moho the sure-footed suddenly slid a few feet down the slope on the slippery pine needles. Derry, jerked out of his thought by the mule's movement, leaped sideways. The mule shook his head and glared at Derry, planting his feet. They were almost at the bottom of the ridge now.

"Sorry, boy, I was woolgathering."

As the slope melted away behind them and the ground became level, Derry waited for the right moment to cross the road into the woods surrounding Emmittsville and circle back toward the outskirts of the town where the Widow Fox lived. He'd sharpened knives for her once or twice, but until three days ago, he hadn't known that Susan Fox and Rachel Pedersen were sisters.

There was a bend in the road where the trees on either side almost met overhead. It would provide good cover and a safe place to cross. He could hide Moho behind the widow's barn while he made sure she was alone. In a year, a lot could change. Maybe she wasn't a widow anymore; maybe she was taking in boarders.

As he crouched in the tall grass of the field across the road from the widow's front porch, Derry waited and watched. Moho was tethered behind the widow's tiny barn, much to the animal's ear-flattened disgust. If not tethered, the mule would follow him. Moho was named for his nature—Mind of His Own.

The Widow Fox had been sitting in a rocker on her front porch for almost an hour. No one had come in or out of the house while Derry watched. He was sure that she was alone. When she got up and went inside, Derry walked around to the back of the house with quiet steps, stopping once to catch his breath and calm his pounding heart.

He walked up the stairs of the Widow Fox's back porch, opened the back door without a sound and stepped inside the kitchen.

The widow was setting a bowl on a table, her back to Derry. He took two steps towards her and slid his hand over her mouth. Her terrified eyes rolled back towards him. Her fear made him miserable with shame.

"It's all right, Mrs. Fox," he began, making his voice soothing and his eyes big and round to reassure her. "I won't hurt you."

She was taller than her sister, Rachel, and scraggily built, but the eyes meeting his in shocked recognition were the same bright blue.

Keeping his hand over her mouth, Derry slid the pack off his shoulders onto the table and single-handedly untied the leather string at the top of it. The widow struggled, but he held her firmly against his chest.

"It's all right, Mrs. Fox. I'm not going to hurt you." He pulled out the vase still wrapped in Olaf Pedersen's shirt. "I brought this from your sister."

At his words, the widow bucked violently and he almost dropped the heavy vase. Quickly he set it on the table and wrapped his other arm around her, holding her still.

"Stop! Stop, please," he gasped.

She continued to fight him. Derry had never held a woman before and he had been in only two fights. The thought of fighting a woman was horrifying. He almost let her go, but then he remembered his reason for being in her kitchen.

He pinned her against the table and said in a rush, "She made me promise to bring it, the vase, the blue vase that was your mother's."

Susan Fox stopped struggling and became still. Under the pressure of Derry's arm, her right hand wiggled and Derry raised his arm cautiously.

The widow reached forward and touched the vase. Through the wrappings she carefully felt its round base and the handles on either side. Then she muttered something under Derry's hand. She looked back at him and nodded. He moved his hand away from her mouth, ready to clap it back if needed.

"I won't scream," she said in a calm voice. "No one would hear me if I did anyway."

He thought she was probably right; her place was on its own at the end of the town.

Derry pulled out a chair from the table and released her, motioning toward the chair. As she seated herself in it, he pushed the vase over to her.

"Go ahead, take it out," said Derry.

The widow began to undo the knots in the twine Derry had tied around the wrapping. He pulled out the other chair and sat down uncertainly next to her.

"They came through town last night and said you killed her. I heard about it this morning at Farnon's store," she said in a flat voice. Her eyes were fastened on the knots in front of her, fingers busily working.

Derry's stomach plummeted. He'd figured searchers would be looking for him; he'd crawled through brush and climbed hills to avoid the possibility, but it was a nail in his heart to know it for sure.

"I didn't kill her," he choked out. "I found her hurt and I tried to help her, but she died."

The widow slewed her eyes toward him as she pulled the last of the twine off the vase.

"They said she was beaten and the house ransacked," said Susan Fox in the same flat voice.

"She was beaten, something awful. She told me Tark did it and then he left her there." The sorrow in his heart tightened his throat and made his voice thicken. "Olaf died in the winter. Did you know?"

She shook her head slowly; a small contained movement, and put her hands in her lap.

Derry reached over and began pulling the shirt away from the vase. "She wanted you to have this and said to tell you that she loved you and she was sorry."

The widow kept her eyes focused on her lap.

The last of the shirt fell away and the vase stood revealed, smoothly round and blue; a thing of glowing beauty.

Susan Fox looked up from her lap to the vase, fixing her eyes on it. In a voice so low, Derry could barely hear it, she asked, "What was she sorry about?"

Derry had had enough. He was hungry and exhausted from lack of sleep. The widow's question was senseless to him. He burst out, "Sorry for lying to you about your mother giving it to her; sorry about taking it. She said she kept it and you knew she was lying."

The widow turned her head and met Derry's eyes. Her eyes, the same color as the vase, the same color as her sister's eyes, were filled with tears.

"Tell me."

It passed belief that she would expect him to sit in the kitchen and tell her what happened as if they were old friends, but he supposed she had a right to know what happened to her kin.

In the next hour, Derry told the widow every detail of her sister's death and his flight afterward. She said nothing while he talked, but her tears flowed in a constant stream and her fingers stroked the vase, following its contours.

When he was finished, Derry stood, eager to get back outside to Moho and leave this place.

Despite his exhaustion and the encroaching darkness, he needed to get moving. Keeping the widow in his sight, he reached for the lantern on the kitchen table. Susan Fox nodded toward a box of matches sitting on the table and Derry lit the lantern.

He wasn't sure what to do next. He needed to get Moho and he needed food and sleep but mostly, he wanted to get out of town as quickly as he could, without the widow giving an alarm. He could tie her up, he supposed, but it went against his grain to treat someone so.

"I've got to go get my mule," he said, not knowing why he was telling her this.

The widow watched him and wiped away tears with the edge of her cotton apron. Then she said, "I'll go out with you to see to the mule. You can put it in the barn and then we'll have something to eat."

Women were a puzzle—she had read his struggle so easily. He thought it might be a trick to get outside and run away, but she didn't seem afraid of him anymore. While he debated, the widow stood up from her chair, picked up the lantern and walked out the back door. Derry bolted after her.

In the dark summer night, cicadas sang and Derry could smell the tomatoes growing in the widow's vegetable garden. They walked behind the barn to the copse of trees where Derry had left Moho.

The mule started nervously at the sight of the lantern, but Derry hurried over to him. Moho gazed solemnly at the woman. She stood still and Derry led the mule over to her. "Put out your hand and let him smell you."

He took the lantern from her and she held out her hand, palm up. Moho moved into the light and sniffed delicately, nostrils flaring. Then he placed his nose squarely on her palm and the widow curved her hand to cup the side of it. Moho pushed his head down causing her hand to slide slid up the bridge of his nose toward his forehead. Startled, the widow pulled her hand away while Moho vigorously nodded his head.

That mule, thought Derry, no matter what happens, he still wants his head rubbed.

"What is he doing?" the widow asked.

"He wants you to rub his forehead."

The widow reached up and found Moho's sweet spot, right between his eyes; she used the pads of her fingers to rub it. Moho closed his eyes in ecstasy. Susan Fox gave a surprised laugh and rubbed a little harder.

They walked Moho back to the widow's tiny barn. While Derry held the lantern, she opened the doors. The barn was empty except for a few old trunks stacked along one wall.

The widow said, "I don't have any oats for him. I haven't had a horse since my husband died."

"He's been eating his head off for the past few hours," Derry said. "He'll be fine after I get him some water."

He picked up an old tin bucket resting just inside the door and motioned the woman over to the well in the yard. While she stood next to him, Derry filled the bucket and then poked it under Moho's thirsty nose. During Moho's next two buckets, Susan Fox remained standing where he indicated, making no attempt to escape. At last, Derry and the widow led the willing mule to the barn and closed him inside.

Inside the cottage, Susan Fox warmed up a meal of beans and corn bread and Derry puzzled over her apparent change in attitude. As she heaped spoonfuls of beans on the plates, he could stand it no longer.

"Why are you doing this?"

"Why am I serving you beans instead of running to the neighbors and screaming for help, you mean?"

Derry nodded.

The widow set down the pot of beans and reached a hand toward the vase, centering it on the table. "You brought Rachel back to me." Her blue eyes bored into his brown ones. "You brought the vase to me instead of getting safely away. Knowing that her last wish was to heal the hurt between us..." she shrugged and looked at him, her eyes filled with tears.

"How do you know I didn't kill her?" blurted Derry.

"And after you killed her, you decided to stop by and bring me a family heirloom while there's a posse of men looking for you?" scoffed the widow, wiping her eyes with her apron. Then she added in a softer voice, "Derry, I believe you to be an honorable man. Stay in Emmittsville and we'll go to the sheriff together. I'm sure he'll believe you if we both talk to him."

Maybe she was right. He was so tired. All he wanted to do was sleep; sleep for hours, for days, until all of this was over. He sat in the chair, the beans and cornbread warm in his stomach, trying to force his exhausted mind to explore the possibilities. Brother Anselm's calm, intelligent face appeared before him and Derry felt comforted. The prior would know what to do.

"I have to go," Derry announced. He started up out of the chair, but the widow gently pushed him back down.

She shook her head at him, but said, "I'll pack some food for you to take." He sat at the table as she cleared up their meal. Worry and exhaustion took their toll and Derry fell asleep.

He awoke with a start, disoriented by the dark and the unfamiliar room. On the table in front of him was a neat package. In the lantern light, he saw the widow sitting across from him with the vase in her hands.

"You've been asleep for more than two hours. The moon is up."

Derry caught his breath at the danger in which his nap had placed him. The widow's face told him nothing. He stood slowly, rolling his neck from side to side and then he picked up the package.

"Thank you."

"Derry, you have a reputation as a good and dependable person. Tark had a bad temper even when he was a little boy," said the widow. "People will remember that. Please go to the sheriff with me. It will be all right."

Derry looked at her pleading eyes, so like her sister's. Could it be a trick or was she genuinely concerned for him? He needed to be with people he could trust. He wanted to talk to Brother Anselm.

"I'm sorry," he said, "I've got to go home."

The widow nodded as though she expected this answer. "What are you going to do with the mule?"

Her question cleared his sleep-fogged mind.

"If you're trying to keep ahead of the posse, you'd be able to move faster without him."

She was right, Derry knew. He'd thought of it, but didn't want to turn Moho loose to fend for himself. Besides, the mule would follow him.

"I could keep him," said Susan. "I could hide him in my barn for a few days until you got farther away."

Derry stared at her. "Somebody would surely recognize Moho and they'd want to know how you got him."

"Not for a couple of days, and then I'd tell them the truth—how you brought me the vase, how you found Rachel and stayed with her," Susan nodded at him. "I could help you, Derry, and I'd take good care of Moho until this mess is settled and you can come back for him."

Somehow he knew that Moho would be safe with her. About his own safety he couldn't be so sure. Finally, he nodded. "I'd appreciate it."

Hours later, Derry fought his way up a slope using trees to stop his backward slide against wet pine needles, a litter of small boulders and rocks tumbling in his wake. He caught hold of a pine sapling and used it to pull himself up, scrabbling at the muddy ground for purchase.

It was early morning. A steady rain blurred his vision and seeped through his clothing, chilling his sweaty skin. Below, he could hear the voices of two men calling to each other as they ascended the slope. Panic spurred him up to the top of the ridge where he turned east and began working his way along the spine, searching for an opening through the thickly grown manzanita bushes. A gap appeared and he threw himself into it, slipping and sliding down the slickening slope, grabbing at branches to slow his runaway descent. They must be close if he could hear them over the sound of the rain.

The two hours of sleep at the Widow Fox's house hadn't been near enough. She'd stuffed food and water into his pack, but it kept snagging on the brush and he'd ditched it somewhere on the way up the ridge when he'd caught sight of the two men following him. He'd come upon them unexpectedly, as they were packing up camp at dawn and had been trying to outrun them for the past two hours. Just his bad luck.

Thunder boomed. A man's voice echoed above him. Derry stopped grabbing for branches and allowed himself to slide uncontrolled down the slope, trying to outpace the searchers on his trail. Twisting and turning, gathering speed through the trees, he took a giant sliding step as the steady rain became a downpour. The tree canopy protected him from the brunt of the rain, but rivulets of water from the top of the ridge turned the slope into a churning mass of mud. Another sliding step brought him up short on the side of his foot, twisting his ankle with a wrenching pain and throwing him off balance. A blast of thunder shook the ground. Derry looked up just as lightning exploded within him and sent his body flying deaf and sightless through the air.

Pain, there was only pain. A buzzing in his head, a strong metallic smell in the air and something incredibly heavy pinning him down. He was on his back, legs twisted beneath him. In the soft black silence surrounding him, Derry saw the Widow Fox. One of her hands stroked Moho's velvety nose as she fed him a carrot with the other. The peace of the scene filled him, replacing the pain. Stars, like beacons, bloomed in the sky and he followed them.

Holy shit. I jerked awake, opening my eyes to blackness. Was I awake or still dreaming? Wake up, wake up. My arms flew out and thwapped against the leather of the couch. There was no tree lying across me, no mud covered slope beneath me.

While I waited for my heart to stop throwing itself against my rib cage, I felt my arms and legs. Everything was where it should be. Nothing appeared to be damaged except that my brains felt fried and I wasn't completely sure if I were David or Derry.

The white digital numbers on the CD player glowed in the darkness. I reached out, feeling for the floor lamp at the end of the couch, and turned it on.

My condo, my jeans-covered legs. The window showed only blackness and the sound of the rain had stopped. The Clive Cussler I'd been reading was still on the floor and the vase I'd thought would make a good gift for my mother was still on the coffee table. Maybe I'd buy her gardening tools instead.

I stood up, grateful to feel my legs under me, and went into the kitchen. The microwave clock said 8:31. I'd been dreaming for almost ten hours.

Chapter Twelve

I ponder insanity and build for the future

I was as wired up as a man with forty lattes; galvanized as if a direct current was blasting through me. I had to do something, go somewhere, and get away from the dream in my head. I had to talk to someone beside myself. I called Steve.

"Hey man, I'm glad you called," he said. "I'm on my way to Katy's parents' house. Their water heater blew and I'm helping her dad put in a new one. What are you doing tomorrow?"

Nothing except imploding, I thought, my plan to spill my guts to Steve foiled. "Nothing planned. What's up?"

"Come over in the morning. I'm building a sandbox for Brian. On your way, can you stop by the Rock Place and pick up a few bags of sand? I'll tell them which ones and they'll load you up." Then Steve was gone and my confessional had to be postponed. Nate and Patrick were at a hockey game, more bad luck.

The condo couldn't hold me—I had to get out. It was after nine when I grabbed a jacket and got into my car. I drove with no destination in mind, still shaking off Derry Tinker. After an hour of aimless turns, I found myself near a Burgerville and went through the drive-thru, ordering a bacon burger and sweet potato fries. The food, eaten in my car in the parking lot, seemed to ground me back in my own reality: Dave Peltier, computer geek, admirer of long-legged redheads and dreamer of curious dreams.

It wasn't a dream; it couldn't be. A dream didn't let you wake up and then go back into it, picking up where it left off. Dreams didn't happen in sequence and give a back-story. I had been inside Derry, knowing his thoughts, his life, sharing his memories—and his death. It had been both frightening and exhilarating, but it hadn't felt like a dream.

Why was this happening? What did it mean? Was I being possessed as Mom feared? Why did I seem to have each experience only once? If the objects from Astrella's caused dreams, why wouldn't I have them every night? I'd had the vase for almost a week—why dream of Derry tonight?

I wanted to drive to Bedlington and confront the old woman for answers, but the fullness in my belly slowed me down enough to realize that hurtling to Bedlington to pound on some old lady's door in the middle of the night wasn't one of my better ideas.

Tomorrow I could talk to Steve. On Monday, I'd be hiking with Melanie and I could talk to the woman in the shop. This time I would get answers.

My cell phone was ringing when I unlocked the door around eleven. I picked it up from the kitchen counter and looked at the caller ID. Mom. How did she always know when something weird had happened to me?

"Hi, Mom." I tried to keep the lack of enthusiasm out of my voice.

"Hi honey, I know it's late but I just had to talk to you."

I had wanted to talk with someone before my burger, but not now and not Mom. She was a good listener but, now that I had calmed somewhat, I didn't want to get back into the dream or talk about metaphysics.

"I just heard from my friend Winona—you know, the dream interpreter I told you about?" Mom sounded excited. "She said objects show up in dreams all the time and usually it's because of the meaning the dreamer attaches to them. Winona suggested that you examine what you believe about each object and maybe that would help you figure out why you had the dreams."

I knew exactly what I believed about the objects. I believed the painting was of a naked woman and it would fill in the blankness of my bathroom wall; I believed the statue head would make a good paperweight and I used to believe that the blue vase was a pretty color and would make a good gift for Mom. None of these beliefs seemed to be the sort that would project me into completely different periods of the space/time continuum or lead to demonic possession.

"Thanks, Mom, I'll work on it." I held back from telling her about the latest dream—maybe to keep from worrying her, maybe to keep from worrying myself.

"Did you talk to the woman at the curio shop yet?"

"Not exactly. She's not very approachable."

"Well, Winona also said dreams carry things in their pockets for us and that you shouldn't buy anything else from the shop, just in case there are psychic repercussions."

"Seriously, Mom? 'Dreams carry things in their pockets?' And what the hell are psychic repercussions?"

"I don't know—Winona was a little vague about that. But she definitely wanted me to tell you not to buy anything else. And if the dreams start bothering you again, put the quartz crystal on the nightstand next to your bed. Quartz is a powerful protector."

A protector against what? Psychic repercussions, whatever they were, old hags selling stuff I didn't need, or maybe burglars after my mountain bike?

The crystal was in the bedroom acting as a doorstop. The dream had occurred in the living room after I'd removed the crystal. Was there a connection?

After promising not to buy anything more from Astrella's, I hung up.

Unable to sleep, I spent the next few hours on the Internet Googling dreams, dream symbology and dream interpretation. I even looked up spirit possession. It was interesting stuff, but nothing seemed to fit the circumstances of what was happening to me. Was I crazy? Were the objects from Astrella's making me that way?

I fell asleep with my head on the keyboard in the middle of reading about the significance of a bee and a pomegranate in a Salvador Dali painting. The morning sun shining on my face through the open blinds in my living room window woke me at 7:40. An hour later, I was on my way to Steve's, the Saturn groaning under the weight of ten bags of sand, a box of doughnuts and two large coffees.

"Come on in," Steve yelled in answer to my knock. I walked through the door carrying the doughnuts and coffee and peering around cautiously for two-year old Brian who usually dropped whatever he was breaking to wrap himself around my knees. The house was quiet—no tiny tots; no pregnant Katy.

Steve's voice came from the kitchen, "Out here—in the garage."

The side door from the kitchen to the attached garage was open. Steve was standing in the middle of lumber, tools, bags of sand, corrugated green plastic and tarps. He said he'd been up since five, preparing the ground and laying out the boards.

"It's a surprise," he said as we unloaded the sand from my car. "I wanted to have this ready for the little man's birthday next Saturday. Katy's parents gave her a spa day as an early Christmas present and they're taking Brian to the aquarium and the zoo today. No one will be home until around seven tonight."

"It will be pretty wet around here for the next few months," I ventured. "Won't he be disappointed if he can't use it?"

Building a sandbox in the middle of winter was a typical Steve project— good idea, great motivation, but bad timing. We'd always made a good team— he would get the bug for something and I would help him make it work. He pointed toward the sheet of corrugated plastic and some two by fours.

"I thought of that," Steve said, "I'm putting a roof on it so he can use it in any kind of weather." He'd also gotten a piece of plywood to serve as a cover for the sandbox to keep out the neighborhood cats.

He showed me the plans he'd drawn up with careful measurements noted on the margins. The plan was doable—much easier than the three-story tree house we'd attempted in sixth grade.

As we carried the materials outside to the square he'd dug out for the sandbox, Steve looked at me out of the corners of his eyes and said, "So what's the deal?

You look like you're working on your last nerve."

I wasn't surprised that he'd already picked up my vibes. Steve knew me better than anyone with the exception of my mother and he was privy to a whole bunch of things that I hoped she'd never find out.

We'd been friends since we were six. We grew up around the corner from each other in Burlingame and decided to go to college at the University of Oregon together when Steve got a baseball scholarship. He was the only one of my close friends who was married. He and Katy had little Brian who was turning three and they were expecting another child in February.

I said, "I've been having some really weird dreams and it's freaking me out."

As we measured, sawed and bolted pieces of wood together, I told him about my three dreams. I showed him the newspaper clipping I still carried in my wallet and told him about the dreamologist's advice.

By the time I finished talking, the coffee and doughnuts were gone and the sandbox was practically completed.

Steve took a step back and used a rotating sander to smooth a rough patch on the edge of one side. Turning the sander off, he looked at me and said, "At the risk of stating the obvious, if you think the objects are giving you dreams, then stop buying them."

I frowned down at the sheet of heavy duty plastic I was unfolding to use as a liner. I'd been hoping for a different response, maybe something to do with a little known medical condition, easily cured.

Steve continued, "It sounds like those stories you used to tell us when we played Indiana Jones. Remember? I was into war games, but you always wanted to search for treasure in your grandparents' back yard. And when we found something, you'd make up a story about it."

Did I? I remembered mock battles in my grandparents' back yard, until my pacifist elders called a halt to them. We became archeological adventurers instead. GPop's passion for antiques ensured plenty of old junk lying around in the yard, ripe for intrepid treasure hunters.

"I remember pretending GMa's iris garden was a jungle, but I don't remember making up stories about the stuff we found," I said.

"Are you kidding?" Steve said, crawling around on the plastic, measuring and marking it. "That was almost the best part. You'd uncover a teapot with no handle or a brass spittoon and tell us some wild story about it. Ask Jeremy."

He was right. The stories I made up with GPop sometimes spilled over into our play. How could I have forgotten? Still, those stories weren't anything like the dream visions I'd been having.

"Well, they are more like stories than dreams, but they aren't anything like our kid stories," I said. "I felt like I was living these things."

"You grew up. Maybe your stories are better now."

While I cut the liner, Steve loaded up the staple gun. Together we wrestled the stiff plastic into the sand box and began tucking and stapling, attempting to pull it tight without tearing it, a chore that absorbed all our concentration and most of our doughnut-fueled energy.

After a few stapled digits, an impressive variety of curse words and some minor repairs, the liner was stapled smooth and taut, ready for the sand. We hadn't yet built the overhead covering, but Steve insisted on filling the box.

"I just want to see what it's going to look like," he said. "When Brian wakes up tomorrow morning, I want him to see that sand."

Steve ripped open a bag of sand and poured it into the box. I grabbed another bag and helped out. There was a lot of empty space to fill.

He said, "You know, I was surprised that you decided to go into computers when we went to college instead of into something like journalism or creative writing. The teachers were always raving about your essays."

I remembered why I chose computer science. History, antiquities and storytelling were ridiculous wastes of time that led nowhere, according to my father. Economics, business, finance and computers were the foundation of the future. My parents weren't yet divorced, but the tension in our house was on a steady increase and fights with my father over my future career added to the mix. Except for treasure hunting, I had no clear idea of what I wanted to do with my life. Computers were the most acceptable of what I thought of as my father's Four Horsemen of the Apocalypse.

"It worked out okay," I mumbled, pouring clean white sand into a corner.

"Sure, dude, better than geology," he said. Steve was a geologist, working for the state and at the bottom of the food chain. Someday he might be pulling down the big bucks, but not yet, and probably not until he got a master's degree.

"Maybe the dreams are your way of telling the stories you want to write," Steve said, strewing sand like sugar in a cup of coffee. I ripped open another bag and glared at him.

"Since when did you become Sigmund Freud?" He and Mom, delving into my psyche. My psyche was just fine.

"Hey, it's just a thought. Makes more sense than magical antiques," he shot back.

Steve knew me well, but there were things that even he didn't know and that I had forgotten until now. One of them was that I hadn't made up those stories.

Chapter Thirteen

In which I take a hike and clear my head

The next morning, after a dreamless night, I took off for Melanie and Bedlington. The closer I got to Melanie's house, the more the balance of niggling memory and anticipation tipped toward anticipation. I blasted Coldplay at top volume to further drown out my worries and sang along as I flew down I-5. A whole day with Melanie shimmered before me and despite Steve's pragmatic view of my dreams and my own wish to let things be simple, I still planned to talk to the old woman at Astrella's.

I left Portland while it was still dark, but by the time I pulled into Melanie's driveway at nine, the sun was shining above flat, feathery cirrus clouds, promising a perfect day for hiking.

She met me at the porch door with a kiss, already wearing her hiking gear—a soft brown sweater, gray water-resistant pants and hiking boots. Against the drab colors her hair stood out like a beacon. I dropped my duffle bag on a chair in the kitchen and hugged her properly.

"Mmm." Melanie snuggled into me for a minute, activating all my synapses in helpless response. Then she said briskly, "Let's get going. We'll take my car."

She grabbed her backpack off the kitchen table and her jacket from the back of a dining room chair and we walked out to her little red Camry. I fetched my backpack from my car, tossed it into her back seat, and we were off.

"The ridge is only about fifteen miles from here," she said, maneuvering the car past cow-studded fields, "but it's a nice hike."

As we tooled along, Melanie told me how she'd ended up working at Betsy's.

"I should have gotten a job in Eugene, closer to the college, but I stopped at the diner on my way back from a skiing trip last December. Something just clicked. They happened to be short a waitress and I needed to get a job and establish residency, so it worked out perfectly. I've been working there since January." She gave me an openhearted grin. "I love working at Betsy's, but next August, it will be law school and part time work in the law library or something like that."

It was all so clear in her mind, as though the future was a well-marked path lying straight and wide right in front of her. My path had never been clear, at least not to me.

I told her about following Steve to the University of Oregon, Corvallis; meeting Nate and Patrick at college; about liking the climate and the scene in Portland; about getting the job with Promise Computers and enjoying the flexible hours and helping people build computer systems that worked for them.

"What about the future? Are you going to stay in computers?" asked Melanie.

It was a reasonable question and one that gave me some discomfort. I'd taken the first computer job that came my way and I didn't have any plans for the future. Beer-fueled philosophical discussions with my buddies would sometimes produce a yearning for a life purpose, but it was nothing I could define. In any case, I always dismissed it in the next day's sober reality. Except for my relationship with Melanie and buying my condo, nothing in my life had been planned.

"I don't know," I said slowly, "I haven't made any long range plans."

Thankfully, any further discussion of my future was interrupted by our arrival at the trail head. Melanie slowed the car, turning right onto a driveway almost obscured by pines and other foliage. The driveway opened up into an empty parking lot big enough for maybe five vehicles. Fifty feet beyond the paved lot, nestled in the encroaching forest, I could see a small cinder block outhouse. A trail sign faced Melanie's Camry. The white letters read, "Herman Falls Trail loop- 2 miles; Tinker's Ridge Trail-3 miles."

My breath stopped. For a second, I felt the slippery wet slope from the dream under my feet and the rough manzanita leaves in my hands. Derry's panic overcame me and my heart suddenly filled my throat.

Melanie's voice called me back. "Dave? Is this all right?

I blinked, took a breath. "Yeah, yeah, sure. It looks great."

In truth, all you could see from the parking lot was the concrete block privy and the woods with a backdrop of gradually ascending trees. The ridge itself was not visible. Nothing looked familiar, but the hairs on the back of my neck told me all I needed to know. I sent Melanie a reassuring look and pointed toward the outhouse.

"Hey, there's even a bathroom. Perfect for the weary traveler."

Melanie gave me a puzzled smile and then opened her door. "You can't see the ridge from here, because of all the trees, but there's an incredible view from the top."

I nodded and got out of the car. I remembered that view.

The trail was a narrow dirt path, packed down by years of hikers' feet. As we switch backed up the steep slope, I asked Melanie if she knew why it was called Tinker's Ridge.

"There's a plaque at the top that explains about the ridge. Something about a guy who was running from the law and got struck by lightning. We can read it when we get up there."

Every hair on my body stood up. I looked for something recognizable from the dream, but the trees were much bigger than the trees I remembered. The slope had less brush than my dream slope and it had been raining then, so I couldn't use today's sunlight to orient myself. I knew for sure that I had never been here before as Dave Peltier. I began to sweat despite the coolness of the air.

Melanie set a good pace, just a few steps ahead of me. I was slightly out of breath by the time we reached the top. A vista point, made for Kodak moments, lay before us, carefully bounded by simulated split rail fencing. Mounted on one of the rails was a brass plaque: "Tinker's Ridge. Formerly Emmittsville Ridge. Known as Tinker's Ridge after an itinerant peddler, known as Derry the Tinker, was suspected of murdering a Bedlington woman and tracked up the ridge by a posse in 1882. Lightning struck the fugitive during the chase. He was later found to have been innocent of the crime."

I reached out to run a finger over the words on the plaque. They were real; Derry was real. I could feel my heart jumping around in my chest as if I had just run the hundred yard dash and it had nothing to do with the hike or the altitude. Melanie stood next to me, curving into my side as she read the plaque. I slipped my arm around her. Together we took in the sweep of ridges before us and the drop to the valley below. Somewhere, down in that valley Derry had seen home and safety. Somewhere, up here, he had died.

Melanie said, "That sign always bothers me. It doesn't say whether the guy actually died here. People don't always die when lightning hits them. Maybe he died years later, of something else. They should have been more specific," added the would-be lawyer.

"Oh, he died here," I said searching the slope for a charred log.

"You sound pretty sure," Melanie said looking up at me. I shrugged. She turned to the expanse of trees and valley in front of us. "Isn't it beautiful?"

My mind was still spinning, but I smiled down at her, "It was worth the hike."

That was an understatement for sure.

I pulled out my camera and took photos from every direction, including a picture of Melanie and me standing in front of the simulated-wood rail with the view at our backs. We climbed over the rail, risking life and limb and the wrath of the Forest Service, to look for a lunch spot. I kept scanning the slope and the valleys below us for anything familiar, but saw nothing that meant anything to me.

We spread out our lunch on a narrow ledge. Melanie broke out two bottles of microbrew and we popped the caps. I made a toast: "To Derry the Tinker and all that he believed in."

We tapped our bottles together gently.

Melanie looked at me quizzically. "What would he believe in, Dave?"

I'd forgotten she didn't know about my dream. It was almost bursting out of me, but I didn't want to take a chance on relating something that sounded other-worldly at best and crazy at worst. I'd been down that road before.

The niggling memories, the ones I had resolutely kept throttled back for so many years, came surging up. Twelve had been a rough year for me. Puberty, middle school, and the reactions of my father and a teacher I had a crush on to demonstrations that, somehow, I had knowledge of things I couldn't know, had made me feel like a freak. As if seventh grade didn't make everyone feel like a freak already. I had no desire to revisit that feeling with Melanie so I pushed away the memories and quoted from Superman instead: "Truth, justice and the American Way."

She grinned and shook her head.

After lunch, which we shared with a few curious squirrels, we hooked up with the Herman Falls trail. Walking side by side down the pine scented trail, I told Melanie that I needed to talk to Mrs. Astrella about one of the objects I'd bought, so, after a couple of hours checking out the falls and enjoying being together, we headed for Bedlington.

As Melanie drove confidently along the winding roads, I filled her in on my plans to leave early on Tuesday to do client visits in Bend.

She circled back to our earlier conversation like a dog with a bone and said, "So, do you plan to do this for a long time or is it something just for now?"

"I like helping people make their business more successful," I said, looking out at the trees and fields flashing by. "But I don't know what else I want to do." I turned back to her, hating to sound vague.

"I bet you do," she replied. "Sometimes what people really want to do sounds crazy and what they think they're supposed to do sounds boring, so they just say they don't know what they want to do." She turned her bright brown eyes upon me and smiled. "So, if it didn't sound crazy, what would you want do?"

This girl was going to make a great lawyer, if she didn't decided to become a psychotherapist instead, I thought. Her smile said, "I'm waiting."

I thought it over for a moment and then hazarded, "Well, when I was a kid, I wanted to be a treasure hunter."

I figured she might laugh and write me off at that point, but I was also curious about what she would say.

She didn't laugh. "Like an archeologist on a dig or like Indiana Jones?"

"Neither one—something different. I thought it would be cool to look for interesting things and find out the stories behind them. And then...well I don't know what would happen then...I guess other people would be interested in the stories too."

"Do you like to collect things?"

I thought about the collection of eggcups I'd amassed with my grandparents, just because they were small and colorful. They were stored in three boxes in my father's garage, something he reminded me about every time I visited.

"Not so much. I don't want to own a lot of stuff. I'd rather pass it off to someone else. The interesting part would be the search and the stories."

Once again, those long buried memories pecked at my brain. I shook myself like a dog and began a spirited discussion about reggae vs. hip-hop.

Maybe, if she had laughed, treasure hunting as a career choice would have been kicked to the curb, buried back under other impossible wishes—like my grandparents being alive again. But Melanie treated my childhood dream with gentleness and it stayed alive in the back of my mind.

We got to Bedlington after four o'clock, but Astrella's was closed. There was a handwritten sign on the locked door that read, "Back on Dec. 5."

Melanie said, "That's weird. I didn't know Astrella's ever closed."

Was I never going to get to the bottom of this?

Melanie must have seen the frustration in my face despite my attempt at nonchalance because she said, "Let's go to Betsy's and have a burger. Maybe Ross will know where she is."

When in doubt, eat. It's a good motto. We walked to Betsy's where Melanie was greeted as if she had returned from a three month journey to the center of the earth with cannibals for guides.

We slid into a booth, sitting opposite each other. I liked seeing her face across from me and I liked having space to move rather than being crowded together on one side of the booth.

I wondered if it might be time to try something from the menu, but Ross appeared from the kitchen and plucked them from our hands. "I made some Whizzbanger Chili. You gotta have a bowl."

Melanie's eyes lit up. My mouth was set for burger, but she looked at me and said, "Dave, you're going to love this."

I decided that Whizzbanger Chili was exactly what I wanted.

Ross nodded and went back into the kitchen. Melanie said, "Ross only makes this chili two or three times a year and he won't tell anyone the recipe, but it's the best, the absolute best."

Ross reappeared bearing two white crockery bowls, which he set before us. A swirl of white sour cream melted into the deep red of the chili. One of the waitresses followed with bowls of shredded Cheddar cheese and sliced green onions, a covered basket and two extra-large glasses of water. The covered basket held two large, bumpy biscuits.

"Beer and red onion biscuits," Melanie informed me.

She sprinkled a tablespoon of cheddar onto her bowl of chili, followed by a spoonful of green onions. I copied her every move as Ross and the waitress departed. Finally, I lifted a heaping spoonful of red, green, orange and white stuff to my lips.

The first spoonful was good, the second even better and it just kept getting better, and hotter, with every bite. The biscuits were a perfect accompaniment. I drank every drop of my water. Melanie savored and smiled. I was warm inside and out.

To slow myself from inhaling the chili, I looked around the restaurant at the photographs adorning the pale yellow walls. With a shock, my eye stopped on one I had noticed the first time I came into Betsy's—the one with the woman wearing a huge hat and standing next to a mule.

Ross appeared next to me. "How's that chili?"

My mouth opened and closed. Nothing came out.

"Not too hot, is it?" he asked anxiously.

It wasn't the chili that had me gasping like a guppy in the desert. Melanie looked at me, concern in her eyes. She put down her spoon.

"The chili is awesome," I managed, "the best I've ever had."

Ross smiled and the concern went out of Melanie's eyes, but she didn't pick up her spoon until I said, "Really, Ross, it's great and so are the biscuits."

Melanie began eating again when I asked, "Is that a mule in that picture?"

Ross looked over his shoulder at the photograph. "Yes, good call. Most people think it's a horse, but it's a famous, or probably I should say, infamous, mule named Moho. The picture was taken in Emmittsville, a little town that used to be near here."

Moho. "Who's the lady?"

Ross laughed. "That's the Widow Fox. According to my grandmother, she and Moho were quite the pair."

At my look of interest, Ross looked around at the quiet diner and then pulled a chair to the end of our booth and sat down. "My grandmother was born in Emmittsville and the widow was an old, old lady when Grandma knew her. Moho was long dead by then, but the stories about him lived on. Old-timers loved to tell about his habit of falling in love with various animals.

"One time he fell in love with a three-legged dog the widow had rescued. The pair of them escaped from the widow's yard and walked down Main Street looking in all the shop windows as if they were shopping. Gave some ladies inside the stores quite a fright."

Melanie and I laughed. Ross' eyes lit up. "The story is that the widow kept pretty much to herself until she got Moho. I don't know how or why she got him, but she started rescuing kittens somebody had tried to drown, crippled dogs, birds that couldn't fly, goats and other animals so he would have plenty of friends.

"Then the widow became a suffragette and she and Moho started showing up in all the town parades, campaigning for women's right to vote. That's what this is a picture of. See Moho's all spruced up and the widow's wearing a 'Give Women the Vote' sash across her chest."

With every word, amazement bloomed inside me. Moho, Derry and the Widow Fox were real; they were part of history, not a story I made up. The chili and Ross' story were untangling the knots of worry in my brain, but now there were a lot more questions.

Ross finished with, "Moho would carry things, but he wouldn't let anyone ride on his back. Not even the widow. She lived just long enough to see the Nineteenth Amendment become ratified. There were rumors of some kind of old scandal—the widow had a nephew or something, who supposedly murdered someone and ran away—but she and Moho were quite the town favorites."

The diner door opened and a gaggle of ladies laden with shopping bags poured in. Ross stood up and began to put away his chair. Melanie threw out a quick question.

"Hey, boss, we stopped by Astrella's and it's closed until December fifth. Do you know why?"

"She closes every year at this time." At Melanie's look of puzzlement, Ross said, "I forgot, you didn't start working here until January. Daria has closed on the anniversary of her husband's death for the past nine years. Always for three days. I figure she probably goes to wherever he is buried to pay her respects."

"Ross, do you know if there is a monastery around here?" I blurted. Melanie stared at me. I couldn't blame her; it was a bizarre question in the middle of this talk of mules, suffragette widows and antique storeowners.

He seemed to take it in stride. "Well, not around Bedlington, but there used to be one about twenty miles from here near Flat Rock. The monastery folded a long time ago, but there's still an old church and a cemetery there." He cocked his head toward me. "Why do you ask?"

"It was something I heard from a friend," I said, looking around the diner so I wouldn't have to meet Ross' eyes. "He's interested in historical stuff and thought I might want to check it out."

Ross pushed in the chair and nodded at the ladies.

"Chili's on the house," he said walking away toward the kitchen. "See you later, Mel."

We downed the rest of his amazing creation, practically licking the bowls clean, before heading back out into the early December darkness. With the monastery only twenty miles away, I was afire with Whizzbanger Chili and the determination to explore just as soon as I could hustle out of Betsy's.

Chapter Fourteen

I take a journey and almost get lucky

It was only Melanie's presence and the darkness outside that prevented me from whipping out a map and bolting to Flat Rock, wherever it was. Where was Derry buried? Had his body been left on that rainy slope? Did Brother Anselm ever find out what happened to Derry? Were there any records at the church? If Derry was real, were the other dreams about real events and people too? Suddenly the newspaper clipping that came with the painting took on new meaning.

As we walked to the car, Melanie broke into my inner cache of questions. "So, are you going to check out Flat Rock tomorrow?"

Tomorrow? I looked down into her eyes, glimmering in the streetlight. The questions stopped swirling around in my head and shaped themselves into a plan. Tomorrow would be fine—tonight there was a warm girl by my side and I was exactly where I wanted to be.

We rented a movie at a grocery store on the way back to Melanie's house and by the time we drove into the wide yard, it was filled with vehicles. All the roomies were home.

They were in the kitchen/dining room when we came in. Melanie introduced me to Gillian, the artist roommate. If I'd been blindfolded, I could probably have picked her out as an artist; she smelled of patchouli and sported about fifty pieces of clunking, jingling jewelry on her arms, her hands, her neck and her earlobes. Her hair was almost the same burnt orange as the walls in the living room and spiked out all around her face. The other two roomies were wearing comfortable looking sweats, but Gillian had on black and white striped leggings, reminiscent of the Wicked Witch of the East, purple high tops, a short purple dress and a black and white striped scarf. Cute, but in a scary way.

Karen looked up from the textbook she was reading at the table, giving me a nod and a smile. Bethany was pulling something out of the oven and asked if we wanted some dinner, but we were still full of Whizzbanger Chili. Gillian's brown eyes bored into me, unblinking, and she said, "So, you're the guy who left his toothbrush in the bathroom."

"Was it green?" I asked. An unblinking nod. "Well, then, that would be mine." I gave her a friendly smile.

"I threw it in the trash. You never know where those things have been."

I felt Melanie's hand tighten in mine. I pressed it gently and said, "Good idea. When I used it on the grout, I figured it was almost time to give it up anyway."

At last, a blink. Then the Wicked Witch smiled.

She had all of her teeth and a nice smile. She nodded at me and jangled her way over to the refrigerator.

Karen peeked over the top of her book and winked. Bethany shrugged as if to say, "What can you do?" Melanie and I went into the living room and pulled off our jackets.

"Sorry, Dave," she whispered. "Jill's a little rough sometimes, but she's really a good person."

"No problem," I said. "I know someone just like her—he's behind bars—but he's just like her."

We laughed together and then Melanie called out, "We rented 'Transformers.' Anyone want to watch?"

Karen begged off, citing tons of homework as her excuse; Gillian had a date in an hour and Bethany said she had to call her mother. It didn't feel like a rejection—more like they were giving us time to be alone and that was fine with me.

The movie was pretty exciting—for the fifteen minutes we actually watched it. Melanie and I discovered better action on the couch in the darkened living room than on the tiny television screen. I heard the front door slam at one point, presumably Gillian going out on her date.

We finally came up for a breather as the ending credits music filled the air. We hadn't made it to home plate yet, but we'd been almost everywhere else.

Melanie kissed me deeply and pulled away.

"You want a sandwich?" she asked as she swept her hair back from her face and straightened her sweater. I made a few adjustments of my own and decided that a break might be a good idea. Maybe I wouldn't be sleeping on the couch after all.

In the middle of our sandwiches, the Wicked Witch flew home and banged in through the front door. She flashed a suspicious look toward our innocent peanut butter and jelly eating selves and stomped upstairs.

"Bad date?" I guessed. Melanie giggled.

Then Karen came downstairs in search of something to eat and we spent the rest of the evening politely learning about the differences between coastal redwoods and sequoias. Any thoughts of returning to the couch except to fix up my lonely bed were shelved, bored to death by Karen's earnest explanations. I suspected she had done it on purpose to save Melanie's virtue and wondered if a fatal accident with a coastal redwood could be arranged for her.

The next morning, after a fitfully frustrated sleep, I was up and dressed by six, with a long day of driving ahead of me. I checked out my map at the kitchen table while waiting for Melanie to come downstairs. It was about ten or twelve miles to Flat Rock on one of those skinny gray map roads—out of my planned route, but doable. If I left in the next hour, I could be there, check out the monastery and still be at my first client's office by ten or eleven.

Melanie came downstairs. At the sight of her, all my plans wavered mightily. Yawning, in her blue Cal Bears sweatshirt, yellow and blue plaid flannel lounge pants, fuzzy blue slippers and all that mahogany hair tumbling around her shoulders, she was a bright spot in a cloudy day. She smothered a yawn behind her hand and said "Hey cowboy."

A cowboy I am not—I don't even own a pair of boots. A horse is an extra-terrestrial as far as I'm concerned. Still, Melanie's greeting sparked some manly thing in my psyche to flex its macho muscle. I gave her a Marlboro Man smile and growled, "Hey yourself."

From somewhere upstairs, I heard the sound of gagging. Gillian the Patchouli Princess. Before the Marlboro Man could slink away, I caught Melanie's eye and we exploded into laughter. The gagging stopped abruptly. Both Bethany and Karen appeared on the stairs behind Melanie who was clutching the banister and giggling helplessly.

Karen slipped by Melanie, giving me a grin.

"Hey Cowboy," she drawled as she went into the kitchen.

Bethany, in full workout regalia and carrying a bulging gym bag, whispered, "Hey Cowboy," with a smirk as she glided past and disappeared out the front door.

I reached up and snatched Melanie off the stairs and we tussled and kissed until she stopped giggling and we were both breathless. She stepped back and said, in a disappointed voice, "You're already dressed."

"I could change that, you know." Already I was calculating how to switch my route.

A cough came from upstairs. The Patchouli Princess being subtle.

Melanie gave me a conspiratorial shrug and whispered, "Next week, at your place?"

I left regretfully, but with the promise of a whole night with my dream girl, actually *with* her, glowing in my heart.

The route I'd plotted toward Bend and Flat Rock reprised part of Derry's summer circuit, and, in the nanosecond it took me to drive through the tiny town of Nimrod, I stared hard, looking for the familiar. Nothing struck me. I took a southerly right at a three way intersection and the road passed Willamette, another of Derry's summer stops, but it just looked like another micro town, interchangeable with so many others in Oregon, just big enough for a Mom and Pop market, a couple of ramshackle houses and either a church or a used book store. I wondered if any of the residents ever got hammered and ended up in the wrong town.

Finally, a green sign showed Flat Rock to be two miles away. The GPS had gotten me to Flat Rock, but it couldn't guide me to the ruins of an old monastery that wasn't on the map. I peered intently through the windows of the car, looking for old buildings or foundations. After a mile or so, I saw a couple of singlewide trailers set back from the road.

The land on either side of the road began to fill in with ancient barns and two-story wooden houses that reminded me of Melanie's house, but with more weathering and less paint.

The world's oldest gas station appeared. There were four cars on the right of the station that were at least a decade older than me, a pickup that might have been dark blue in the 1930's and a big red Dodge Ram truck from the current millennium. I pulled in and parked.

A kid who looked like he might still be in high school slouched out of the dingy office. I got out of my car and met him halfway. "Do you know where I could find the old Catholic church around here, the one that used to be part of a monastery?"

"There's only the one church. I don't know about it being part of a monastery," said the kid. "It's down this road on the right side a few hundred yards. It won't be open, though. Father Gregory's been sick."

"Thanks," I said. "I won't bother Father Gregory."

He looked at me doubtfully, waited while I walked back to my Saturn, and raised a hand when I pulled out of the station and back onto the road.

I found St. Benedict's Catholic Church a minute and a half later—a largish, white wooden building with a rock foundation on the corner of Main Street and Monastery Road. Monastery Road went back into the hills flanking the town and I decided to check it out before trying the church. Either the kid at the gas station couldn't read or he'd never connected the dots.

The road was a narrow chip and seal thing that inclined up into the hills. At the top, it curved to the left, paralleling the town and, as I followed it, I could see the back of the church and a little white house behind it as well as a cemetery and the backyards of a couple of houses. The town side of Monastery Road was pastureland with golden brown grass. On the hill side of the road, pines, oaks and manzanita jostled each other for space.

I hadn't gone far before I realized the road was going to a long, low, brown house and it looked to be ending there. There was no place to turn around on the narrow pavement, so I decided to tough it out and turn around in front of the house, hoping that the occupants wouldn't emerge with shotguns.

As I made a looping turn in the graveled drive in front of the house, the front door opened and a burly man in jeans and plaid flannel coat emerged. He seemed surprised to see me, but raised a hand to wave me down. I stopped, feeling like a trespasser, which, of course, I was.

The man stumped over to the driver's side window. I rolled it down and he bent down to lean in.

"Hey there, what can I do for you?" His voice sounded friendly, but his narrowed eyes were wary.

"Sorry about turning around in your driveway. I was following the road and didn't realize that it stopped in front of your house," I said.

"No problem. Are you looking for someone?"

"I was looking for the monastery that used to be somewhere in Flat Rock about a hundred years ago," I said.

His eyes lit up. "Well, then you're in the right place." He pointed back at the house. "That's it—that and the barn. My great grandfather bought the property, a hundred acres of it anyway, from the Church when the monastery closed and he turned the monks' quarters into this house."

I had anticipated stone ruins covered with moss and the remains of arched walkways, so this prosaic looking house sitting above fields of cows and horses was a surprise. The barn, weathered but still sturdy looking, loomed up behind the house.

The rancher must have seen the doubt on my face because he took a step back and straightened his back. "There's still the church down on the road that the monks built, and the cemetery, but this is where they lived."

If his family had owned the property for a long time maybe they would know something about Derry.

"I was looking for someone who lived near the monastery and might be buried around here," I said.

"I know everyone who's buried in the cemetery. Who're you looking for?"

"A man named Derry the Tinker."

The friendly crinkles around his eyes disappeared as he rocked back on his boot heels. "There's no Derry or Tinker buried in that cemetery," he said with a voice that sounded like granite. "Why are you looking for him? You a relative?"

"No...," How could I explain that I was looking for a man who died miles away from here, with a connection that few would know about?

"What made you think he'd be buried here?" The rancher's face was now so stiff, that it was hard to believe he'd been able to get the words out. I didn't know what his problem was, but it was obvious he wasn't feeling friendly any more.

I looked into his rock-like face. My brain doesn't work quick enough to lie, so after an endless moment, I told him the truth.

"I had a dream about him—that he came from this monastery where he spent the winters and he traveled around during the summers with a mule named Moho. And he was trying to get back here when he died. I was hoping that somebody brought him back."

The rigidity remained in the rancher's face as he stared into my eyes. Then he said, "He's buried up there, on the knoll behind the house. Come on, I'll show you."

The sudden shift of the rancher's internal weather caught me by off-balance, but I got out of the car as fast as I could, and trailed behind him as he stumped away with his stiff-kneed gait back toward the house. We skirted it, following a pathway that ran around up behind it, up past a yard with what was left of a vegetable garden, some flowers and a covered back deck, and up a slope behind the house. At the top of the oak covered knoll, there was a small squared-off clearing with four stone grave markers. The rancher stopped and emitted a phlegmy, rolling cough that went on forever.

Red-faced, he shook his head as he said, "I get winded easier than I used to." He pointed to one of the grave markers. "He's there."

The four loaf-shaped stones stood in a row and on the third one from the left, I saw Derry's name.

"Derry Tinker, 1862-1882" was etched into the stone. It didn't look like a professional job. Maybe one of the monks did it. There was a word under the dates and some other carving. I knelt down and peered at it, but the stone was too worn and the letters too lightly etched for me to make it out.

"It says, 'John 8:32.' Bible verse. It used to be easier to read," came the rancher's voice from behind me. He quoted, 'Ye shall know the truth and the truth shall make ye free.'"

I ran my fingers over the words on the headstone, unwanted tears blurring my vision. They had brought him back and someone had believed in his innocence. I wondered if it had been Brother Anselm, the prior, and then realized that it had to have been.

I turned my head. The rancher was looking out over the house and pasture below us. The knoll wasn't very high, but from the clearing I could see beyond the pasture to the town and the valley beyond it and beyond that to the dark ridges in the distance. The colors of the landscape were muted up here, the edges of the ridges blurred and softened. The silence and the view seemed limitless and restful. It was a peaceful place to be—maybe why the monks chose it for their dead.

Looking back at the clearing, I noticed for the first time that the gravestones were free of lichen and moss, the clearing carefully trimmed and mowed.

"Brother Nicholas, 1842-1879," read one stone. With a start I recognized the name of the monk who hit his head on the root cellar door. Another read, "Brother John, 1841-1873." The last marker, on the right side of Derry's, read "Brother Anselm, Prior, 1837-1890."

Only Derry's stone had an inscription and it spoke of a belief in his innocence. I knew that unshakably, although there was no proof. The tears threatened again.

The rancher cleared his throat. "I used to come up here all the time, even when I was a little kid. Most kids would be skittish of graves, but it was always peaceful to me. I liked keeping the grass mowed and the stones clean. Nobody made me do it; I just wanted to."

He continued to stare out into the vista spread before us. I stood up and breathed. Every breath felt like a banquet, rich and satisfying.

"I'm glad to know that he's here," I said. "This is where he wanted to be. Someone cared enough about him to bring him home and bury him."

The rancher looked over at me. "You know where he died, then?"

I nodded.

"It don't say on the plaque where he was from. You get that from your dream?"

I nodded again.

"That must have been some dream." He stuck out his hand. "I'm Ed Chessari."

We shook hands as I introduced myself.

"Come down to the house and have a cup of coffee. I'd like to hear more about your dream. I'll tell you what I know about Derry."

Chessari didn't sound like he expected me to refuse and although it would put a dent in my schedule, I wanted to know everything I could.

I took a last look around and pulled out my phone. I held it up so Chessari could see my intent. He shrugged and I took a few pictures of the graves and the view before following him down the narrow track that led to his house.

The house had a stone foundation but was otherwise plain, painted a light brown with teal trim; a color I doubted had been original. We went in through the back, through French doors that opened from the deck into a peach painted kitchen and dining area. It didn't look like a monks' abode on the inside with its wainscoting paneling and modern appliances. Only the addition of a back deck and front porch marred the original long narrow profile of the building.

Chessari poured two cups of coffee from a half-filled carafe he took from a coffeemaker. He put them in a microwave and pulled out two kitchen chairs, indicating that I should take one.

"My great grandpa bought the place a few years after the prior died. I guess it had never been a big concern, only half a dozen monks or so. They tried to keep things going. Some of the townsfolk helped them in the fields, but after a while they sold everything except the church and the cemetery and they left."

The microwave beeped and he took the cups out of it and set them on the table. He pulled a quart of Half and Half out of the refrigerator and two spoons from a drawer and put them on the table next to a round blue sugar bowl. Host duties completed, Chessari lowered himself into his chair and looked at me.

"Tell me about your dream."

I tried to make it as short as I could, being mindful of the time, but the rancher's narrow eyes stayed fixed on me, pulling out every detail. Finally I was done, a little hoarse, and glad to ease my throat with the now cold coffee.

Chessari was silent, looking down at the oak table. He moved a spoon around. Then he said, "When Grandpa added bedrooms onto the end of the house, he found the prior's journal. I don't know how the brothers missed it when they packed up—it wasn't like they had a lot of stuff.

"I don't have it anymore; it got ruined in a flood we had years ago. It was mostly a record of what the monks did and how the crops were, but the prior wrote about being notified by the sheriff after Derry died and going by himself to fetch the body. It was a sad thing for him to have to do. I think he loved that boy like a son.

"By the time he picked up the body, it seems the sheriff was having his doubts about Derry's guilt. A bunch of Derry's customers came forward to speak for him. One of them," the rancher turned to me, a light of excitement in his eyes, "was a widow from Emmittsville. And then, while Brother Anselm was still in Bedlington, the son of the woman Derry was supposed to have killed ran away—before the sheriff could question him."

"Tark Pedersen," I said and the rancher nodded.

He sat silently for a minute and then said, "My great grand-dad told me the whole town of Flat Rock turned out for Derry's funeral service. I always wanted to know about him—who he was and why the monks would bury him up there with their own." Chessari looked into my face. "When you said the mule's name, I wanted to hear your story, but when you knew that Moho meant Mind of His Own, I knew you were for real. In the journal, Brother Anselm said he had named the mule—nowadays no one would know what it meant. I read that journal a million times trying to figure out what really happened to Derry. Now I know."

I looked back at him, nodding. My questions about whether someone cared about Derry and believed in his innocence had been answered as well. I glanced at my watch, needing to be on my way.

"Thank you for showing me Derry's grave," I said.

"I don't know where your dream came from, but I believe it was a true one," said Chessari. "You should pay attention to things like that."

We stood and he walked with me through the living room and out to my car.

Looking at the barn behind the house, the barn where Moho and Derry lived during the winter. I wondered if there were any buildings or fences still standing that Derry had helped build. Then I realized that I didn't care. I didn't need to see the church or the cemetery—everything I wanted to know had been on that knoll.

Chessari held out his hand, "I'm glad you stopped by, young man."

I nodded my agreement, too full of thought to speak, and turned my car down the road, still filled with the peace I'd felt at Derry's gravesite.

Chapter Fifteen

The neighbor takes a bathroom break and I learn to love

cold pizza.

The rancher gave me directions for a local short cut. Despite the problems I associate with directions from people who say, "You can't miss it," I followed them, still feeling that curious sense of peace. I arrived at my first client's office only fifteen minutes late.

The rest of the week passed in a blur of driving, client visits and fast food. Nightly calls to Melanie livened things up considerably, but there was still plenty of time to wonder about the dreams and the people in them. If Derry and the Widow Fox were real people who'd lived in Oregon, what about Edmund and Katharine from my second dream or the naked woman from my first? This wasn't making up a story; it was, at least in the Derry Dream, reliving it. How could this happen?

I still wanted to talk with Mrs. Astrella from the curio shop, but my client schedule and Melanie's imminent arrival in Portland precluded a visit there.

Saturday afternoon, an hour after I arrived home from trekking around the state, there was a knock on my front door. I opened it to find my next-door neighbor hopping up and down on my steps.

"Hi-Dave-glad-you're-home-can-I-use-your-bathroom?" she jerked out, still hopping, with her arms wrapped around herself. I blinked and opened the door wider. She sprinted in and disappeared into my bedroom, presumably in pursuit of the bathroom. Our condos were mirror images, so I didn't think she'd have a problem finding it.

Looking out into the parking lot, I noticed a white truck I hadn't seen before. The red lettering on the side read, "Redman Plumbing-We'll bring peace to your pipes."

I had been in the middle of dumping the clothes from my duffle bag to the pile growing on the bedroom floor when Mrs. Browning knocked, but I didn't want to spook her by going back into the bedroom. Instead, I stayed in the living room, plugged in my laptop and checked emails.

My boss had sent along the description of a new computer system. After looking it over, I was crafting a reply when it occurred to me that my neighbor hadn't yet emerged from the bathroom. Fifteen minutes had passed. It seemed like a long time, but maybe middle-aged ladies take a long time to do whatever it is they do in the bathroom. I went back to my email, finished my questions, sent it off and emailed Melanie.

Mrs. Browning still hadn't made an appearance. I didn't know what she could be doing or whether I should knock on the door and ask if she was all right.

Just as I resolved to start making a lot of noise to remind her that I was still in the condo, I heard the toilet flush. A few minutes later, the door opened and Mrs. Browning came through the bedroom doorway.

She walked slowly, as if she was feeling her way through fog. Her face was the color of oatmeal—not a good color on her. I jumped up and went over to her. She looked at me, but her eyes, wide and dark with some kind of emotion, couldn't seem to focus.

"Mrs. Browning...," I struggled to remember her first name. "Barbara, are you okay?" I touched her elbow.

Her eyes gradually focused and she laid her hand on my arm as if she were steadying herself. "Oh. Dave. I'm fine. Fine."

Barbara Browning took a breath and stood a little straighter. She took her hand back and gave me a weak smile. "That's an interesting painting you have in the bathroom."

All this because of a painting? She didn't seem the type to freak out about naked people, but then, I didn't know her very well. Maybe she was part of some religious sect. I thought back to the weekends I'd fed their cat, trying to remember any religious décor in their condo.

She swayed slightly as she stood there in her pink cardigan and jeans. My neighbor was clearly not doing well.

"Barbara, would you like to sit down?" I indicated the couch, the only place to sit except for the floor or my computer chair.

She seemed to give herself a mental shake and drifted over to perch on the couch.

"Where did you get the painting?" she asked.

"I bought it in a little town near Eugene," I said. "It didn't offend you did it?"

"No," she said slowly. "No, but I think I know the woman in the painting."

How could anyone identify someone from a painting of a naked back?

Barbara Browning twisted the bottom of her sweater in her fingers. Light brown hair fell limply down her cheek as she looked toward her shoes.

"I know this sounds weird, but could I…borrow the painting for a day or so?"

It certainly did sound weird, but at this point, I had about a hundred million things to do before Melanie arrived. If taking the painting would get my neighbor off the couch so I could do them, it was all right by me. Still, I wondered at the effect the painting had on her.

"You aren't going to…uh…do anything to it, are you? You know, like paint clothes on her or anything like that? You look kind of upset."

The color came back into her face, making her look a little healthier. She smiled a little.

"No, it has nothing to do with her being naked—the reason I want the painting—and I'm not really upset, just…surprised. I can't really explain, Dave, but I just want to look at it and see if it has anything more to tell me."

I didn't think it was possible that she could have had a dream in the bathroom, but weird things had been happening since I first got the painting. Maybe I wasn't the only one susceptible to objects from Astrella's Antiques & Curio Shop.

"Who do you think the woman might be?"

"I'm not trying to be rude, Dave, but I can't talk about it yet."

What the hell had happened in my bathroom? And why would she need the painting? The questions died on my tongue at the pleading look on Barbara's face.

I went to the bathroom and picked the painting off the wall. It would leave a blank space, but it was possible that Melanie might object to it anyway.

I brought it out to Barbara who took the painting with trembling hands. Then I reached into my wallet and brought out the newspaper clipping. "This came with the painting," I told her, "but I don't know how they are connected."

She took the clipping and looked directly into my eyes.

"Thank you, Dave," she whispered. Then she left.

Melanie arrived on Monday morning around eleven. For two days my thoughts had circled around Barbara Browning's reaction to the painting, my dreams, the visit with Ed Chessari and what to do and say when Melanie arrived. It wasn't a casual visit and both of us knew it. There's a difference between shagging someone in the back of a car or at a party and actually planning for time together. None of my thoughts were easy ones and I was ramped up to a high state of jitters by the time the doorbell rang.

I took a breath and opened the door. Melanie stood on the step, a shy smile on her face and a pizza box in her hands.

"I brought snacks," she said.

"Then you may enter," I said in my best Darth Vader voice, trying to cover my nervousness.

Melanie walked into the living room. I took the pizza box from her and placed it on the breakfast bar. She gave a quick glance around and turned toward me, brown eyes questioning. I pulled her into my arms and felt the solid warmth of her arms around me. For a moment we stood there, just holding each other, as if we had finally arrived home after a long trip. In that moment, my nervousness melted away.

We pulled apart. Melanie reached up and pulled my willing face down for a kiss. With slow deliberation we moved into a dance of touching and kissing, stroking and caressing from the kitchen to the bedroom, shedding clothing and inhibitions along our route.

Hours later, we untangled ourselves from the sheets and looked around. I felt as if we were floating together on a gentle sea; the bed, our ship. Every time I looked at the sheet-rocked ceiling I expected to see puffy white clouds. Melanie cuddled into my side and I felt her smile against my skin. My own smile was too all encompassing to be only something my mouth did.

Melanie popped her head up. "I'm starved."

"I know where we can find some cold pizza," I offered.

The next thirty hours flew past in a whirl of lovemaking, food and lots of laughter. I don't remember what we laughed about, only that we did. Once, I spared a brief thought for Barbara Browning, hoping that her pipes were being peaceful and that she wouldn't need to return the painting or use my bathroom for a few more days, but I needn't have worried—my time with Melanie was uninterrupted.

Melanie left at five on Tuesday after a couple of thousand last, last, okay-this-is-really-the-last kisses. My cell phone rang as she drove out of the parking lot.

Chapter Sixteen

Jeremy takes a powder and the painting returns

"Have you heard from Jeremy lately?" my father's voice demanded. From Dad's peremptory tone it sounded like my little brother had gotten himself into trouble again, a frequent occurrence. I didn't know anything that could either save or incriminate him, so I spoke the truth.

"I got an email from him a week ago and I talked to him on Thanksgiving, but nothing since then. Why?"

"He's supposed to come home for Christmas in the next week or so. I emailed him last Friday to find out when he'd be coming in and he hasn't responded. He's not answering his cell phone. I called that dive where he lives," there was an aggrieved pause, "and his roommate, that Greek guy with the funky name, whatever it is, finally told me Jeremy had left for the United States on Saturday."

Even given the time difference and possible delays, Jeremy should have been in San Francisco by Monday, at the latest. It was now late Tuesday afternoon. The email I'd received a week ago contained a few pass along jokes and a sentence saying he'd see me at Christmas and warning me to be prepared to lose my ass at pool. There was nothing in it about when he was going to show up.

Christmas was still two weeks away, unusually early for Jeremy to come home. He arrived one or two days before the holiday, did his shopping on Christmas Eve and showed up on Christmas Day with a hangover and some bizarre gifts at whichever parent's house was hosting Christmas that year.

"Did you check on the flight?" I asked.

"I'm talking to you first," said my father. "Don't bullshit me—do you know where he is?"

Always the kind and gentle approach. Since my high school days, Dad's method was to fire questions at me, usually not listening to the answers, and to hold me responsible for Jeremy.

"I told you—I haven't heard from him in almost a week." My Melanie afterglow was fading fast, replaced by the truculence my father could inspire in me almost instantly.

"Don't take that tone with me. Call your mother and find out what she knows." The phone went silent.

I wasn't about to take his orders. Jeremy was probably hanging out with friends. Why was Dad so determined to find him anyway—he was twenty-three years old, for Pete's sake. Twenty-three and Dad was still paying his way, a nasty voice in my head piped up. Twenty-three and totally irresponsible and impulsive. Twenty-three, with a history of stupid stunts that I usually caught some sort of parental flack for, and generally had to rescue him from.

I brushed aside the thoughts. Maybe I'd call Mom a little later, after I caught up on my emails.

Five minutes later, I was on the phone to Mom, my email chores as unfinished as my thoughts.

"Dave! What's happened?" my mother's voice sounded worried.

"Nothing, what do you mean?"

Did she know something about Jeremy? Had Dad called her? My stomach took a dive.

"Well, you don't usually call," Mom said matter-of-factly, "so I thought something might have happened."

Mom isn't the guilt-trip type, but a couple of pounds of the stuff wrapped around my neck and made me hang my head. I was glad that she couldn't see me.

"Nothing exciting," I hedged. "Just wondered what your thoughts are about Christmas this year."

"Isn't this the year you guys are at your father's for Christmas?"

"Oh, yeah. I forgot. Do you remember when Jeremy was supposed to be coming home?"

I was congratulating myself on my subtlety when Mom said, "David, you know perfectly well that Jeremy never arrives before Christmas Eve. What's up?"

Damn that Mom Radar anyhow. I told her about Dad's call. She didn't seem worried.

"Sounds like Jeremy has overextended himself again and your father wants an explanation…"

"RIGHT NOW," we both said at the same time.

Mom laughed, "He probably snuck home and is hanging out at a friend's house until Christmas. And he's not answering his cell because he knows your father is P.O.ed."

That was my thought as well. Mom hadn't heard from Jeremy in a week and she was probably right about his predicament. It had happened before. We talked for a few minutes and then we hung up. I culled my brain for the names of Jeremy's friends.

The cell phone rang again.

"Your brother arrived in Los Angeles on Sunday," my father said, "according to the airlines. Who does he know in Los Angeles?"

It was on the tip of my tongue to say "I'm not my brother's keeper," but I refrained.

"Dad, he's a big boy. At least you know he's in the States. He'll call in a few days."

The tirade that followed had me holding my phone as far from my ear as my hand could get and ended when my father hung up on me before I could get a word in. I stomped around the condo for a few minutes, slamming cabinet doors and muttering curses before I realized that someone was knocking on the door.

I flung open the door, half expecting to see my recalcitrant brother on the doorstep. A startled Barbara Browning took a step back, hand still upraised. Her other hand held my painting.

"Uh… Dave, I brought your painting back," she said. "Is this a bad time?"

It was, but it wasn't. Anything that pulled me away from rehashing all the things I wished I'd said to my obnoxious father was a good thing. I took a breath and opened the door wider.

"No problem, Barbara. I'm just recovering from a phone call from my dad. He's a little annoyed with me."

I smiled and shrugged. She stepped through the doorway and handed me the painting.

"I know how that can be," she said. "I wouldn't disturb you, but I think I owe you an explanation and, actually, I really need to talk."

Every cell in my body screamed, "Run away!"—my usual response when a woman says she needs to talk, but I fought my instincts and stayed put. I even gestured towards the couch.

Barbara took a seat on the couch while I leaned the painting against a wall. The picture looked just the same—the girl was still naked in the turquoise water with the gray boulders looming over her.

I pulled up my office chair and waited. Barbara sat primly, looking like an L.L. Bean ad in her white pullover, blue fleece vest, jeans and brown loafers. She took a breath and said, "It must have seemed strange to you that I wanted to borrow the painting." She waited a beat, looking at me with a question in her round blue eyes. I gave a little shrug.

She looked down at her shoes. "Well, if you don't mind, I have to tell you a little bit about myself before I tell you why the painting was so important to me." Her gaze flickered up to my face and back to her shoes.

"When I was fifteen, my half-sister, Marla, disappeared. She was twelve years older than me, but we were close. We lived in Sacramento. Marla worked for the state as a secretary and had her own apartment over by Sac State. I spent a lot of time there, trying to elude my parents."

She shrugged her shoulders. "My dad and Marla didn't get along, but Mom thought she might be a good influence on me. Marla was a big health food and exercise nut and she was always trying to get me to run or bike with her."

Barbara looked up from her shoes and met my eyes. "My dad said Marla was a whore, but she was nothing like that. She hardly even dated. Once in a while, she'd be with a guy, but it wouldn't last. No one ever did. She was really pretty and smart, but sometimes you could see another side, a cold, secret side that was a little scary. She was always sweet to me and I loved her, but still, I could understand sometimes why guys might back away."

She glanced at the painting. "Marla was very independent. She biked and jogged down the trail near the college by herself all the time. In the 1970s, there were a series of disappearances and attacks along the trail and I was afraid for her, but Marla just laughed. My mom wanted her to get a roommate, but she didn't want one. She said she was safe.

"Mom saved the clippings from the newspaper every time there was an attack and she would show them to Marla, trying to get her to be more careful. Marla laughed about it, but those attacks, mostly on women, really creeped me out.

"Then, all of a sudden, Marla stopped going out, except for work. She stayed in her apartment all the time and she seemed tense to me. She wouldn't even go out to get groceries. I'd have to pick up food for her and Mom would take me over. She shrugged off our questions. After a few weeks, Marla told me that she was going on a two-week vacation to Mexico. I wanted to go with her and tried to talk her into waiting until school was out in June. Marla said it would be too hot then and she needed a break now.

"Marla left at the end of April." Barbara was back to looking at her shoes. "I never saw her again." Tears tracked slowly down her face and in the silence I heard one of them drop onto my leather couch.

Barbara produced a Kleenex from the pocket of her vest and went on with her story. The telltale hairs on the back of my neck, so often in action since the painting first came into my life, were standing at attention once more.

"Marla was always secretive so we didn't know exactly where she was going in Mexico or when she would be home, but, after two and a half weeks, my mom and I were pretty worried. My dad said that she was probably off with some man, but I didn't think so. Her office called, wanting to know if we had heard from her. My mom was hysterical.

"We talked to the police, of course, and they tracked Marla down to Mexico City through the airlines. But, Mexico City is huge. They lost her trail after that. Her rental car was found in a gully in the desert with most of the parts stripped off. I spent days searching her apartment for any clue about where she might have been headed, but like I said, Marla was always secretive.

"Mom wanted to go to Mexico to look for her, but Dad said it was a waste of money, that the police would handle it, and that she probably got what she deserved. I hated him for that."

I remembered the dream woman's thoughts in my head, the secret life she lived and the pride she took in never being suspected for being the killer she was. Now I was looking at the little sister who had loved her and who still missed a woman she didn't really know. I sat in my chair, transfixed, my heart pounding.

Barbara looked back at me. "They never found her. All through high school and college I kept waiting for Marla to show up. I looked for her at every event, even my wedding, years later. I knew that if she were alive, she would be there. But when she wasn't, I knew that she was really gone.

"Then, the other day, in your bathroom, I saw my sister for the first time in thirty years. In that." She nodded at the painting lying against the wall. "I knew, when I saw her back, even before you handed me the newspaper clipping. Because she spoke to me! I heard her voice…right there in your bathroom." Barbara held my eyes, pleading for understanding.

This might have been the point at which I suddenly remembered an urgent errand across town or maybe in Cleveland, but I knew how the painting could speak to someone. I took a breath to still my pounding heart, stayed in my chair and said, "Barbara, I believe you." And I did.

She didn't ask why, but the look in her eyes changed as if she'd received the right answer. "When I heard Marla call my name, I had to take that painting home. And now I know that she is the woman in the painting and she died in the grotto, looking for the light and the voices of the angels. And I know why."

Tears rolled down Barbara's face. "I don't want to believe what she told me, but I have to." Her face contorted and she wiped the tears from her cheeks even as more of them poured forth. After a moment she said, "She did some really bad things and, in that place, she received justice for them. In a weird way, I'm relieved—it's like the jagged and unfinished pieces in my life that were Marla have been smoothed into place."

I considered telling her about my dream, but it didn't sound like she needed my corroboration. Then too, if my neighbor realized that I knew exactly what her sister had done and how she felt about her actions, it might be more horrifying than helpful.

"It probably doesn't make any sense to you, Dave," Barbara smiled at me through her tears, "but the feeling of peace I have now is amazing. I loved my sister and I still love her no matter what she did. What happened to her in that grotto was something she wanted and needed." She looked down for a moment and whispered, "I just wish my mom could have known."

She stood up, still twisting a button on her sweater. "Thanks for sharing the painting, Dave…and for listening." She looked up at me, waiting for my response, her eyes red-rimmed but clear.

Barbara had taken a big chance, telling a relative stranger about her dead sister talking to her from a painting. I appreciated her courage, but I was thunderstruck that the woman from my dream had a real name and an actual family.

I came to myself and walked Barbara to the door. "You can keep the painting if you want it, Barbara," I said. Now that the woman in the painting had a name, I wasn't sure I wanted her in my bathroom any more.

"Can I take a rain check on that, Dave?" She gave me a rueful look. "I need to sift through this first. It feels like my life might move in a different direction now that my questions about Marla have been answered." I nodded, not really understanding what she meant, but willing to give her the time to figure it out.

After Barbara left, I sat on the couch and stared at the painting. Too many feelings in a too short a period of time—from euphoria with Melanie, anger at my father, concern about Jeremy—I didn't know what to feel about Barbara's story and the part the painting had played.

Chapter Seventeen

The prodigal son returns

Melanie called as soon as she arrived home that afternoon. We did a good job of recapturing some of the magic we'd shared during her visit, but I longed to touch her. As trite as it seemed, words just weren't enough. The phone call was long, filled with unfinished sentences, and when I hung up at last, all thoughts of Jeremy had vanished.

The next morning, my father called again.

"I'm going to LA to look for Jeremy. I've waited long enough. Start calling his friends. Call me if your mother hears from him."

I'd spent a mostly sleepless night, replaying Barbara's bizarre story. Dad's announcement frayed a few more nerves. The role of concerned parent was out of character for him. I was more familiar with the distant and dictatorial guy who emailed from his office. His transformation raised my level of concern about Jeremy to Henny Penny status and I started making calls.

By afternoon, phone calls and emails turned up empty and my stomach was clenched with worry. None of Jeremy's friends or even friends of friends knew where he might be. As I picked up the phone once more, it rang in my hand.

"Davy? Hello?"

"Mom, I was just about to call you."

"Your father called and said he was at LAX taking Jeremy's picture around to taxi drivers. He's already given a copy to the CHP. Dave, what's going on?"

This was bad—Dad hadn't called Mom directly in the five years since their divorce was final. Every communication between them was relayed through

Jeremy or me. My stomach tightened. I didn't even know he had her number. Dad's anxiety level must be off the charts if he actually called my mother and was accosting cabbies in LA.

"I don't know, Mom. He called me this morning to say he was going to LA and he wanted me to call Jeremy's friends. I did, but nobody knows where he is."

"Did you call Piper or Brendan?"

"Yeah, they started sort of a phone tree but so far, no one has heard from Jeremy. You called just as I was about to call you to find out if you'd heard from him yet."

"Last time he was home, he emailed a few people from my computer—I'll check with them. He's got me worried."

I knew which "he" she meant. Jeremy had been AWOL before, but it was Dad's reaction that was causing concern to mount.

"I'll check with Dad and call you if there's any news." I hung up and called my father, but his cell was busy and every time I called during the next two hours, the phone went to voice mail.

Unable to focus on work, I called Melanie. We made plans for our next time together, but I didn't share my concern about Jeremy—no sense in bringing up something that might not be a real problem.

Hearing Melanie's voice allowed my stomach to relax a bit, but as soon as I hung up I started feeling anxious again. I tried to catch up on some work without success. Then I switched to a Trailblazers game on TV, but found myself listening for a phone that wasn't ringing.

Thursday morning wasn't any better. I'd had less sleep and more time to imagine worst-case scenarios. At 11 a.m. the phone rang.

"The CHP found him," my father said. My heart suddenly filled my throat. "He's in Barstow Community Hospital. I'm on my way there now."

"How …" I managed to croak out the single word before Dad interrupted.

"I talked to the doctor on call. Jeremy is in fair condition with a broken leg, a concussion and a few broken ribs. He was a passenger in a car accident yesterday somewhere in the Mojave Desert. Barstow was the closest hospital." I heard him take a breath. "He wasn't conscious when they brought him in, didn't have any identification. They couldn't figure out who he was until this morning. He'll be there for another few days."

My heart moved back where it belonged, but it was beating erratically. "I'll call Mom," I managed.

"I already did." Another unprecedented event. "She wants to come down here to see him." Then, slowly, as if he were reluctant, Dad said, "Sandra's on her way too."

I spared a tiny bit of empathy for him. Current wife and ex-wife in the same small hospital room. No wonder he sounded reluctant.

"I'll make sure Mom gets there."

"Good. Barstow Community Hospital." He hung up.

Mom was calm when I called, having already decided we should drive. It would take longer, but not much longer than waiting for a puddle jumper at the Weed airport, flying to Sacramento, taking another flight to LAX, renting a car and driving to Barstow.

Hours later, I pulled into the driveway between the Alchemy Rock Shop and Mom's dark green bungalow. The red front door opened and Mom flew out. She hugged me as soon as I got out of the car and said, "I'm ready to go. Your father called again. Jeremy was awake and talking when he got to the hospital. His vitals look good."

My heart beat a little less raggedly at that news. Mom hugged me again as we walked to the door. While I stretched to work the kinks out of my back, she insisted on feeding me a snack—organic tomato soup and veggie chips. I survived the infusion of healthy food long enough to fit Mom's red bag into the trunk of my car, between my hastily packed duffle and the box with the blue vase. At the last minute I had put the vase in the trunk, planning to give it to Mom for Christmas after all. I knew she would love it, especially if it brought a dream.

We reached Barstow just after 9:30 Friday morning, made a pit stop at a McDonald's to clean up, and headed for the hospital. When we walked into Jeremy's room, the look of relief on my brother's face and my father's, was identical. Mom made a beeline for Jeremy, leaving me to greet my father and Sandra who were parked in chairs by the window. They stood up and Dad extended his hand to me across Jeremy's cast-covered leg. Sandra gave me the nervous smile she usually gives me, as if I'm a large dog with a reputation for chewing the furniture, but extended her hand as well. I gave Dad's hand a quick shake and took the boneless one that Sandra offered, pressing it once.

"So you finally got here," Dad rasped out. The hairs on the back of my neck bristled at his tone. He looked like crap, with bags under his eyes as if he hadn't slept in a week. He was wearing his version of casual attire—a sports coat over a button down shirt with no tie and a pair of pressed khakis—but the lines on his fifty-year old face showed up against his pale skin like crevasses on a snowy slope.

Sandra looked better, no surprise there, but tired. She was decked out in an orange jacket and black slacks with a gold cuff bracelet on one wrist and a big diamond studded watch on the other. She muttered something that sounded like, "more chairs" and scuttled past me out of the room.

If Dad looked pale, Jeremy was a kaleidoscope of color. Against the background of dark blue and purple bruises, dark red scratches, yellow antiseptic, and the bloodshot veins in his eyes, his blue eyes were almost colorless.

Jeremy managed a weak version of his "I don't believe I did this" grin. I smiled back, grateful to see that stupid grin, but too afraid to reach forward through the tubes and stuff taped to his arms to hug him. I gave him a gentle squeeze above the tape on the hand Mom was still holding.

"Looks like you've still got all your teeth buddy," I said.

Dad made a noise. When Jeremy turned his head toward him, I saw a bandage on the back of his head, startlingly white against his blonde hair. Sandra clumped back into the room on high heels, carrying a metal chair. I took it from her, said thanks, and waved her off from fetching another one. I scooted the chair behind Mom. She sank into it, not taking her eyes off Jeremy.

While we all stood or sat around staring awkwardly at Jeremy, a doctor and a nurse came into the room. Jeremy had one half of the room and no roommate at the moment, but it was very crowded with the two of them standing at the foot of his bed. Between the sight of my little brother hooked up to monitors and the crowd in the room, it suddenly felt as if there wasn't enough space for me to breathe. I wanted to stay and find out what the doctor could tell us, but when he touched the bandage on Jeremy's head, I started to see little black things before my eyes. I mumbled something about finding coffee and left the room. Mom could fill me in later.

Out in the corridor I tried to call Melanie on my cell, but had no reception. A nurse in purple scrubs with pink flamingos on them gave me directions to the cafeteria. After a few missteps that detoured me to Radiology, I walked into the cafeteria and located the coffee urns. I wasn't in any hurry to get back to Jeremy's room. I bought a Coke and sat down at a small table by the window. In front of the window there were enough bars on my cell phone for reception, so I called Melanie again. Her cheery voice mail came on—I'd forgotten she was mid-shift at Betsy's. I left a message telling her I was in Barstow with my family and I'd tell her all about it when we talked.

As I snapped the phone shut, an elderly gentleman at the table nearest me asked, "How well do those things work in here?"

"Works okay near the window here, not good at all in the corridors," I told him.

There was a cup of coffee beside him along with the remains of a pastry on a plate. "They make good cinnamon rolls here," he said, "It's the only perk about eating in the cafeteria—damn good cinnamon rolls."

He introduced himself as Bob Kerwin, retired engineer with a wife, Edie, who was recovering from gall bladder surgery.

"She was supposed to go home after two days, but there were some complications. It's giving me a chance to store up on the cinnamon rolls because I think they might be on the forbidden list when Edie gets home. Might have to load up on Kentucky Fried and some Del Taco too. No telling how healthy I'm going to have to start eating." He grinned. "What brings you here?"

The guy was a talker, but seemed harmless.

"My brother was in a car accident. He has a broken leg, some busted ribs and a concussion."

"I'm sorry about your brother. Are you from around here?"

I told him where we were from and Kerwin nodded as though he'd suspected we were out-of-towners. He said, "We're from Iowa originally, but Edie and I moved here in 1949 when I got taken on as an engineer for the Santa Fe Railroad. They used to have a pretty fancy depot here, did you know that? Now we're known for the world's biggest thermometer. Edie and I had a little ranch off I-15, but we sold it a couple of years ago. Moved into a mobile home park because Edie likes having neighbors—especially since our daughters and grandchildren are scattered around LA and San Diego."

I finished the Coke and began plotting an escape.

"You look about the age my son was when he died. He was only twenty-seven."

Kerwin looked down and moved the pastry remains around a little with his fork. "You know, I always did things by the book—rode out WWII in a destroyer escort, had a couple of years of college on the G-I Bill, got a job and then got married. I had a family and a mortgage by the time I was thirty—the steady type, you know." He shook his head. "Dale bounced in and out of college; didn't seem to know what he wanted to do. He always had something new going on—taking pictures, roaming the world, going to strange places. I tried to make him stay in one place and get a real job, but he just couldn't stay put." Kerwin paused to take a sip of coffee. "He was killed in a motorcycle accident up near Point Mugu. I had to go up and identify the body…"

I drifted off a bit while he was talking, thinking about Astrella's. In the excitement of Melanie's visit and the drama of Jeremy's accident, my dreams had taken a step back. Now that I knew Derry and the woman from the painting were real, I wanted to know more. During Kerwin's monologue, I had a sudden, clear vision of a silver jar gleaming dully on the dark shelf behind the counter in Astrella's. Before I could do more than register the vision, the metallic clang of silverware dropping on the floor brought me back to hear Bob Kerwin's last few words: "It was a long, long time ago. I wish I'd known what he wanted. I miss that boy every day."

Sadness lingered in his eyes. Then he smiled and said, "Well, I've bent your ear long enough. Edie's going to be wondering where I am so she can kick my butt in Scrabble again."

He stood, back curved like a question mark, and picked up his tray. I stood and he held out a hand for me to shake.

"Bob Kerwin. Desert Oaks Mobile Home Park. If you or your family need anything while you're here, you let me know." Then he shuffled off to drop off his tableware, greeting a doctor and teasing a pretty nurse along his way. The silver jar in Astrella's flashed into my mind again as I watched him leave—I couldn't imagine why.

When I got back to Jeremy's room carrying three coffees, Mom, Dad and Sandra were standing stiffly with folded arms outside the door.

"They took Jeremy down for some tests," Dad informed me. "He'll be back in a little while. What do you say we find somewhere close and talk?"

It should have been a question, but it wasn't. Mom told me the doctor's assessment as we followed the nursing staff's directions to a vacant waiting room. "He has a fractured right leg, a concussion and two broken ribs, but Dr. Singh says he should make a full recovery with no complications," said Mom. The relief I felt almost caused me to drop the coffees.

The tiny room had an L-shaped couch and a matching chair. Magazines, at least a year old, filled a rack on the wall. Mom took the chair, Dad and Sandra took the couch and I leaned up against the wall. No one wanted the coffee, so I tossed it into the wastebasket next to an end table.

"When they release Jeremy, we're flying him home with us," announced Dad. "He can recuperate in his old room at the house."

Mom blinked once. "He might need help at first. If you and Sandra are both at work, will there be anyone around if he does? If he came home with me, the rock shop is next door and I'm right there."

"He's coming home with us," said Dad. "He'll be fine."

Mom said nothing, but she gave him the same look she'd given me when I had a temperature of 104 and insisted I was going to Steve's last high school football game—as if she couldn't believe that anyone that stupid had managed to live this long. Dad looked back, chin jutting out.

Sandra ventured, "I guess I could stay home…"

Mom broke the stare long enough to give Sandra a brief dismissive smile before she returned to giving Dad the treatment.

Dad's chin went down. He shot a look at the door. Then he said, "I can work from home for a few days. I'll see to Jeremy if he needs it."

Mom nodded once. After a minute of awkward silence, Dad announced he and Sandra were going out and would be back in an hour.

We hung around the nurse's station until Jeremy was returned to his bed. We took up positions on either side of him. The orderly dropped off a lunch tray with a turkey sandwich, vegetable soup, a fruit cup and some packaged cookies. I realized I was starved when I found myself eyeing the fruit cup.

While Jeremy picked at his lunch, Mom and I tried to liven up the atmosphere with jokes about the accommodations.

Jeremy joked with us for a few minutes, but I could tell his heart wasn't in it. He pushed the tray with its uneaten food away.

"Mom, can you find out how Carol is?" Jeremy's voice sounded worried. "She's the girl I was in the accident with. Dad said she was in ICU, but that doesn't tell me anything."

I hid my surprise. It was the first I'd heard of a girl being involved, except that Dad said Jeremy had been a passenger in a car accident. The look of concern on Jeremy's face was a surprise too—he never admitted to any kind of worry. "Whatever" was his mantra. I'd sometimes envied his laid back approach to life. No one would ever call him "Henny Penny."

Mom squeezed his hand and gave him a smile. "I'll go check now," she said.

He closed his eyes. "Her last name is Peneman, Mom."

After she left the room, I asked, "So who is Carol?"

Jeremy opened his eyes and said, "We met in Crete while she and some friends were there on vacation and we kept in touch. She's a geology major at UC Irvine and knows all about this area. It's got some amazing rock formations. We decided to hook up when I came home."

"Since when are you interested in rocks, little bro?"

He closed his eyes again and gave a faint smile. "Since Carol started explaining about them in person."

"Did she pick you up from the airport?" He nodded. "Then what happened?"

Jeremy opened his eyes and squinted at me. "When did Dad come back into the room?"

I chuckled at his attempt at sarcasm. "Just curious, that's all. I'm a little fuzzy on how you ended up in the Mojave Desert. I've heard of wrong turns, but LAX to Barstow is kind of a doozy."

He relaxed back against his pillows. "Like I said, Carol knows about the desert. It sounded cool to spend a few days camping out in the middle of nowhere together. So we dropped off my stuff at her place in Irvine and the next morning we headed for Needles and the Rainbow Basin. She had the Jeep packed with food, a tent and blankets—everything we'd need. It was cold at night but we had a blast, hiking in Owl Canyon, off-roading it, exploring, sharing a little ouzo. Then it got super cold and we decided to come home Wednesday morning."

Jeremy licked his lips. I handed him a cup of water from his tray and he drank most of it before continuing.

"We left the campground around eight that morning and Carol was jamming along the dirt road, kicking up dust. We didn't see this big tortoise in the middle of the road until we were almost on top of it. She swerved and we flew off the road and down an embankment. Then I woke up here."

Against the backdrop of purple and blue bruises, a single crystal tear made a slow path down his cheek. "I feel so bad—she was the one wearing her seat belt and now she's…"

I squeezed his arm gently. "It's okay. Mom will find out what's going on. If you're going to be okay, then so is Carol. She'll be fine."

I hoped my words were true.

Chapter Eighteen

Wheelchairs and magic beads; Jeremy takes a turn for the better

I was telling Jeremy about hiking up Tinker's Ridge, leaving out the part about Derry the Tinker, when Mom came into the room behind an orderly who removed the tray. Mom laid a hand on Jeremy's arm.

"I met Carol's parents outside the ICU," she said. "She's still there with head trauma from when the Jeep rolled. Her chest was compressed by the steering wheel or the air bag or something like that, too. Her mother, Iris, said she's wakened up a few times on her own and she responded to them, so those are good signs."

Mom nodded at Jeremy who relaxed back against his pillows. "Her doctors are already talking about moving her out of ICU and into a regular room in the next day or so if she keeps making progress." She stopped for a second and then continued, "The Penemans are the nicest people. But they didn't know you existed until the doctor asked them if they knew the name of the passenger in Carol's car."

Mom cocked an eyebrow at Jeremy who closed his eyes. I couldn't blame him. For a woman with an open mind and an easygoing manner, Sioux-san has definite opinions about wearing seatbelts and communicating with family members.

"When they let you get up and move around, you can probably go down to see her," she said, relenting.

Jeremy nodded and said, "Thanks, Mom."

She peered at his face, then caught my eye and shrugged.

Dad walked in, minus Sandra. Jeremy kept his eyes closed as if he wanted to sleep. I suggested to Mom that we check into a motel. To my surprise, Dad glanced over at Jeremy and nodded agreement. I leaned over and gave my brother an arm squeeze.

"We'll be back in a while to watch you slurp down your Jell-O, bro."

Jeremy nodded slightly, eyes still closed, but his hand caught my arm and squeezed back.

Dad walked with us out of the hospital and into the parking lot. While Mom continued on to our car, I hung back with my father.

"Dad, Jeremy's gone off on little trips like this before. Why were you so concerned this time?"

My father looked toward the rows of cars. I wasn't sure he would answer me, but I persisted. "You know, you called to tell me that you were going to LA around 8 a.m. Jeremy said that's when the accident happened."

Dad stopped his inspection of the cars and looked directly into my eyes. He said, "I know." Then he walked off toward his rental car.

Over a late lunch, Mom and I talked about Jeremy's accident and our next steps.

"Dr. Singh wants him to get up and move around," said Mom. "Then he can go home in the next day or two. I'd like to make sure he gets settled in Burlingame before we go home. Are you okay with that?"

It meant pushing back some work I needed to get done, but knowing Jeremy was safe was definitely worth it. "No worries."

We found two rooms at the Barstow Motel. I fell across the polyester comforter on the bed as soon as I came into the room, sleeping in my clothes, too tired to give Dad's "I know" more than a passing thought.

Mom called a few hours later. After I had a quick shower, we took off for the hospital. While I'd slept, she had been meditating and doing yoga. She looked a lot more rested than I felt.

I picked up a 3x3 burger off the secret menu at an In-N-Out Burger for Jeremy. When we got to his room, the physical therapist was helping him back into bed. Dad stood white-faced in the corner. Sandra stood close to Dad, holding his hand. It looked as if watching Jeremy maneuver in and out of bed had been almost as painful for Dad as it had been for my brother. It was a side of my father I hadn't seen for a long time.

Dr. Singh came into the room and checked Jeremy over. "We will try again tomorrow morning. You need to be ambulatory before we can release you." If Jeremy could maneuver, Dr. Singh was willing to release him on Sunday.

We stayed until Jeremy fell asleep and then headed back to the motel, after a stop at Del Taco. Mom looked exhausted and hugged me hard before turning in with her bean and cheese burrito. I called Melanie the minute I got inside my room. Hearing her voice was like seeing the sun after a rainstorm.

"Are you okay?" she asked, concern in her voice. I told her I was, even though seeing my little brother in a hospital and wondering if my father had psychic abilities had left me feeling off balance. I told her about Jeremy's condition and Carol being in ICU.

"It sounds like Jeremy was pretty lucky," she said, "and the docs are probably watching to see if there's any swelling in Carol's brain. That's one of the major complications of a head injury."

Apparently some of the family medical knowledge had rubbed off.

"So, what happens next?" she asked.

"We'll be hanging out with Jeremy until the doctor releases him, probably on Sunday. Then Dad and Sandra will drive him to the Ontario airport to fly him up to Burlingame. Mom and I will follow them up in the car."

"Then you'll be at your dad's house on Monday?"

"Yes, but I'm not sure when we'll be coming home."

"Think you can stop by here on your way back to Portland, Cowboy?"

"Absolutely. Neither snow, nor rain, nor heat, nor gloom of night will stay me from showing up on your doorstep."

She giggled. "Okay, Mr. Postman. I'll be waiting…with something from off the menu."

On Saturday, I watched with my hands tucked securely into my armpits as Jeremy wrestled himself into a wheelchair. Then we set off for the ICU, with me pushing. He'd already called once that morning to check on Carol, but told me he needed to see her for himself.

Outside the ICU, Mom had her arm around a blond woman whose red eyes and nose testified to recent tears. I slowed the wheelchair, but Mom motioned us forward.

"Iris, these are my sons David and Jeremy," said Mom. The woman looked over at us, focusing on Jeremy. He wheeled himself closer and put out his hand. She took it after a slight hesitation.

"I'm really sorry about Carol, Mrs. Peneman," Jeremy said. "When I called this morning, they said she'd had a good night. How is she?"

Before she could answer, the door to the ICU opened and a tired looking middle-aged man wearing a University of Michigan sweatshirt came out. He made straight for Iris Peneman. "Honey, she's awake."

Mrs. Peneman hugged her husband and introduced us to him. Dick Peneman gave Jeremy an appraising look—the one guaranteed to make most young guys think twice about dating their daughters. Mrs. Peneman hugged my mom and pressed the intercom to request entrance to ICU. As the doors slowly swung open, she turned back to Jeremy. "Would you like to come in with me? They only allow one at a time, but I think they'll make an exception." She waited.

"That would be great." He wheeled himself toward the open doors, but Mrs. Peneman came around behind him to push. Together, they went inside and the doors closed.

Mr. Peneman shook my mom's hand, murmured something about coffee and left. While Mom and I waited for Jeremy, I caught sight of Bob Kerwin, my talkative friend from the cafeteria, at the end of the hall. He was pushing a silver-haired woman in a wheelchair toward the hospital lobby. He noticed me and raised his hand in a thumb-up sign. I returned it with a smile. A little parade of women and teenagers bearing vases of flowers and stuffed animals followed behind.

The ICU doors opened and Jeremy wheeled himself out alone. His face was grim, but he gave us a small smile before propelling himself silently down the hall. We had to run to catch up.

Jeremy was determined to leave the hospital and while he practiced getting in and out of the wheelchair and became adept at speeding down the corridors, the rest of us practiced being in the same space. It was the longest amount of time my divorced family had spent together in five years and it brought up a complex stew of unfamiliar emotions in my gut.

I felt raw inside as if the dam I'd walled against my feelings had been breached and I was being flooded with feeling. It occurred to me that I'd been experiencing some of this before Jeremy's accident—since I met Melanie. No, since the dreams. I wasn't used to feeling so much, so often. Had the dreams done this?

Jeremy seemed different, too. I'd never seen him so concerned about someone, the way he was about Carol. His uncharacteristic silence made me think that he might be doing some reflection. When we were taking a lap around the nurse's station, I let him know that Dad would be available to him 24/7 once they got to Burlingame.

Jeremy rolled his eyes. "That's the best incentive I could have for healing." He glanced over at me walking by his side and shook his head. "Sorry, that sounds pretty rude. I'm trying to grow up a little. I really appreciate all of you showing up and being here for me—even Sandra." He gave a wry smile. "But Dad, 24/7, might just push me over the edge."

I thought of our father watching Jeremy being helped into bed, of the sound of his voice when he called to tell me he was going to LA before the rest of us knew that Jeremy was in trouble.

"You know, bro, he was really worried about you. At first I thought it was because maybe you'd done something flaky again." Jeremy winced in pretended discomfort at my words. "But this has hit him hard. He couldn't even watch when you first got into the wheelchair."

He was quiet for a minute. "Yeah, okay. I'll try to roll with it. But if all this parental supervision gets to be too much, can I come to Portland?"

"I'll rescue you in my trusty Saturn."

He groaned. "Oh man, that would be embarrassing," and propelled himself away.

Dr. Singh gave orders for Jeremy's release on Sunday morning. Dad made all the flight arrangements and sent Sandra on ahead to Burlingame. Mom covered Jeremy's emotional bases by keeping in contact with the Penemans. Her report that Carol was awake and responsive and scheduled to be moved out of ICU Sunday afternoon brought a relieved smile to his face.

Carol's older brother was in Irvine, planning to drive his van down to pick her up when she was released. Mrs. Peneman told Mom that he'd let us into Carol's apartment if we wanted to pick up Jeremy's things.

On Sunday, we got to the hospital early. Jeremy wanted to see Carol again before he was released. This time, Mr. Peneman took him in. Either Jeremy's obvious concern for Carol won him over or he just wanted to make sure he knew what they were saying to each other. Jeremy didn't enlighten us when he came back to the room, but the worry in his eyes was almost gone.

As Mom, Dad and I accompanied Jeremy in his wheelchair out of the hospital, I reflected on how strange it felt for the four of us to be together again—almost as if the past five years had had never happened.

We placed Jeremy carefully in the front seat of Dad's rental, reclined so far that it might as well have been the back seat. Once he was ensconced inside, and Mom had tucked pillows and blankets around him, he said, "I gotta pee…"

The three of us must have sported the same horror-struck look because he started laughing. "Just kidding."

Mom smacked him gently on the shoulder and then pulled a tiny pair of scissors and a bracelet made of black, red and gold beads out of her purse. She snipped off Jeremy's hospital identification bracelet and put the bead bracelet on his arm.

"Obsidian, carnelian and amber. Amber guards against infection and pain; carnelian is good for wounds and obsidian helps bones heal and enables the wearer to surrender negative habits and pathways." Mom looked into Jeremy's eyes and said, "I gave Iris a fluorite, amethyst and chrysoprase bracelet for Carol to speed healing and protect her from negativity." She kissed him and tucked the pillows in more securely.

Jeremy squeezed her hand and whispered, "Thanks." Then he grinned. "At least I'll get to sit in the front of the plane this time." It was beginning to look like his own grin again.

Jeremy and I exchanged the series of complicated handshakes we'd developed through the years—our own fraternal code for all the mushy stuff neither one of us could say. Then I walked around to Dad's side of the car as Mom gently closed Jeremy's door.

Dad was belted in, looking impatient to be off, but when I looked inside his open window and said, "We're going to pick up Jeremy's stuff at Carol's place and we'll follow you up," he turned and extended his hand out the window.

He gave my hand a warm squeeze and said, "Thanks for coming down. You're a good brother." His voice was husky. "Plan on staying a few days." It could have been a command, but this time it wasn't. "We can have an early Christmas."

An early Christmas in the old family home with both parents and my step-mother didn't appeal to me, but I nodded. We'd be there.

Chapter Nineteen

On the road again and into strange country

Mom and I met up with Carol Peneman's older brother, Hugh, at Carol's apartment in Irvine. We scurried inside and located Jeremy's stuff in a heap on the floor in Carol's bedroom. I tried not to blush as I pulled his things from the trail of entwined clothing leading from the door to the bed, but Mom blithely made sure his wallet and passport were in the duffel bag we stowed in the back of my car.

Once we were out of LA and onto I-5, the spine of California, traffic became uneventful and we settled into the long drive. It was four p.m. and already getting dark. We'd agreed to share the driving again, trying to drive straight through to Burlingame. Mom was going to stay with friends there, but I would be going on to Dad's.

As the dark settled down upon us, Mom was quiet, thinking perhaps, or maybe snoozing. My thoughts drifted and then focused on what was really bothering me: the niggling memory I'd had since the dreams began and Dad's "I know"–two words that packed a powerful punch in my memory. For the first time in many years, I allowed myself to remember the first time that I "knew" something.

I was eight and on an antique hunt with my grandparents. GPop and I had been cruising the perimeter of the "His Junk and Her Treasures" store while GMa checked out the contents of a glass-topped case that held jewelry, watches, spectacles, lighters and a bunch of other small, fragile objects. She was looking for sugar tongs, most likely, or maybe a brooch to add to her collection.

GMa wore brooches on her hats, sweaters and blouses. She even sported a pair of matching brooches on the tops of her Keds.

"Her" side of the store had a lot of china and Depression-era glass. "His" side was a hodgepodge of stuffed wildlife, farming and automotive tools, porcelain advertising signs, jugs and crockery bottles. Her side was relatively dust-free; His was awash in rust and dust. It was safer to hang out on the His side since there was less to break.

As we shuffled past a pile of rusted metal toolboxes and old tackle boxes, GPop made a sudden stop and reached into the heap. He pulled out a teardrop-shaped lead weight the size of an egg and dropped it into my hand, saying, "So, Davy. What's the story on this one? Tell me the first thing that comes to your mind."

I wasn't prepared for the weight's heaviness. My hand dipped down to the ground, almost dropping the thing, before I adjusted for it.

"Heavy," I said.

"Yes, it's heavy," said GPop. "But tell me what it makes you think about." He peered into my face as if I were going to be sick. "Close your eyes if it helps you think."

I closed my eyes, feeling a little silly, standing there holding a fishing weight. I wasn't sure what he wanted, so I decided to play our story game. I opened my mouth to say "A big whale swallowed this weight…" but what came out was, "A man is looking for this weight…."

I opened my eyes in surprise and GPop was looking at me, nodding. He raised his bushy eyebrows, encouraging me to continue. I had no idea what would happen next, so I closed my eyes again and heard myself say, "It was the one he always used when he went bottom fishing with his cousin, Pete. Pete's in 'Nam and he's afraid."

"Who's afraid?" I heard GPop ask.

I remember the weight in my hand feeling warm and flexible like a living thing instead of a lump of lead. "The man's afraid because Pete got hurt there and now it's the man's turn to go to 'Nam." I opened my eyes.

The heavy weight dropped out of my hand and clunked on the linoleum-covered floor. I shot a look toward the front of the store where GMa was talking to the owner of Her side. GPop dived after the weight. The shopkeeper glared in our direction, but GPop held it up with an ingratiating smile. GMa frowned and GPop gave me a tiny push. We edged toward the door, GPop stopping to put the weight on the counter next to GMa along with some money. Outside in the May sunshine, we stood on the sidewalk.

"Where's 'Nam?" I asked GPop.

He fished in his pants pocket and pulled out a pack of watermelon BubbleYum, our new favorite. While he tore open the package and pulled out two cubes of gum, he said, "It's a place called Vietnam and it's near China."

"Is it hot?"

"I've heard it can be," he said handing me the gum.

I took off the wrapper and GPop held out his hand for it. We put the gum in our mouths, savoring that first bite into the cube, the one with the flavor burst that made all the juices in your mouth flow like Niagara. "I felt hot when I was holding it."

"You did well, Davy."

The shop door opened, GMa emerged, and we took off in their Corvair.

After that, GPop would often hand me little objects and ask me to tell him what I saw or felt when I held them. Sometimes I didn't feel much; other times there was a whole story. With practice, I got better at being quiet enough inside that I could see the story unfold. That was the good memory. The other happened four years later.

I came home from baseball practice one afternoon and, after grabbing a glass of milk and the partial bag of Cheetos I'd squirreled away in the pantry, I headed for the living room. Jeremy was sitting on the floor, watching a *Dukes of Hazzard* rerun and rolling a black eight-ball along the hardwood floor. It made a lot of noise.

"Where'd you get that?" I asked.

"Found it," he said, holding out his hand for some Cheetos.

I ate a few more orange curls and then shook two out into Jeremy's upraised palm. I held out my hand for the ball. He turned it toward me but kept it just out of my reach.

"Let me see it."

"Give me the Cheetos first."

I handed him the bag with one hand and snapped my fingers with the other, palm held out for the ball.

"You gotta give it back," he warned, handing the ball over.

"Don't eat 'em all, pig," I warned back.

The black billiard ball had been bored out to use as a gearshift knob, which was why it didn't roll smoothly. I'd seen knobs like this before, only they weren't real eight balls; they were gearshift knobs made to look like eight balls. This was the real thing and it was pretty cool. After swiping my hands across my shirt to get rid of the Cheetos dust, I rolled the ball around in my palms. It was heavy and solid. I hefted it in one hand and concentrated the way I did with GPop.

Jeremy waited. He was used to this. The sounds of Cheetos crunching faded away and I said, "The guy that made this has an old blue VW—a slug bug. He's not cool, but the bug makes him feel cool, especially when he's wearing the new shirt his girlfriend bought him. He's getting out of this place to go to California and be a disc jockey."

The ball was snatched from my hands. My father, his face red as my baseball shirt, stood over me with the eight ball clenched in one fist.

"Where did you get this?"

I stared back at him, my mind still with the guy tooling around in the Volkswagen.

"I asked you a question, David. Where did you get this?" Dad's Don't Mess With Me tone of voice, the one that meant we'd stepped over the line. I looked over at Jeremy whose face was hidden behind the bag of Cheetos.

"I found it."

"You went through my closet, didn't you? Who have you been talking to?" He was seriously angry and if I survived, Jeremy was going to pay for this.

"No one, I haven't been talking to anyone. Sometimes I just…know stuff."

"Then stop…just 'knowing' stuff," he mimicked me. "Stop it right now. I don't want you to ever try to 'know' again or even pretend to 'know.' It's not normal. My son is not going to be a freak. No more of this, do you understand me?" His eyes bored into me, their intensity frightening. I nodded.

"And," he whirled back to my brother hiding behind the Cheetos bag, "you stay out of my closet and put that rock in your pocket back on your mother's desk. You hear me?"

We both nodded and Dad left the room as suddenly as he had entered, the eight ball tucked into his hand.

After a moment when we could be sure he wasn't going to reappear, Jeremy pulled Mom's hunk of obsidian out of his pocket and looked at it. Then he held up the bag. "Want some Cheetos?"

Dad's saying that "knowing" made me a freak kept me awake at night, especially those nights when he worked late and I could tell Mom was upset. It became one of a thousand things I held against my dad, along with his focus on work and away from us; the look in Mom's eyes when he called and said he wouldn't be home for dinner again; the way we never went fishing or did anything with him anymore; the way he was always impatient and angry with Jeremy and me; the arguments I could overhear from my parents' bedroom.

Was I a freak? With GPop, "knowing things" was just something fun to do; something I was good at. But Dad made it seem bad—something not normal.

When Steve, Jeremy and I played Indiana Jones, I hadn't been making up stories about the objects we found in GPop's yard; I'd been telling them the impressions I received from the objects. They thought they were stories and I never thought it was important to tell them otherwise.

Reeling from Dad's reaction, I looked back at times at school where I'd gotten impressions and shared them, once with disastrous results. I didn't do it anymore at school and we were getting too old to play Indiana Jones, but I had felt comfortable in my own home—until Dad said I was a freak.

After that, I stopped trying to receive impressions from things unless I was around GPop and even then, it began to seem like a silly game, one that nobody else played. GPop didn't make a big deal out of my growing reluctance to make up stories or receive impressions. Sometimes I said I was tired and he seemed to understand and didn't push. We started spending more time going to the movies or exploring in San Francisco instead of antiquing. And then, suddenly, GPop and GMa were gone, killed in a pile-up on a foggy morning.

The puzzle pieces I'd stuffed into a dark place in my memory started to assemble a new shape. Dad had known about Jeremy before the accident happened; he'd known it was Jeremy, not me, who had found the eight ball. He knew that Mom's obsidian was in Jeremy's pocket.

Maybe some of those many times when Dad seemed to be the smartest man in the whole world were times he had "known" things. Maybe the look I'd seen in his eyes when I was twelve had been more fear than anger—fear that came from realizing that he'd passed along something to me that he'd been hiding all his life.

This new thought took my breath away. Driving the dark road, I culled my memories, looking for evidence and pulling out instance after instance when Dad had seemed to know things that he couldn't have known. Like the time I'd fallen out of a tree in Tommy Burke's back yard and fractured my elbow. By the time I stood up, cradling my elbow and trying not to cry in front of Tommy and his mean older brother, James, Dad was at the backyard gate. He hustled me out to the car and sped to the hospital. Tommy's parents weren't home and none of us had called him. He was just there.

It was possible there was more to the distance between my father and his sons than his preoccupation with a job. Perhaps the wall had been created by a secret.

Mom's voice broke into my thoughts. "How about a bathroom break?"

Startled, I looked at the clock on my dashboard radio. It had been almost two hours since we'd spoken and now we were in the middle of nowhere on I-5.

"Okay. Do you need me to find someplace right now or can you wait for a town?"

"I can wait," she assured me. "You looked like you were far, far away."

"Just thinking."

"Me too. Road trips are good for that," she looked at me and smiled.

We were silent for a minute and then I said, "Mom, Dad knew about Jeremy's accident before it happened—he told me. Did he ever do that before? Know about things, I mean?"

She shot me a quick look before fixing her eyes on the dark road ahead. "People often get precognitive flashes about their loved ones."

"I didn't. You didn't. Just Dad. I think I remember him having those kinds of flashes a number of times when we were growing up. Is Dad, like, psychic or something?" I was putting it badly, but, suddenly, it was important for me to know.

"Why are you asking about this? Does this have something to do with those dreams you had?

"Yes. No. Well, it might," I hedged. I had been thinking more in terms of Dad's possible psychic ability being the reason for my own long ago aptitude, but maybe there was a connection to the dreams. One thing at a time.

"Dave, if you want to know about your father, then he's the best person to ask." She turned her head toward the window and snuggled into the seat as if she were going to take a nap.

I couldn't believe she was blowing me off. Mom was the most straight-up person I knew. She'd answer you with the truth even if it wasn't in her best interest to do so—like the time I asked her if she'd ever smoked pot.

A road sign showed Kettleman City sixteen miles away. I pointed to it silently. Mom nodded and after a few moments she turned to me.

"Look honey, it's not my story to tell—if there's any story at all," she said. "Talk to your dad. You don't do enough of that, anyway."

I rolled my eyes.

"Okay, okay, he's a little tough to talk to, but, you know, I think he's changing."

I shot her a look out of the corners of my eyes.

"He called me himself instead of getting you to do it and that's a huge step," she said. "And I noticed at the hospital he seemed less armored, more vulnerable. Maybe Sandra has something to do with that—I think he's happy with her."

Her words swizzled around inside my head. It sounded as if she was relieved, not upset. Her next words confirmed it.

"Thank God for Sandra because otherwise I'd be worrying about your dad as much as I worry about you and Jeremy."

At the trembly tone of her voice my head swiveled towards her. "Mom, we're…"

She wasn't finished. "Neither one of you is close to your dad anymore; Jeremy is a perennial party boy and, although you're responsible and a great guy, I think you're drifting."

Sioux-san was a great shot when she decided to take aim. Her thoughts about Sandra as Dad's savior instead of as her own replacement were a shock, but I hadn't realized how much she fretted over Jeremy and me. I tried to reassure her.

"Mom, I think Jeremy might be changing. The accident made him think. Didn't you see how determined he was in the hospital?"

She nodded.

"Look, I'll try to talk to Dad, even though I'm not sure he's as open as you think. And I'm not just drifting…I met someone."

Mom sat up straight and turned to me. I could see her raised eyebrows in the dash light. The exit for Kettleman City came up and as I swung into it, she said with a touch of impatience, "Well?"

I decided to make her sweat a little, in payback for not telling me about Dad. Just a little.

"Let's find that bathroom and get something to eat." I drawled. "Maybe I'll tell you over dinner."

Chapter Twenty

Change is good?

It was over chicken-fried steak at Mike's Roadhouse Cafe that I realized I loved Melanie. As I described her to Mom—her sense of humor, her plans for the future, the way she cared about the people she worked with at the diner, her family and her roommates, I felt her presence next to me. I stopped in mid-sentence, suddenly overwhelmed with a warm and unfamiliar joy, wanting her there, with me, always.

Mom was listening attentively, eating her garden salad and garlic bread and watching my face. She smiled and her eyes filled as she put her hand on mine, resting on the table. "I'm glad, Davy. She sounds wonderful. Do I get to meet her soon?"

I did want Mom to meet Melanie—I wanted everyone to meet her. I wanted to fly over the miles between us and swoop her up, wrap myself around her. I wanted to hear her voice and see her smile. Suddenly I missed her with all my being.

Mom picked up the check. "I'll settle up here. Meet you at the car."

I didn't protest. I had a call to make.

Outside, I waited for Melanie to answer her phone. My cautious, non-committal self disappeared as soon as I heard, "Hey Cowboy."

"I miss you," I blurted.

There was an intake of breath and then, "I miss you too."

Just a few words from both of us, but it felt like a lot of other things were being said. I told her I'd call tomorrow and be there as soon as I could. It was enough.

I dropped Mom off in San Mateo around midnight and made it to our old house in Burlingame just after one in the morning. Dad greeted me at the front door as I was fumbling for my key. He still looked tired, but better than he had in the hospital.

He walked me upstairs to my old room. Jeremy was bunking in the den downstairs.

When Mom moved out, Dad left the house pretty much the way it had been—he was always at work anyway. But, after he and Sandra married three years ago, he had Jeremy and I pack up our rooms. At that time, we had nowhere to put our boxes of kid paraphernalia since Jeremy was living in a dorm and I was still sharing an apartment with Nate and Patrick. The boxes had gone to the garage where they had been ever since. Our old rooms were bare except for beds and a dresser, but it was understood that, one day, even that would change. I didn't know how Jeremy felt about it, but I didn't care. At least, I didn't think I cared until Dad turned on the light in my bedroom and the light reflecting off the now butter-yellow walls almost blinded me.

Dad seemed a little surprised himself. Possibly he'd forgotten the paint job. In any case, after the initial blinding, he set down my duffle bag and said, "We've been doing a little remodeling." He blinked once or twice. The room needed a lower wattage light in the future. It might be hard to sleep in there, even with the lights out, unless you were as exhausted as I was.

I said, "It looks good." Then I caught his eye and we started laughing. It felt good, laughing with my dad. It had been a long time. Still chuckling, he waved goodnight and left. I turned off the light, threw off my clothes and slid into bed.

I woke up the next morning surrounded by the yellow glow of sunshine despite the overcast gray skies outside. On a sunny day with the blinds open, it might feel as if you were inside the sun. As the smell of coffee drifted upstairs, I noticed the formerly scuffed baseboards had been painted a bright shiny white and so had the trim around the doors and windows. The window blinds had been changed out too—from wood slats to a high tech white vinyl version without any visible cords.

The shared bathroom between Jeremy's bedroom and mine was the next shock. It was also painted butter-yellow, but the shiny blue-tiled counter had been replaced with gray and gold-flecked marble with a greenish thread through it. Larger tile in the same marble covered the floor and the fluffy rug in front of the double sinks was sage green. I opened the adjoining door to Jeremy's old room. It had undergone a transformation from the purple that Mom let him paint it in ninth grade to sage green, just like the fluffy rug. With two computers, cream painted furniture and watercolor paintings on the wall, it had become a tidy home office, probably Sandra's.

I followed the smell of coffee downstairs to the kitchen wondering what other changes were in store.

"Hey Sleeping Beauty," Jeremy called from a wheelchair parked in the breakfast nook. It was only 8:30, but everyone was up. Dad leaned up against the kitchen cabinets, a coffee mug in his hand, while Sandra, dressed for the office, buttered a slice of toast at the butcher block. She gave me a nervous smile as I came in.

It had been six months since I had last been in this kitchen, but magic had been wrought. There didn't seem to be any other explanation for the total change from sunny French provincial to ultra-modern sleek. Everything was stainless steel, granite, or black except the dark cherry wood glass-fronted cabinets. Our family gathering spot was now a marvel of technology and testosterone. I looked at Sandra in some trepidation. It appeared she was a little bolder than the upstairs office would indicate.

Dad handed me a mug of coffee. "What do you think of my kingdom?" he asked waving his hand around the room. Before I could answer, he pulled down an omelet pan from the rack above the butcher block and set it on the stove. He kissed Sandra and handed her a to-go cup. She bundled her toast into a napkin, nodded to Jeremy and me and left for work.

Dad opened a refrigerator the size of Rhode Island and started pulling out eggs and veggies. Then he asked, "What kind of omelet do you want?"

Who was this man? Jeremy and I exchanged an incredulous look before my brother buried his head on the granite-topped table and began to shake with silent laughter. Dad had been known to barbecue and he could make a peanut butter sandwich, but that was the extent of his culinary interest and skills as far as we knew.

Dad was waiting, fancy ceramic knife in hand.

"Whatever you want to make is okay with me," I managed.

Jeremy opted for toast. I made it and poured him a glass of milk while Dad went to town—chopping up chives and mushrooms, beating eggs and expertly slipping them into the omelet pan. In less than ten minutes, he slid a beautiful omelet filled with cheese and garnished with chives onto a plate and handed me a fork. I was impressed and said so.

"When did you take up cooking?"

"A while ago. I designed the kitchen remodel too." That explained the schizophrenic difference between the softly glowing upstairs and the masculine downstairs.

Mom's friend Frieda brought her over just after Dad disappeared to complete his grocery shopping for the next day's Christmas dinner. Mom digested this information with a straight face, even after I told her that he was planning to cook it too.

I poured her a cup of Dad's coffee while Jeremy and I talked about the marvels of Dad's omelet and the changes upstairs. Mom walked around her former kitchen and peeked into the gleaming living room where a dark hardwood floor reflected taupe leather furniture and crystal lamps. It was a far cry from Mom's comfort-and-color style, but she nodded approvingly and said, "Looks like he's moving on—making space in his life for something new to come in."

That thought was way too metaphysical for me.

In the afternoon, Jeremy and I took Mom for an hour of Christmas shopping at the mall. I bought an iPod Nano for Melanie and Jeremy and I collaborated on an iPod Shuffle for Dad.

"Are you sure he'll be okay with this?" Jeremy demurred from the depths of his wheelchair. "It seems sort of modern for a guy who still has cassettes."

"C'mon, have you really looked at that kitchen? Trust me, he'll like this," I said, thinking about Dad's youthful disc jockey dreams.

While we waited for Mom to emerge from REI, Jeremy asked, "Who's the Nano for?"

"Not you."

He looked disappointed for a second but brightened up as the implication hit him.

"Your hiking friend," he smirked knowingly. I knew I was in for a bout of fraternal investigation, but Mom arrived, laden with bags.

When we got home, Dad was outside hanging Christmas lights in the early darkness. I helped him while Mom took Jeremy inside.

"Dad, I could do this tomorrow morning when we can see better," I said as I wobbled perilously on the ladder and felt around under the eaves for the hooks.

"I want the lights to be on when Sandra comes home tonight," he said tersely. "They would have been up last week, but…I didn't have time."

I caught a glimmer of the tightrope Dad walked, balancing re-connection with his first family, while being mindful of his wife's feelings and needs. Whatever Mom felt about hanging around her ex-husband and his wife in her ex-house, she was keeping to herself. I couldn't even imagine what Sandra was feeling.

As we worked, I thought this might be a good time to ask Dad about his precognitive ability, but Sandra pulled up into the driveway. As she lugged her briefcase out of the car, Dad flicked a remote and the lights blazed on. Sandra's tired face lit up brighter than the white lights we'd wrapped around the catalpa tree trunks as she dropped the briefcase and put her arms around Dad. I disappeared into the garage with the ladder and tools.

Mom was already walking out of the kitchen as I came into the house from the garage. "I'm having dinner with Frieda tonight and baking a pumpkin pie. I'll see you both in the morning. Can't wait for Christmas dinner," she said with a wicked smile.

She kissed Jeremy and me, nodded to Dad and Sandra as they came in and continued on to the front door. Frieda's Prius drove up and Mom waved goodbye.

Dad announced that we would be decorating the tree and sent me to the garage for the fake Noble fir and ornaments while he ordered a pizza. I found myself stringing lights and remembering past Christmases when it was Mom, not Sandra, Dad lifted up to put the star on the top of the tree. As Christmas memories flashed through my mind, I searched them for anything that would indicate Dad having paranormal abilities, but could remember only the year he'd brought out the fire extinguisher from the kitchen and set it on the mantel. Jeremy and I wondered what the fire extinguisher was doing there, but later, when the heat from the Christmas lights caught our dried out tree on fire, Dad put it out in a few minutes, much to our awed delight.

Had Dad passed along some sort of paranormal ability to me—something that made me able to receive impressions from objects I touched? Something that made me susceptible to dreams about other objects? My long-forgotten talent with impressions was something I had always associated with GPop, not Dad, because GPop had encouraged my abilities. Dad wanted nothing to do with them. If my father had passed along some psychic ability to me, why would GPop, my mother's father, encourage it? How were the dreams connected?

As I took the ornaments Sandra passed to me for the upper branches of the tree, my thoughts wandered to the people in my dreams. Had Barbara Browning's Christmas memories of her sister had undergone any change now that she knew her sister was a serial killer? What would Derry's Christmases have been like in a monastery? Would I ever know the reality of Maude's story?

They were strange thoughts, but the dreams were like wiggling a loose tooth, popping up constantly in my thoughts which never circled too far from them. I planned to make a stop at Astrella's on my way home.

As the tree began to transform from fake fiber to Christmas miracle, we began to feel like a family. Not my family exactly, but a family nonetheless. Jeremy, utterly exhausted from the day, fell asleep in his wheelchair with an ornament in his hand. Did he have some paranormal ability of his own?

"Next year we'll have a real tree," Sandra said, standing back next to Dad, scrutinizing our handiwork. They exchanged a look and smiled into each other's eyes. He put his arm around her.

A year earlier, I would have gagged; a year earlier Dad wouldn't have been so open about touching Sandra. Maybe it was my feeling for Melanie that caused the change in my perspective. I didn't know what to attribute Dad's change to, other than Sandra, but it was a change for the better.

I looked over at Jeremy who had wakened and was watching Dad. He looked back and smiled—not the sarcastic grimace we'd always exchanged before when Dad and Sandra occasionally touched—just a smile that said it was okay.

Chapter Twenty-one

Santa brings a gift

Dad's Christmas feast the next day was amazing—and edible. Before we launched into his turkey, cornbread stuffing and bourbon-laced sweet potatoes, Sandra's green bean casserole and Mom's pumpkin pie, he insisted on a toast.

"To my family," he said, raising a glass of red wine. As we raised our glasses in return, my eyes flicked around the cherry wood table. Dad was at one end proudly viewing the fruits of his labor, both culinary and human; Jeremy was in his wheelchair at the other, a prisoner of his injuries, but learning to overcome them; Mom sat between Jeremy and me, exchanging a smile with Sandra while squeezing Jeremy's hand and Sandra sat next to Dad with her glass of water upraised in one hand, her other held in Dad's. The previous night, she'd declined a beer with her single slice of pizza—maybe she was swearing off alcohol as an early New Year's resolution.

After dinner and cleanup, Dad presented Jeremy and me with the usual Christmas check, but my check was accompanied by the boxes of vintage egg cups I'd stored in his garage for the past three years.

"Merry Christmas," he smirked, obviously enjoying the joke. I rolled my eyes and laughed, wondering how I was going to fit them in my Saturn.

Mom gave Sandra and Dad a "hostess gift" of gourmet coffee beans and herbal tea from Peet's. Jeremy and I had gotten each other web cameras— a similarity which caused some laughter. Sandra seemed pleased with the Barnes & Noble gift certificate we'd gotten her, saying she already knew just what books she planned to get.

Dad opened the iPod Shuffle and looked at it curiously. I had put a few tunes from the Seventies on it and Jeremy planned to teach him how to load it. Dad pushed the power button and smiled when "Jeremiah Was a Bullfrog" blared out.

Dad and Sandra made it clear they would exchange their presents to each other on the actual day of Christmas, so Mom, Jeremy and I excused ourselves to Jeremy's temporary room in the den to open our gifts. Mom was thrilled with the chalcedony cameo necklace that Jeremy brought her from Greece. She opened the box with the vase and pulled it out, its deep blue glaze a startling contrast to the mahogany den, drawing the eye like a magnet. She explored its contours, one hand tracing a handle, the other cupping the fat base.

"It's beautiful, Dave," she said smiling.

Later that evening, I drove Mom back to Frieda's. When I returned, the house was quiet. Dad sat alone in a designer recliner in the living room. The television was off and a single floor lamp kept the room from darkness. Flashbacks from high school curfews filled my head.

"Hey, Dad. Where is everybody?"

"Sandra's gone up to bed and Jeremy's on the computer in the den, emailing every human being in Greece."

He got up and walked over to the wet bar in the corner of the room. "Have a drink with me?"

Without waiting for an answer, he set two snifters on the bar and poured an inch of Courvoisier XO into them. Cognac isn't my drink of choice, but it was clear he wanted to talk. That was fine with me; I had questions of my own to ask.

Dad settled back into the recliner. I moved into its twin next to him. He pushed the leather ottoman between us. We both propped our feet up and swirled the liquid in our glasses, warming it in our hands. It was very weird—almost as if we were posing for a GQ ad for male bonding. Silence closed in.

After more swirling, I took a sip of cognac. It burned a trail down my throat and into my stomach where I felt it smoldering its way through my Christmas dinner. It was now or never.

"Dad, do you remember telling me once when I was about twelve, that you didn't want me to 'know' things?" I focused on the amber liquid in my glass. Even so, I could feel him beside me, tightening up.

"I used to play a game with GPop where I would hold something and close my eyes and then I would 'know' about it. After a while I stopped doing it because you told me you didn't want me to be a freak."

I caught his wince, but continued. "But I think you know things too. Like the time I fell out of Tommy's tree and broke my arm and the time you wouldn't let us go river rafting with Ellen's family and her uncle fell out of the raft and drowned."

"Her uncle was drunk," Dad said dismissively. He peered into his snifter, watching the swirling liquid as if reading something in its depths.

"But you knew something was going to happen, didn't you? Like with Jeremy?"

He dragged his eyes from the glass and stared at the darkened window facing the landscaped backyard. I saw his shoulders lift as he took a breath.

"Yes, I knew." He turned towards me, shoulders hunched. His blue eyes were cloudy with what looked like sadness. I realized that he was afraid—of me, of what I might think. I felt a rush of adrenaline that didn't come from the cognac.

"Have you always known things that will happen?" I looked into my glass and took another fiery sip.

Minutes went by. Then, as if he were pushing a boulder uphill, he said, "My first memory is the look from my parents when I told my Uncle Lew to stay out of his barn. I was three. Later, I found out that my father was embarrassed because he thought I'd overheard them talking about the way Lew went out to the barn to do his secret drinking. I didn't know about any drinking, just that the barn was a bad place for Uncle Lew that day. When my father spanked me for eavesdropping, I couldn't understand why. Uncle Lew fell onto a pitchfork in the hay and it punctured his chest. He didn't die, but he wasn't ever the same."

Dad took another deep breath. "When I was seven, my sister, Rosie, drowned. She was only four."

My head reeled. Dad had never talked about his family. Now, he had an Uncle Lew and a baby sister?

Dad continued, "I was playing over at Kenny Hassler's house under the porch that day and suddenly I knew something was wrong with Rosie. I headed for home, only a few blocks away, with Kenny trailing me. When I got to our house, my mother was already outside, surrounded by neighbor ladies. She ran to me and asked if I knew where Rosie was. I blurted out that Rosie was in the creek. I heard gasps from a few of the neighbors, but I couldn't look away from my mother. Some of the neighbors ran toward the creek, but Mother just stood there, staring at me, with her hand over her mouth."

He put his hand over his eyes and his voice roughened. "It seemed like a long time before Mr. Torgerson came up from behind the house, carrying Rosie. Water was dripping off the skirt of her little red dress. Leaves and sticks stuck to it from where he'd pulled her out of the creek and tried to pump the water out of her lungs. It's been more than forty years, but I can still hear my mother's screams." Dad stopped talking.

In the endless moment of silence that followed, I sat completely still—paralyzed by the mixture of sorrow, pity and horror that filled me. Finally, Dad's dry voice cut into the morass of emotion threatening to swamp me.

"After that, the neighbors kept a distance from me. I was the weird kid, the one that 'knew' things. My mother treated me as if I were an unwanted guest in her house."

I could hear the resentment in his voice after all this time.

"Even after she knew that I was at Kenny's house, she blamed me for Rosie, as if my knowing about it meant that I could have stopped it. But, until she asked, I *hadn't* known anything—just that I needed to be home because something had happened to my sister."

He took a breath, held it, and released it with a sigh. "My father treated me differently too—like I was a survivor who'd stayed alive through cannibalism. Sometimes kids teased me at school about being a freak, wanting to know if I could predict the Kentucky Derby winner or the color of the teacher's underwear." He grimaced and took another sip of cognac. "I never wanted you or Jeremy to have to go through that. I didn't want you to be like me—I just wanted you to be regular kids, not kids who had strange thoughts. But, after that day with the gearshift knob, I couldn't pretend anymore."

We were silent, Dad sipping his cognac in the darkness, me trying to process his words. More pieces of the Dad puzzle moved into place. I could understand his need to keep my brother and me from knowing anything about his bitter childhood, but to shut us out completely from his family seemed drastic. We'd been to Iowa only once to see Dad's parents. I never thought of them as my grandparents—I wasn't even sure if they were still alive.

Sorrow and shame radiated from my father, making me ache for him. After a moment, I said, "I get it, Dad, I do, but…You were there to take me to the hospital the time I fell out of the tree and you started the search for Jeremy because of this ability, so it can't be a totally bad thing. Maybe you didn't stop what happened, but you got us all in place so we could be there for him."

"Maybe." Dad was still looking into his glass, but his shoulders seemed more relaxed. Then he said, "Do you still receive impressions from objects?"

I didn't know how to answer this. Did the dreams count? Would Dad have some advice about them?

"I haven't let myself do it in a long time. I don't know what use it could be. Lately, I've had a few dreams about things…" I trailed off. Talking with Dad about this felt amazing, but I wasn't sure how the dreams were connected to our shared abilities, if at all. I wanted to stay in this moment and not drag other things into it, so I finished with a lame, "Well, they've been pretty real and I don't know what they mean."

He waited for a moment. When I didn't say anything further, he said, "Maybe you're right and there is a purpose to all this. Maybe you'll be the one to find out. Do you think Jeremy has any abilities like this?"

I could tell that he wanted me to say no. "I don't know Dad. He's never said anything."

"Neither did you," Dad reminded me. Then, abruptly, he told me what he'd been waiting up to say. "Sandra's pregnant."

The air rushed out of me. "Wow," I said, struggling for composure. "And I thought she just didn't like alcohol."

He was startled for a second and then burst out laughing. I grinned weakly, still trying to get my head around the implications. Mom was hoping he would move on and now he had. But what kind of father would he be this time? He was still smiling, but his eyes looked anxious. I knew what I had to say.

"Congratulations, Dad. Have you told Jeremy yet?"

He shook his head. "Will you tell your mother for me?"

I nodded. Some of the anxiety left his eyes. Silence settled around us like a blanket, broken at last by Dad's hesitant voice.

"I've missed you, son. I started missing you when you were a teenager and you pulled away from me. I missed you when you stood by your mother during the divorce, but I admired it too. I watched you pull Jeremy's fat out of the fire time after time and I kept pushing, just to see what you would do; where you would draw the line, but you never did. The only line you drew was between us. And that was my fault." He looked over at me. "You and Jeremy mean the world to me. I'll be a better father this time."

Walls began to crumble inside me; the barriers I'd constructed to protect myself from my father's distance trembled and fell. I'd missed him too, the dad who played tag in the front yard, the dad who'd shown me fireflies in Iowa, the man who liked to fish and had taught me to bait my own hook.

It felt as if I'd been given permission to explore—permission I hadn't even realized I was waiting for. Whether the dreams and my long lost abilities were connected; whether I still had those abilities; whether I even wanted to find out, was all in front of me, waiting.

Chapter Twenty-two

Secrets are shared

The next morning, in spite of my early start, Dad and Sandra were already waiting in the kitchen. Dad had a one-armed hug and a couple of to-go cups of coffee for me. Sandra gave me another hug as I whispered, "Congratulations," in her ear.

Jeremy swung in on the crutches Dad had brought home with the Christmas groceries and caught me on the way to the door. "Tell Mom I'll be up to see her before I go back to Greece. I'll be up to see you too—I want to meet the owner of the Nano."

We did our handshake thing and added a hug. Then I was out the door, in a sweat to get to Melanie and Astrella's.

I'd planned to drive Mom home to Mt. Shasta City and then continue on to Melanie's house, but a storm set in and the rain we encountered in the Bay Area became snow after we passed Redding. As the rain fell and gradually thickened to flakes, I told Mom about my conversation with Dad, leaving the part about the baby until last.

My stomach clenched when I finished—I'd just told her that I had some sort of paranormal ability as a child; that Dad had family members we'd never heard about and that he was going to be a father again. There were a lot of secrets packed into that conversation.

Mom was silent for several minutes. I snuck a look at her face, but couldn't tell what she was thinking. Finally she said, "He was always so guarded, even in our closest moments. I knew his childhood was miserable, but he never told me about his sister. How can you have a real relationship with someone who can't share themselves with you?"

My stomach tightened again, thinking of all I was holding back from both her and Melanie. The snow began to stick to the road. It was getting harder to see.

"I'm glad he talked to you and that he's getting a second chance to be a dad," she said slowly. "Maybe this will be what he needs to finally open up and let go. I hope so. It rolls away a little stone of that guilt I carry around about the divorce."

Always a surprise, my mother.

As if reading my mind, she continued, "I've worried that leaving your dad after you two were out of high school was selfish, that maybe I wasn't making the right choice—right for me, but maybe not for anyone else." She shook her head. "I had gotten to a point where I thought that things would always be the same and then, suddenly, it was like a window opened up and I could see possibilities all around me. I just couldn't stay any more. I'm sorry if it hurt you and Jeremy."

We were almost to Dunsmuir and the snow was coming down thick and fast, almost a whiteout. There were things I wanted to say, but between the snow and the increasingly dangerous road conditions, I decided to wait until we got to Mom's house. Both of us leaned forward, trying to see past the blanket of white.

Safe at her house an hour later, Mom set about making potato soup while I built a fire in the woodstove and brought in her bag. Later, we watched the snow fall, eating our soup and enjoying the warmth of the fire. The blue vase glowed in its new home on Mom's bookshelf.

"Is that beautiful vase from the curio shop?" she asked.

I didn't want to tell her about the blue vase dream, partly because I wanted her to enjoy the vase without knowing its history and partly because I was curious to see if she might have a dream of her own. Still, it was hard to lie to my mother.

"Yes, it's from Astrella's." I left it at that, hoping she wouldn't ask. She did.

"Did you have a dream about it?"

"Well… yes. But I'm not going to tell you about it. Maybe you'll have your own dream."

"Oh good. I can't wait," Mom was as excited as a little kid at Disneyland. "I'll put it in the bedroom, right now." She hopped off the couch, picked up the vase and carried it away.

When she returned, she said, "Are you still having the dreams? Is that why you're so interested in your Dad's precognitive skills? Do you think there's some connection with your ability to receive impressions from objects?" She slipped in the questions casually.

In the car, she hadn't seemed to react to news of my childhood paranormal skills; now, I realized she'd probably always known about them and had told GPop.

"I don't know if there's a connection—I thought the dreamologist told you I was supposed to look for meaning in the objects."

"She also said you shouldn't buy any more things from the shop," Mom grinned. "Winona told me dreams come when you're ready. Maybe that's why you're having them now—because you're ready for your life to go in a new direction."

Was I? What direction would that be? What if I didn't want to go in that direction? My life was fine the way it was. Then I recalled the conversation in Melanie's car. Maybe there *was* something within me that wanted more.

A minute went by, and then Mom said, "You know, GPop knew about your dad's ability. He wanted to help you and Jeremy if you ever developed the same ability because he knew that your dad wouldn't. He didn't want either of you to feel scared or unnatural about it."

I felt a pang, thinking of the way I had shut down practicing with GPop and then he was gone before I could change my mind.

"I haven't tried to do it since GPop and GMa died, Mom. I don't know if I still can, or if I even want to."

I looked at my mother, sitting cross-legged on her comfortable couch, her eyes locked on mine, and circled back to our conversation in the snowstorm. I remembered Katharine and the hope and courage she'd needed to leave her abusive husband. Mom's circumstances were different and my father wasn't a wife beater, but it had taken courage all the same.

"I miss the way our family used to be, but I love you Mom. If you needed to go, then I'm glad you were brave enough to do it."

It was more than I'd ever said to her, or to anyone else, about the divorce, but it was what I needed to say. Mom's eyes filled and she gave a brisk nod, saving us both from a bath of emotion.

Chapter Twenty-three

Pie and Frustration

The next morning, I brought in wood and stalled around until Road Conditions said the interstate was open without chain controls. When I took off for Bedlington, snow covered the peaks and valleys, and the bright sun blasted the whiteness into shocking brilliance.

I hit Bedlington about 2:30, my questions about the dreams keeping me company. Jeremy's accident and my growing relationship with Melanie had split my focus, but the closer I got to Astrella's the more questions came to mind. Did the objects cause the dreams? Was there a purpose for my dreams? Could they be controlled? Were they, somehow, dangerous?

Now, added to my dream questions were questions about this ability I had as a child. Were the two connected? Was there some purpose for the ability to get impressions from things I touched? Could I still do it? Did I want to? Daria Astrella probably wouldn't be able to answer those questions, but I couldn't wait to talk to her and find out what she did know.

I made Astrella's my first stop since Melanie would be working at Betsy's for another hour and a half. Parking off Main Street, I walked over to the curio shop. I'd left the snow behind in California, but it was bitterly cold and leaden clouds filled every inch of sky.

The windows of the shop were even darker than usual. I turned the handle, but the door was locked. There was no "closed" sign; no note on the door giving a time of return. I knocked on the door and peered into the window, but could see nothing. I stepped back into the street and looked up at the second story, but that was dark too. For a lady who supposedly never went anywhere, Daria Astrella sure seemed to be gone a lot.

I waited for a few minutes, knocked again and then wandered around downtown for a while before returning to Astrella's. The door was still locked and it appeared likely to stay that way. I wanted to kick down the door and howl in frustration, but a glance at the Christmas shopper-filled street sent me stomping down to Betsy's, hoping the sight of Melanie and working my way through a sampling of Betsy's pies might burn off my angst.

She heard the turning of the shop door handle through the open door of the apartment and went on spooning soup from the crockpot into a bowl. The handle turning stopped and the old woman walked over to the window to watch the boy walk down the street. She could tell from the set of his shoulders and the way he walked, that he was angry. She felt bad about it, but it was the way it had to be. Her winter cold had given her the excuse to keep the shop closed today, but she would have closed it if she'd known he was coming, anyway. He wasn't ready yet.

It was after three when I stalked into the diner. The lunch rush had cleared out; the early bird diners hadn't yet appeared, and the place was dead. With my choice of seats, I sidled into the gangster's booth at the back, giving a nod to Bridget, the waitress cleaning the counter.

Melanie was refilling condiments at the back of the diner. She broke into an enormous soul-saving smile at the sight of me and brought her refill station over to my booth. After a look around the diner, she swooped a quick kiss on my lips. We beamed at each other. Now, it felt like Christmas.

"How's your family?" she asked.

I watched her quick, sure hands refill the catsup and mustard bottles, wiping them down and cleaning the caps while I filled her in about our family Christmas and Jeremy's progress. Every time our eyes met, I felt a thrill of warmth. It was all I could do to keep from grabbing her up and waltzing around the diner.

My story and Melanie's refills ended about the same time. She reached out and squeezed my hand.

"I'm glad your brother is up and moving around. Everything sounds good," she said.

Ross the boss came into the diner through the chrome kitchen door. Melanie gave me another smile as she picked up the tray of condiments and began setting them on the tables. Ross poured himself a cup of coffee from the pot behind the counter, noticed me, and started over.

"Hey Ross," I said. "What's the best pie today?"

He trotted back to the counter, cut a slice of pie from one of the offerings in the pie case, slid it onto a plate and walked over to place it in front of me.

"Sour cream apple," he announced as he sat down opposite me. "It's one of my grandmother's recipes."

I dug into the pie, in perfect faith that it would taste as good as it looked. It was better. Melanie caught my eye and grinned. She dropped off a cup of coffee for me before whisking away to refill sugar containers and saltshakers.

"Is your grandmother the one who taught you to cook?" I asked Ross between bites.

"Yeah, sort of. She was the original Betsy. My father opened the diner with her in 1952, when he got back from Korea. Grandma had her family recipes and a rep for being an awesome cook," said Ross. "I learned to cook by hanging around."

I took another bite and made satisfied noises. When I could speak, I said, "I stopped by Astrella's this afternoon. The store is closed again."

"That's strange," said Ross. "Usually she only closes in early December and she already did that. She was open last week."

"Have you known her long?"

"Ever since she and Padgett came to town in 1963 and bought Grandpa's old hardware store. They traveled all over the world, but Padgett developed a heart condition so they decided to settle down. I don't know why they picked Bedlington," he said as he gulped some coffee. "Padge and my dad were good friends. I spent a lot of time with the Astrellas in their apartment over the store when I was in high school."

"Did you ever buy anything from the shop?"

Ross tilted his head slightly and looked at me as though appraising my intentions. "I do have something from the store—it's a set of carving knives with decorated silver handles. The box they came in has a bullet hole in it. It was the only thing that Padgett ever let me buy from the shop."

He sipped his coffee as I wolfed down the rest of my pie. "The set came to me at a time in my life when I was in a lot of turmoil. I'd just returned from two tours in Vietnam and I couldn't settle down. After the drama over there, I kept looking for something else, something bigger, more exciting than a small town diner. I drifted around for a while. Caused my dad a lot of grief.

"After one three-month walk-about, I came home, still full of anger and unrest. Had an argument with Dad about thirty seconds after I blew in and stormed over to Astrella's. They had a lot more merchandise in those days and Padgett had a sympathetic ear." He shrugged. "During my recital of woe, I saw this wooden box with a hole in it and picked it up. I hadn't seen it before. Something about those beautiful knives called to me, but like I said, Padge never let me buy anything from the store. So, when he told me I could have the knives for five bucks, I fished out that money out of my jeans as fast as I could—just in case he changed his mind.

"I had no plans for them—wasn't planning to go into the family business; wasn't planning to stab anyone. But I brought them home and took them up to my room, sneaking in the house to avoid another confrontation with Dad. I'd already decided to hit the road again."

Ross gave a wry smile before continuing.

"That night, I had a crazy dream that I still remember. There was a woman dressed in black with tears streaming down her face and she was standing in front of something. It was so dark I couldn't see what it was. People came to stand next to her. Each one of them was dressed in dark clothing as if they were mourners. Some were crying, like the woman."

Ross gazed down at the green Formica tabletop. "The first few people touched the woman—held her hand or put an arm around her. The next few people stood next to the first people and connected with them in the same way. Soon, there was a chain of people that seemed to go for miles, all of them touching each other in some way. And every time someone joined the chain, the darkness of the room lightened a little."

He took another gulp of coffee. Melanie stopped by to give him a refill and he gave her a nod of appreciation.

"There was this intense feeling of fellowship and love, like all these people were part of a huge family. The feeling intensified each time another person joined the chain. It was so long, I couldn't even see the end of it. And I wanted to be part of it; to join that enormous family. Gradually the darkness lifted until I could see that the woman was standing in an old-time restaurant kitchen and there was a box of knives, like the one I'd bought, on a table in front of her. I woke up about then thinking how weird it was to have a dream where nothing really happened. When I looked over at my desk, the box of knives on it was glowing like a night light."

Ross cocked an eye in my direction as if checking my reaction. I took a sip of coffee and kept my face neutral.

"I picked up the box to see where the light was coming from. When I touched it, I felt something...a welcoming. As if I had just joined that chain of people in my dream." Ross' thin, bearded face was radiant, remembering. "The box stopped glowing. Later, when I thought about it, I wasn't positive that it actually had.

"I didn't leave the next morning—in fact I haven't left since that night. The dream made me realize just how disconnected I felt from the world. I hadn't been giving myself much of a chance to reconnect with all my stomping around. My family and the diner suddenly seemed like the best place to start." Ross stood up. "Been here ever since and I've never regretted a day. Drama can happen anywhere, but the connection I feel in this place with the people who come into it is something I never want to lose."

"Did you ever tell Padgett about your dream?" I could barely breathe.

"No, but I did ask him where he got the knives. He told me he'd bought them from an old woman in France. They had belonged to her brother."

Ross smiled an embarrassed sort of smile and looked away. "I can't think why I just told you that dream. I've never been sure that there was any association between the dream and the knives. I use them every day. They make me feel at peace—like I'm in the right place, doing the right thing. And this," his glance swept over the nearly empty diner, "is my community, my family and my connection to the world. I take care of everybody the best way I can to keep that chain growing."

He stood abruptly and passed through the chrome kitchen doors, reappearing just as quickly with a flat rectangular box that he handed it to me.

I opened the box to an array of chef's knives resting on red velvet, each in its own niche. Picking up the carving knife, I studied the ornate detail on the handle. When Ross turned away to answer a question from Bridget, I closed my eyes.

I was in a huge restaurant kitchen. Men were shouting outside and I heard a woman's screams. The double doors to the kitchen blew apart and two men hurtled through them. One held a knife, a slender, lethal-looking thing. As the two men faced off, each screaming things in French, the one without a knife reached behind his back and pulled a handgun from his waistband. A group of workers stood frozen in the acts of plating food, chopping vegetables, stirring sauces. A big man in chef's whites stopped carving a cut of beef and, at the sight of the revolver, he motioned to the others to get down. They ducked behind cabinets or slid under the worktable. The chef stepped in front of the table, blocking the combatants' view of the people cowering under it. The man with the knife lunged just as the man with the gun pulled it clear of his waistband. The shot he fired went wild and he fired again as the man with the knife darted past the chef toward the back door. The chef crumpled to the floor, still holding the carving knife in his hand, while both men ran out the back.

I opened my eyes, heart pounding. Ross was staring down at me.

"He was shot," I heard myself say, before realizing the connotations of letting someone know what I'd seen. "The guy who owned the knives, I mean." I tried to cover my words with more words. "I mean, look at that bullet hole in the box."

Ross wasn't fooled. "You saw this?" he asked under his breath. It was an opportunity I wasn't sure I was ready for, but Ross had trusted me with his dream, after all.

"Look, I don't know if this is really what happened or if it's just my imagination…," I disclaimed. Ross shrugged impatiently, his eyes leveled on mine. "There was a fight between two restaurant patrons and it spilled over into the kitchen. The man that owned these knives was the head chef and he was trying to protect his people when one of the fighters pulled out a gun and fired a couple of shots. One of them killed the chef."

Ross shifted on the balls of his feet. His eyes were riveted to my face. Melanie floated by with a sheaf of menus in her hand and a concerned look. I sent her a reassuring smile.

Ross said, "I don't think it was your imagination."

My attention shifted back to him. The diner door opened and an elderly couple came in. Ross turned and nodded to them and then turned back to me.

"Have you seen things like this before?" He was asking the question, but he looked at me as if he already knew the answer.

"I've had a few dreams myself," I said. "That's what I was hoping to talk to Mrs. Astrella about."

The door opened again and three lumberjack types walked in. They looked hungry. One of them called out, "Ross-man. We've come to take a few burgers hostage." Ross grinned at the trio and waved.

"I've got to get back to the kitchen," Ross said, "but we should talk. What you said about the knives feels right, but I'd like to know more. I'll get your number from Melanie, if that's okay. Maybe I'll be able to help with some of the information you want from Daria."

I nodded.

He turned back toward me just before going through the kitchen door. "Hey, if you want, come to our New Year's Party. I always hold it here at Betsy's and there's plenty of food and drink. The whole town will be here—literally. It's my way of touching base with everyone all at once."

Ross nodded again and disappeared into the kitchen, leaving me wondering about the reappearance of an ability I hadn't used in the eleven years since my grandparents died.

Chapter Twenty-four

I receive a Christmas surprise

Melanie's shift was over at four. I was working my way through a second piece of pie, pumpkin this time, and replaying my conversation with Ross, when Melanie slid into the booth next to me and said, "Ready to go?"

I swallowed a last gargantuan bite and nodded. While she grabbed her coat and purse from the kitchen, I paid for my pie.

"Ross said he'll call you tomorrow," she said as we walked out to her car. "What's that about?"

We exchanged a lingering kiss at her car before I said, "He's filling me in with a little history of the area."

Melanie looked up into my face, started to say something and then smiled and shook her head. "See you at home," she said starting the car.

I trudged back down the street to my car as she drove out of Betsy's parking lot.

Following behind Melanie's Camry, I thought about Ross' dream. I knew that the young woman in his dream was the chef's sister and the chain of mourners had been all those whose lives the chef touched in some way. What intrigued me was Ross saying the knives brought him peace—almost the same words Barbara Browning had used about the painting of her sister.

Jeremy's accident, the snow and Astrella's closure—it felt like something was holding me back from getting the answers I needed. I hadn't felt this frustrated since high school calculus.

The house lights were on by the time I turned into Melanie's driveway. The windows and screened-in porch were a-twinkle with white Christmas bulbs. With Christmas only five days away, the roommates had scattered—Karen and Beth were Christmas shopping in Eugene and Gillian was attending a Christmas party at the art gallery where she worked. We had the house to ourselves.

A six-foot Christmas tree in the living room sparkled with more tiny white lights and a plethora of vintage glass ornaments.

"Sorry it's not a real tree," Melanie said as I took off my coat, "Karen is adamant about not cutting down trees for ornamentation." She grinned and wrapped herself around me. "I missed you."

Exactly what I needed to hear.

It felt as if I had been away for a long, long time. Throughout the lengthy drives, the anxiety about Jeremy and our early family Christmas, Melanie had been in my thoughts like a softly glowing beacon to a place I wanted to stay for the rest of my life.

We held each other and kissed until the need to be closer overcame us. Taking my hand, Melanie started up the stairs. I leaned down and grabbed my laptop case off the chair where I'd tossed it and followed her.

She led me into her blue and green bedroom and we sank down into the bed, kissing and touching.

Later, after the first wave of passion was spent, we spooned under the down comforter, our naked bodies curving around each other.

Melanie pulled two small gift-wrapped packages from under her pillow. "Merry Christmas, Dave," she whispered as she put them into my hands and pulled me over for a kiss.

I reached across to my laptop bag on the chair next to the bed and pulled out the little box with the iPod Nano.

"Ladies first," I told her. Melanie pulled off the wrapping and opened the box, squealing with delight when she saw the Nano.

"Check out what's on it," I said. She put in the ear buds immediately and began to play with the buttons, her mahogany hair falling over pearly skin. I tore my eyes away to open one of my packages. I found a New Wine double CD with a collection of the reggae band's greatest hits, just about the time Melanie found the reggae I'd loaded onto the music player. We looked at each other and laughed.

"Great minds…" we began at the same time and laughed again.

I reached into the laptop bag again and pulled out another package. Inside was a framed photo of the two of us on top of Tinker's Ridge. I laid it gently on her chest as she lay back against the pillows. Melanie slid off the gift wrap to reveal the picture. Against the background of trees filling the ridge and valley below us, my dark brown hair and hazel eyes were almost invisible, but Melanie's red-brown mane stood out like a flame. She stared at the picture and then gave me that glorious smile again.

"I love this," she said, reaching up for a kiss. Then she nodded excitedly at the package that still lay between us. "Open it."

I unwrapped the small box. Inside was a cut-glass ashtray. The last time I'd seen it, three weeks earlier, it had been sitting on a shelf in Astrella's Antiques & Curios. The circular dish had a glass post. Perched on the post was a little enamel matchbox with a sepia-toned photograph of Grand Central Station on the front.

I was speechless. It was a beautiful little thing and I was touched that she had thought of getting me something she thought I would really like because it was antique. On the other hand, it was from Astrella's and I was still freaked out about the dreams I'd already had about the objects from that shop. And what about the "right person getting the right object?"

"I love this, but I can't believe she let you buy it," I said.

Melanie frowned slightly, "Well she wasn't going to let me buy it until I finally told her it was for you. She knew who you were. You're right, that old woman is strange."

I nodded and kissed her, thinking fast. I didn't want any weird dreams tonight, of all nights.

"Let's clear the deck here," I whispered in her ear. We swept the gift-wrap and boxes off the bed and while Melanie propped the photograph on her dresser facing us, I put the ashtray and CD in my laptop bag.

Then I said, "I left something downstairs. I won't need this anymore tonight, anyway," as I swooped up the bag. I raced downstairs, dropped it off on a chair, and was back upstairs again before my side of the bed had gotten cold or the roommates came home to find a naked man sprinting up the staircase.

The next morning we were awake early—Melanie had to go to work and I, after trying unsuccessfully to distract her into lingering, was anxious to make that last long drive to be home.

Our goodbyes were passionate, enough to keep me toasty without the car heater despite the rainy, cold weather. Melanie was flying out of Eugene after work on Sunday, to spend Christmas with her family. She wouldn't be returning until the Wednesday after Christmas. Eleven days would pass before we could be together again on New Year's Eve. It was getting harder and harder to be apart. I already missed her.

On the drive home, I realized that Melanie's gift had given me an opportunity to find out how the objects worked. I plotted out an experiment to put into action.

Chapter Twenty-five

Another Christmas gift

As soon as I got home I put the ashtray in the living room and the hunk of quartz on my bedroom night stand. I slept well and dreamlessly. On Saturday and Sunday I brought the ashtray into the bedroom and put it next to the quartz. No dreams those nights either, or at least none I could remember.

Monday was Christmas Eve. I put in a full day of work, called Mom, Dad and Jeremy to exchange Christmas greetings and reassured Steve that I would be at his house bright and early for Christmas Day breakfast. I had a whole box of sand toys for little Brian.

I hauled the piece of quartz into the living room into the corner farthest away from the bedroom door, but kept the ashtray on the night stand. The stage was set. Then I climbed into bed and called Melanie. On Christmas Eve, hers was the voice I wanted to take into my sleep.

She answered her cell right away, her voice full of excitement. The family was opening Christmas presents.

"We always open a few just before we go to bed on Christmas Eve. Then we sleep in and open the rest in the morning. Dad just opened the mono-grammed golf towel I got him—with the set of rubber tees."

Her giggle was infectious. We talked for a few more minutes, sharing how much we missed each other and swearing that next Christmas we would be together. I hung up with a smile on my face, ready for whatever might come next.

They picked the babies first. Ladies always want the little ones; I don't know why. They are more work than us older kids. They picked girls next and the pretty kids–the ones with big eyes and curly hair, both boys and girls.

Tom and me ain't girls and we ain't pretty. My little brother is five and skinny. He's got skin like our mama—so white it makes him look like he's sick even when he's not. He's still got some scabs on his face left over from falling off his cot in the orphanage.

We don't got hair, neither. A while ago, when Cousin Etta bringed us back to the orphan place, they shaved our heads and puffed powder all over us to get rid of cooties. My hair is growing back in little patches, but Tom is still bald and he's got a bumpy head.

He's got a good smile with little, white baby teeth, only most people don't get to see it. My smile ain't so good because some of my teeth is gone. The new ones that come in look too big next to the baby teeth and the holes. I don't smile much.

We both got skinny eyes like Pop, but Tom's are blue and mine are greenish. I have freckles too, lots of them.

They picked the bouncy kids next; kids that looked out at everyone and smiled. At one of our stops, I heard a man say that he wanted a kid with some sap in him and he picked out Jimmy B., who never could stand still, but was always moving and looking around and grinning at everything.

Every time the train stops, I look at the people in the depot and the places where they line us up and I try to see what they see when they look at us. I can't make out what they want from us.

We're used to lining up, Tom and me. All the orphans are. In the Foundling Hospital, we line up for meals; we line up to go outside; we line up to come inside; we line up so Matron could see if we washed our faces and behind our ears.

This lining up is different. We all get off the train, happy to be outside, but we don't know what will happen next. There are always people waiting for us.

Sometimes they line us up right in the train station; other times they walk us down to the town hall or to the courthouse or a church and we line up inside. When we are lined up, the people look at us like we were in a store window and can't see them.

"They know we're coming, Barry," Jasper told me this morning. "I saw a poster on the wall in the train depot. It said 'Homes for Children Wanted' in big letters and then in small letters it said, 'A company of Homeless Children from the East will arrive at McPherson, Texas, Friday, September 16, 1912.' That's today—I asked Mr. Stuart."

Jasper is eight, a year older than me, but he's smaller. He's got jumpy eyes and he twitches, but he is real smart and he already knows how to read good. He came from the Foundling Hospital too, riding the streetcar with us to the train station. Jasper talks about everything except about how he came to the orphan place.

When we started out from New York City Mr. Stuart counted out twenty-three of us kids. This morning there was only six of us left.

We have a car to ourselves at the back of the train and Mr. Stuart and Mrs. Renfro have charge of us. We eat in our car and sleep there too, and when the train stops in a town, we get off and meet people.

On the first day, Mrs. Renfro told us that we were going across the country to find new homes with mothers and fathers that would love us. A couple of the kids already had new mothers and fathers waiting for them, she said. The rest of us would find new homes along the way.

When Mrs. Renfro said this, Tommy frowned and said, "We already got Mama and Pop. We don't need any more." He started to cry.

Mama is dead and Tom knows it, but he won't believe it. He always acts like she's out at her sewing job and will be back. Pop works far away and he only comes home once in a while.

What if Pop comes home and we ain't at the Foundling Hospital where Cousin Etta put us? How's he going to know where we're at? I started to ask Mr. Stuart about how Pop would find us, but he was talking to a little girl who was crying and Mrs. Renfro was looking for medicine for Sylvia's cough.

On the train, we ate peanut butter sandwiches that Mrs. Renfro made for us. Sometimes she bought fruit at the stops and we had that too. There was milk on the train and, one time, Mr. Stuart picked me to help him bring it back from the dining car. Only the boys and girls who were good helpers got picked to go with Mr. Stuart. I couldn't wait to see the dining car.

It was a sight with fancy tables, flowers in vases, glass ashtrays and white table cloths. The afternoon that we went for the milk, the sun was coming through the windows and everything was shining, like Mama's little crystal box that used to sit on the table at home.

There was no one in the car when we passed through. I was walking behind Mr. Stuart and when we got just past the last table, I swiped an ashtray into my pocket, quick as a wink. It made a bump, but my jacket helped hide it.

The ashtray has three little dents for holding cigarettes and a glass thing with a metal matchbox slid down over it. The cover of the matchbox is a picture of a train on one side and the train station where we got on the train in New York City on the other. There's real matches inside too.

I got something from everywhere we've lived; a button I found on the floor of our flat from Mama's blue dress—the one she wore when Pop took us all to Coney Island; a rock from the yard at the Foundling Hospital; a leaf from the tree outside Cousin Etta's flat—all the places I can remember. Those things is easy to hide, but the ashtray is heavy and as big as my hand. I put it in the suitcase between my show clothes and Tom's. I got to be careful with our suitcase so it doesn't thump when we walk.

A week ago, Mr. Stuart loaded us onto the streetcar, each one of us carrying a little cardboard suitcase with our extra set of clothes in it. I call them our show clothes because the only time we put them on is when they show us off to the people. My suitcase has Tom's clothes in it too because he is too little to carry one.

All eight of us from the Foundling Hospital crowded together near Mr. Stuart. I sat down on the seat next to Tom, with the suitcase on my lap and watched the city go by.

The last time we was on a streetcar, it was because Cousin Etta bringed us to the Foundling Hospital. We had been there for a while when she came and got us because Pop was coming home. Then, after he left, she bringed us back.

Tom remembered the streetcar ride with Cousin Etta too, I could tell, because he looked at me and said, "Are we going home?"

I didn't think so; not with all of us carrying suitcases, but I said, "Maybe." I know Cousin Etta don't want us.

The streetcar bell clanged and clanged and finally Mr. Stuart told us it was time to get off and we all climbed down, big ones helping the little ones, and Mr. Stuart lining us up.

The train station was big and loud. People were pushing and shoving everywhere and there were men pushing carts loaded with trunks and boxes and suitcases much bigger than our little ones.

I held onto Tom's hand and the suitcase with all my might and tracked Mr. Stuart through it all. He walked us through the station to a place where some ladies and a lot of other children holding little cardboard suitcases were already waiting.

When the train came, screeching and puffing big clouds of steam, we climbed aboard one of the last cars. All the ladies left, except Mrs. Renfro, and all the children stayed. She and Mr. Stuart got us settled on the hard wooden benches with our suitcases under them.

The first time the train stopped and we got off, none of us knew what would happen. Mr. Stuart and Mrs. Renfro and some people who came to the train station walked us down the street behind the depot to a big building. Inside, there were a lot of grown-ups and we had to walk up an aisle between them and up onto a stage. People came up and looked at us and some of them picked kids to go home with them. Then we got back on the train and left.

Since then, me and Tom have got to know the other kids, like Emma who is our friend. Every time the train stops, we all get off, but only some of us get back on when the train leaves.

This morning, when the train stopped, Mr. Stuart said that it was the end of the line here in Texas. I didn't know what he meant, but it didn't sound good. Ending never sounds good.

First the train slowed way down. I could feel it in my feet and when I looked out the window, it got easier and easier to see the fields and houses. Mrs. Renfro hurried around picking up things and Mr. Stuart hung up the blankets so the girls could change into their show clothes. Us boys changed into ours right there in the open.

Then Mr. Stuart took us to the lavatory to wash our faces and hands. When we come back, the girls were dressed and Mrs. Renfro took them to the lavatory.

Mrs. Renfro combed our hair—the ones that got hair—and fussed our clothes around. Then we got off the train—me and Tommy, Emma, Jasper, Sylvia and Daisy who was coughing again. We took our suitcases with us because we might not be coming back.

What do they want us for? Yesterday, Jasper said he heard that some of the people who get us are cannibals. I asked him what a cannibal is. He looked at me like I was a bug, even though I'm bigger than him.

"If you learned to read, you wouldn't ask such dumb questions," he said.

"Well, how's reading going to help you if I punch your nose in?" I was mad.

Emma turned around from her seat in front of us and hushed us both. She looked grumpy, but she is the nicest person on the whole train except for Mrs. Renfro and Mr. Stuart. "I don't know what a cannibal is either," she said, "and I'm twelve."

Jasper looked surprised, but he said, "A cannibal is a person who eats other people."

Emma and I both moved away from him and Tom started to cry against my shoulder. It made me mad that Jasper would scare him, so I said, "Take it back, you take it back."

Emma said at the same time, "That ain't true," but her eyes looked like they might believe him.

I'm glad he didn't say it when Mary was here. She was a scared look-ing little girl with curly blonde hair and the biggest brown eyes. Her new mother and father were waiting for her two stops ago. She would have screamed if she'd thought they would eat her. But they looked friendly and the man brought a piece of candy for each of us. The new mother had brown eyes that smiled when they saw Mary.

Whenever we get back on the train, we are always quiet. We are the ones that don't get picked and we don't know why. We don't know if it's better to be picked or to stay on the train. What if the new family don't like you after a few days? Would they put you on another train?

Emma always walks with Tom and me and she holds his other hand. I think this makes both of them feel better. She helps Mrs. Renfro with Daisy and Sylvia too and she always makes sure they get the best pieces of fruit.

At this morning's stop, the End of the Line, we walked to a church. An old man come over to Tom and me where we stood between Jasper and Emma. He looked at me like I was a pork chop on a plate. I didn't like his eyes.

He was wearing big, old boots that dropped little pieces of straw on the wood floor when he walked. He bent down to look in my face and I could smell sweat and a bad smell coming off him.

The man grabbed my arm, the one that wasn't holding Tom, but he didn't haul me anywhere, he just squeezed my muscle and let go.

"I'll take this one," he said real loud.

I backed away from him when Mrs. Renfro came over to us.

"Me and my brother, we go together," I told the man. I pulled Tom in front of me.

"I only want the one," the man said to Mrs. Renfro.

She frowned and then she said, "Barry and Tom are brothers. They need a home where they can be together."

"I only want one," the man said real loud again. Mr. Stuart went to talk to him.

A sad looking lady in a blue dress was talking to Emma. Emma looked down at her shoes and she kept looking at them when she answered the lady. The lady talked to her some more, then Emma looked up with a smile on her face. It made her look a lot less grumpy. Then the lady took Emma's hand and they walked over to Mrs. Renfro.

The old man left Mr. Stuart and stood in front of Jasper. I could hear Sylvia cough. Funny how you can tell who's coughing after a while without seeing who it is.

Daisy and Sylvia wasn't coughing when we all got on the train together in New York City. The rest of us thought they must be sisters, but Mrs. Renfro said no. They only talked to each other. When Daisy started coughing the first night, Mrs. Renfro gave her some medicine, but the coughing didn't go away. Then Sylvia started in. The sound of them coughing at night when we go to sleep made me think of Mama.

Emma and the lady started to leave. It meant Emma had a new home and I wouldn't see her again. I looked down at Tom and saw that he was staring at something across the room. I looked where he was looking and saw a man and a lady holding hands. They were looking back at Tom and smiling. Then the man saw me looking and and he kept smiling. The lady did too.

Then Emma was back, standing in front of me and Tom. She bent down and gave Tom a hug and then she stood up and shook my hand. "I'm going to go live with my new mother now, Barry. Take care of Tom."

What did she think I'd been doing? I started to sass her, but then I thought about not seeing her again.

"What did that lady say to you, Emma?"

Emma smiled. "She asked me if I liked kittens. She's got three of them." Then she kissed me on the cheek and left.

We're going home with the Franklins now—the people that was smiling at Tom. Tom is propped up against the grain sacks in the back of the wagon and almost falling asleep. I'm sitting next to him with the ashtray in my hand and the Franklins are sitting up on the wagon seat with their backs to us.

Mr. Franklin says we can ride the horses on their ranch. Mrs. Franklin says we can have a big dinner when we get there. They have nice eyes, but I still don't know what they want us for. Mr. Stuart promised me that he will tell Pop where we are when he comes for us.

I didn't get to say goodbye to Jasper. The old man took him. Only Daisy and Sylvia didn't get picked. I guess they have to go back to the orphan place because Mr. Stuart said the End of the Line means that the train goes back where it came from.

The wagon is bumping along. Everything here is hilly and brown with no people or buildings like in New York, but there's a lot of sun

and it's making sparkles on the wagon, on Tom's face and on the back of Mr. and Mrs. Franklin where it comes through the ashtray. It makes me think about Mama and good things coming.

I woke up slowly, the dream images and Barry's thoughts mixing with disjointed memories of Jeremy and me at our grandparent's house; tenting out in our backyard; his high school graduation night when we'd celebrated with a lot of alcohol.

My face was wet, the pillowcase damp. I rolled over on my stomach, buried my face in the pillow and cried. Like a kid. I didn't care. The load of fear, grief and worry I'd been damming up since Jeremy went missing, maybe even since Mom and Dad broke up, burst through me. I hadn't cried since second grade when Bobby Gruber beat the crap out of me, not even when GMa and GPop died. Tears for Derry, tears now—what were these dreams doing to me?

After a while, I got up and went into the bathroom, feeling slow and heavy. I ran cold water in the sink and splashed my face over and over until the water's icy sting began to shock the weight from my eyes. Rubbing the towel roughly over my face, I began to feel alive... and better.

I walked back into the bedroom, my eyes going to the ashtray on the nightstand. There was no return of sadness at the sight of it; instead I saw the ashtray through Barry's eyes once more, with the play of sunlight glowing through the glass even though there was no sun coming through my condo windows. I felt again Barry's joy in the beauty of the light; his hope that beauty meant something good was coming. The sense of hope and resolution that filled me made me think of Barbara Browning and Ross and what they had said about their objects. Maybe these objects had a purpose.

It was 4 a.m. Christmas morning. I didn't want to go back to sleep. I didn't want to watch TV or read. I just wanted to let whatever the dream let in stay there for a while. Without family, stockings or a feast, it still felt like Christmas inside me.

A few hours later, driving over to Steve and Katy's, something pinged inside my head. I had been thinking of my divorced family like a big bowl that had been shattered into pieces that could never be reassembled—four damaged pieces. But, as I thought about my mother with her phalanx of friends, my father with his hand in Sandra's, Jeremy whose accident was bringing out his determination, it seemed to me that we were more like a quartet of instruments. The quartet had disbanded, but each of the instruments still made music, unique and individual, able to be combined with other instruments to create new music or to play alone.

Maybe it was only me who was still holding on to a picture of my family that was long in the past. It was time for a new picture—one that included Melanie, Steve, Katy and Brian, Nate and Patrick, my clients scattered throughout Oregon and the businesses I was helping them build. The dreams and the freedom to explore my own psychic abilities might be part of this new picture.

A rainy gray dawn with diffused light creeping up from the horizon supplanted the dark night. Introspection was not my style. It could have been a result of Jeremy's accident and all the time our family had just spent together or the conversations with Dad and Mom. Possibly there was another catalyst—a glass ashtray with the light shining through it.

The day after Christmas, Ross called. "Sorry I didn't call sooner," he said. "It's always busy around here up until Christmas and in the next couple of days I'll be getting ready for the New Year's bash. You and Melanie coming?"

I told him we were.

"Astrella's is open again," he said. "Matter of fact, the day you were here was the only day she was closed, except for Christmas."

I picked up the ashtray from the counter and held it up to the light. "Ross, what do you know about that store and the objects in it?"

"Well, like I said, Padgett and Daria bought my grandpa's hardware store and stocked it with things collected in their travels. When they were new to the area, they'd go to yard sales and other antique stores on buying trips, but it got too hard for Padgett to get around, so they just sold the stuff they had."

There was a pause and then Ross continued in a thoughtful voice. "Padgett had a way of knowing which objects might be right for people. Sometimes he'd gently steer them out of the store towards another antique store on the block; other times he'd deliberately show them something different from what they were interested in and they'd end up buying it. He always knew somehow."

He let a few seconds go by. "Daria doesn't have the same touch, so sometimes purchased objects actually end up back at the shop."

"How would that happen? Mrs. Astrella said she doesn't add to her inventory."

"One time she sold this beautiful little soapstone box," said Ross. "Then, about a year later, a guy came into the shop with a bunch of antiques and junk he was trying to sell and the box was in his pile. Daria bought it because she figured it had come back." He cleared his throat. "Twice, she's found an object she'd sold on the doorstep in the morning, as if the person who bought it had dropped it off in the middle of the night."

"Have you ever heard of people having dreams about the objects they buy?" I asked.

"Dreams? No, I never heard of any dreams except the one I had." Ross paused for a moment and then asked, "You been having dreams about the stuff you've bought?"

"I've bought or received four objects and dreamed about every one of them," I said. "That mule in the picture on the wall at Betsy's was part of one of the dreams." I quickly told him the outline of the blue vase dream and of my meeting with Ed Chessari at the monastery. There was a silence after I finished, long enough for me to ask if he was still there.

Then I heard, "Wow. When I was a kid, some geologists were exploring a cave on an old farm a few miles from here. They found a couple of old leather saddle packs, full of small household items and tools from the 1800s in the cave. It was a big deal around here. Made the front page of the Bedlington News and everything. I think the packs ended up in the state museum."

Though I knew my dream of Derry and what happened to him was real, this additional proof took my breath away. Barbara Browning and her serial killer sister; Derry and his untimely end; Ross and the knives—real people, real events. I looked over at the statue head holding down a stack of folders on my floor and wondered if, someday, I would know that her story was real too.

"Man, you've got a gift," Ross said. "How long have you been able to read objects like you did with my knives?"

Read objects? I'd never thought of it as reading, but it fit. Seeing and interpreting, isn't that what reading is? But what did being able to read objects have to do with dreaming about them? And what purpose could a "gift" like this have?

I answered Ross almost absently, with my mind still turning over question after question. "Since I was a kid, but I hadn't done it, didn't even think I could, until the other night at the diner."

"Well, you haven't lost it, my man," Ross assured me. "You know, Padge told me that he was looking for someone like himself to take over the place— not advertising, you understand, just keeping his eyes open. But then, he had the heart attack and Daria insisted on keeping the place open and running it just the way it was. The stock's slowly been dwindling, but Daria won't sell it off in bulk and she won't sell the shop. The city fathers have been itching to get her out of there because the shop looks blighted and she won't renovate. I thought she might be waiting for something, but now I wonder if she's been waiting for someone."

That question made my heart stop. What did I see for myself with this ability? Whatever it was, it wouldn't include being cooped up in a dark, little shop in the middle of a dinky town. With a start, I remembered how fast news could travel in a small place.

"Hey Ross, I haven't told Melanie about any of this yet, so please don't say anything."

"Melanie doesn't know?" There was an exasperated puff from the phone. "I suppose you've got your reasons, but you should tell her. She won't let you down."

Ross said he had to go and we hung up. I ran my fingers over the matchbox on the post of my ashtray, my thoughts confused. If all the dreams were real, what was I supposed to do about them?

Chapter Twenty-six

A crisis occurs and a guardian appears

The theme song from *Rocky* filled my bedroom. When my sleep-befuddled brain finally figured out it was the cell phone, I scrambled to answer it. Phone calls at four a.m. are rarely good news.

"Dave, I'm on my way to the hospital. Katy's having some problems and I'm following the ambulance." Steve's voice was hurried, his words clipped. I tried to focus. "Can you come over and take care of Brian? Katy's parents are away on a cruise."

"Where is he?"

"Still asleep at our house. The lady next door is watching him for now."

"I'm on it, bro."

"Thanks bud. I'll call."

His need galvanized me into action. In five minutes I was dressed and out the door.

Steve's neighbor lady answered my quiet knock and let me in. Brian was still asleep. He'd slept through the whole episode, according to the neighbor, despite the flashing lights that had wakened her. She seemed disposed to stay, but I thanked her for her help and promised to call her if I needed anything or heard news from Steve.

The baby monitor in the living room showed the ghostly outline of Brian's sleeping head, but I checked on him anyway, tiptoeing down the hall and peeking into his darkened room. A sliver of hall light fell on Brian's outflung arm as he lay on his back in his race car bed. I tiptoed back to the living room and turned on the television.

I surfed infomercials, trying to keep my mind from worrying about Katy and Steve. A mop that could purportedly suck up anything on the planet had captured my attention, when I felt a presence in the room. Brian, in his Spiderman pajamas, was standing at the intersection of hallway and living room, watching me. A scruffy yellow blanket was wrapped around one arm and trailed on the carpet.

A silent Brian was unnerving.

"Hey Bri! How you doing, buddy?" I patted the couch beside me. He took a few steps forward, giving me a wary look.

"Where's Mommy?"

Good question.

"She and Daddy went to see the doctor. They'll be back soon." I hoped that's the way it would work out.

He advanced a few more steps. I checked the channel guide for the Disney channel, wondering how soon cartoons started.

Brian shuffled closer. The strains of some sort of happy sounding music came on and he climbed up on the couch next to me.

"Sponge Bob," he directed.

I was flipping through channels, desperately seeking Sponge Bob, when I became aware of a powerful odor. Apparently my little friend wasn't housebroken.

He survived my attempt at diaper changing with great forbearance but refused to go back to bed. We ate bowls of cereal at the coffee table, watched cartoons and built forts in the living room until Steve called at ten.

Katy had given birth to a little girl but the baby was four weeks premature and had some sort of heart problem. Katy was in ICU with an infection. Steve sounded like he was working on his last nerve, but he asked to speak to Brian.

Brian took the phone, more interested in the buttons and the screen display than in communication. He listened, with one eye on something called *Yo Gabba Gabba* lighting up the TV, and then informed his father that he was eating breakfast in the living room and he wanted chocolate milk. Then he handed the phone to me.

"I'll be here all day, till I know what's going on," said Steve. "It's snowing over the pass and I-5 is closed at Yreka, so my parents are stuck in Burlingame until they can get a flight out tomorrow. Can you deal until then?"

"Sure, we'll have fun," I answered bravely.

"You're gonna have to change him—sorry to do it to you, bud. All the stuff is in his bedroom. And he likes the aquarium and the zoo if you need to get out. I left the SUV for you because it has his car seat in it. Keys are on the kitchen table."

"We already practiced the changing thing. No problem. Do what you need to do for Katy and the baby."

I clicked off the phone. My New Year's plans with Melanie were probably trashed and I needed to find some chocolate milk.

The aquarium was closed on Mondays so we opted for the zoo, not the best choice since it started to rain twenty minutes into our visit. Still, we didn't get too wet at the speed with which Brian was moving. I stood beneath a covered area at the polar bear habitation to catch my breath and call Melanie. I was miserable about not seeing her after eleven long days. I could hear disappointment in her voice, but she rallied and told me that she was proud of me for being there for Steve and Katy. Melanie's vote of confidence soothed a little of my misery, but then Brian almost took a header into the polar bear pool and I had to go.

I brought him over to the condo to pick up my laptop and a change of clothes. He trooped inside while I wondered how childproof my place might be. I told him to stay away from the computer, then turned on the television and found ESPN. While NFL highlights flitted over the screen, I plopped Brian on the couch and went to the bedroom to pick up what I needed.

My packing was completed in three minutes, but when I returned to the living room, Brian was no longer on the couch. A quick look around the room didn't turn him up. I was starting to panic, already visualizing him wandering around the condo parking lot and hearing the screech of brakes in my head, when I heard his voice coming from my corner office.

Brian was crouched behind a stack of files, running his fingers over the statue head holding them in place. My thundering heart began to return to its normal pace.

When I reached him, he was muttering something that sounded like, "Endolady."

I bent down to him.

"This, Endolady," Brian said as if he were introducing me to the statue.

"It's Maude, buddy. She keeps my papers safe."

Brian shook his head. "No. Endolady."

"OK, whatever." I picked up my laptop, put it in the backpack and slung it over my shoulder. "Time to roll, buddy." I reached for his hand.

He screeched and wrapped both arms around the statue, trying to pick it up.

"C'mon, Bri. It's time to go. Let Endolady guard the papers; we've got things to do."

"Endolady! ENDOLADY!" Brian shouted, glaring at me and nodding his head for emphasis. He kept a firm grip on the statue. I couldn't tell whether he was correcting my pronunciation or attempting to pass along valuable information, but it was time to get moving.

I reached for his hand again. He erupted, throwing his little Baby Gap covered body over Maude and bursting into tears. His howls reverberated around the room. I hoped Barbara Browning wasn't home; in fact I hoped no one in the entire condo complex was home. Anyone with normal hearing within a five mile radius would be dialing Child Protective Services.

Dropping the backpack, I knelt beside him and made soothing sounds. Brian was making too much noise to hear me. I couldn't hear myself. Finally, I patted his back, still curved protectively over the statue, and the noise diminished slightly. Encouraged, I kept patting and the noise kept diminishing until finally there were a series of hitchy breaths and I could slip in a few words.

"Hey, Bri, we have to go. Don't you want to see your mommy?"

More hitchy breaths and then I heard, "En...do...la...dee," and a quavering sob. I had an inspiration.

"We can take Endolady with us," I said in a cheery voice. "Do you think she would like a ride in the car?"

The little blonde head, turned away from me, nodded.

"Well, then you'll have to stop crying and let me pick her up."

He stood up then, huge blue eyes still filled with tears, mouth turned down. He kept one hand on the statue's face as though suspecting a trick from horrible old me. I retrieved my duffle bag, unzipped it and hefted up the statue head. Brian watched me carefully as I slid the head into my duffle. When I zipped it shut, his face clouded over. Another hurricane was coming.

Hurriedly I said, "It's just for carrying, Bri. We have to take her out to the car. We can unzip it when we get there."

He looked from the backpack to my face. I felt the verdict could go either way, but, finally, he took my hand. Before he could change his mind, I threw the backpack over one shoulder, picked up the now heavy duffle and headed for the car.

Out in Steve's SUV, I buckled Brian into the car seat in the back and unzipped Maude from the duffle. I set her up on the seat next to Brian so that he could see her and told him he could play with her when we got to his house.

When Steve came home for a quick shower just before six, I thought he might say something about a fifteen pound statue head being a weird thing for a kid to play with, but he didn't seem to notice. Katy was still in ICU but responding to the medication. The baby, Rebecca, was scheduled for surgery to repair a heart defect the next day. The poor guy had been running ragged between ICU and the neo-natal ward. He might not have noticed if Brian had been playing with an atomic bomb. Steve threw together a sandwich after his shower, kissed Brian and left again to spend another night at the hospital.

Brian and I played Hide and Seek until seven. The busier I kept him, the less opportunity he had to ask about his mother, I figured, especially since I didn't know what to tell him. At bedtime, he fell apart, wanting Katy and Steve to tuck him in, wondering where they were. I told him they were at the hospital getting ready to bring his little sister home. He didn't care; he just wanted them home.

Brian was working up to a real doozy of a tantrum. It was hard to blame him, faced with a guy who couldn't find the chocolate milk fixings or change a diaper in under twenty minutes. Finally, I thought of the statue head lying on the coffee table in the living room and went out to fetch it. I put it up on Brian's dresser, facing his little race car bed.

"Hey bud, look who's here helping me take care of you until Mommy gets back?" I cozened.

Brian sighted on Maude at once and his tears stopped like a turned off faucet. Under her calm gaze, he settled down into his bed, pulled *Curious George and the Puppy* from under his pillow and handed it to me. It was like magic. With my ears still ringing, I started to read, but Brian fell asleep in the middle of the story. Now, I'll never know how it ends.

I took a breather on the couch to call my mom, Nate, and Patrick to let them know about Katy and the baby. Nate and Patrick each went to voice mail, but Mom was home, snowbound in her little house. Steve was like her third son and she was still good friends with his mother. Mom said she would add Katy, Steve and the baby to her prayer chain and she gave me some tips for quicker diaper changing.

"Taking care of Brian is good practice for you," she said. It was practice that I didn't think I would be using for another ten years or so, but I didn't mention that to her.

An hour later, my cell rang. I hoped it was Steve with an update, but it was better.

"Hey Cowboy, what'cha doin'?" Melanie's voice was sweet balm to my ears.

"Just put the Brian to bed and I'm hanging out. What are you doing?"

"I'm hanging out too—outside your condo. How do I get to Steve's house?"

She'd driven the two and a half hours to Portland through snow, rain and darkness just to be with me. My heart swelled as I gave her directions.

When Melanie's little red Camry arrived twenty minutes later, I met her at the door with a bear hug that lifted her into the air. As we held each other, she said, "I told Ross we'd have to pass on the New Year's party. You're a good guy, Dave—too good to be spending New Year's without me."

I liked the proprietary air with which she said this, and when she produced a sleeping bag out of the gear she'd brought in, we turned the couch into our own nest for the night.

In the morning, Brian woke us out of the nest. He stared at Melanie, but she was equal to it. She said, "I know how to make chocolate milk."

That was all it took for Brian to fall in love, that and the Hershey's chocolate syrup Melanie had thoughtfully brought along.

Steve called to give me his parents' flight number and arrival time. Katy's parents had jumped their cruise in Mazatlán and were coming in around the same time, so we bundled Brian into his car seat and went to The Bagel Place for breakfast before heading over to the airport. Melanie followed me in the Camry so we'd have enough room for people and suitcases.

Back at Steve's house, Steve's mom took charge and Melanie and I were off the hook. Except for the utterly disgusting task of changing poopy diapers, it hadn't been too bad and Melanie and I still had the opportunity to start the

New Year in each other's arms. I hoped Steve, Katy and the baby would have the same chance.

It was late afternoon and the rain had settled in, steady and cold.

"We still have time to make that party at Betsy's," I said to Melanie as we walked out to our cars.

She looked up at me from underneath her parka hood as rain fell between us. "If you want to go, then sure. But I'd be happy just to be warm and dry here with you."

We stopped at a store to pick up supplies before going back to the condo and then spent a few hours jumping each other's bones before dinner. While I put together my specialty—Dave's Killer Chicken Nachos, Steve called.

Katy was doing better and the surgery for the baby had gone well which added some extra cheer. We fell asleep on the couch, waking up just in time to watch the ball drop in Times Square and toast the New Year with the last two Droptop Amber Ales left in my refrigerator. It was the best New Year's party I had been to in my life.

In the morning, waking up next to Melanie was the way I wanted every New Year to begin. I wrapped myself around her, spoon fashion and whispered in her ear, "I love you." Part of me was hoping she was still asleep—not that I wanted to take the words back, but because I didn't know what the next step might be and that scared me.

Melanie rolled over in my arms, her eyes wide-awake and questioning. I looked back, the answer in my eyes. Almost nose to nose, she whispered, "The man with the killer smile, yummy nachos and sexy hazel eyes." Then, she rolled me over, cuddled into my back, and whispered into my ear, "I love you."

I had to laugh—she'd mocked me so perfectly, but sweetly too. There are times when you laugh because something is funny, times you laugh because something is not, and times you laugh because the world is just a damn fine place. It was a great way to start the new year.

Chapter Twenty-seven

Mom has a dream

Over the next two weeks, Melanie and I took turns driving back and forth to spend Sunday evenings and Mondays together. Steve updated me weekly, first that Katy was home and baby Rebecca was holding her own; then the baby was doing well at the hospital; and finally that she had come home and the family was together. I knew he had a lot going on and tried not to bug him. With the uptick in my relationship with Melanie, I suddenly didn't have much time, either, not even to check out Astrella's.

I kept the glass ashtray on the nightstand and although I often played with it, turning it over and over in my hands while talking on the phone to Melanie, there were no more dreams. Melanie filled most of my thoughts instead.

One Sunday afternoon when I was getting ready to drive to Bedlington, Steve called.

"Sorry I've been a recluse, bud, but since the baby came home, it's taken a little while for the dust to settle. All the parents went home and it's just us now. The baby is doing fine and Katy is amazing. Stop by when you can."

It was good to hear him sounding so cheerful.

"I'm on my way to Melanie's but I'll stop by later this week."

"Sure, that would be great. So things look kind of serious with Melanie, huh?" There was a smile in his voice. "Brian already thinks she's the bomb. Oh, by the way, the statue thing… is that the one from your dream? Do you mind if we keep it a while longer? Bri is really attached to it. He made me bring it into our bedroom—to make Mommy better, he said."

"No problem. You guys can have her. Mom made sure I had another paper weight."

Steve laughed and then said, "He says she loves us and watches over 'Becca and mommy.'" His voice dropped. "You know, it's weird, but it kind of feels that way to me and Katy too. When I brought Katy home from the hospital, she really had a hard time sleeping because she was so worried about the baby and she still had some pain. Brian made me put the statue on Katy's nightstand. When she couldn't sleep, Katy would run her fingers over it again and again. She said it helped her relax and then she could feel hopeful that things would be okay. Now that the baby is home, the only time she sleeps soundly is if the statue is next to her crib." He gave a snort. "It's like a good luck charm. Everyone knows you don't mess with a streak. Maybe those objects from the curio shop are special after all."

His thought echoed mine. I remembered Katharine drawing hope and courage from the statue and wondered about Brian's connection to it. "Like I said, I've got another paper weight. You're welcome to Maude."

My curiosity got the better of me. "Do all three-year olds have a thing for statues? And what's with Brian calling her 'Endo lady'?"

Steve laughed. "Brian's not quite up to speed with all of his words yet—that's 'Angel Lady' in three-year-old speak. And, no, he doesn't get excited about statues—just this one." His voice became serious again. "Hey, thanks again, bud. You're the best."

I was almost out the door when the phone rang again. It was Mom calling to check on Steve and Katy. I let her know that all was well.

"I'm so glad. I made a rose quartz baby bracelet for the little one and I'll mail it up," she said. "Oh, I keep forgetting to tell you. I had a dream the other night."

I sat down immediately, hoping this wasn't bad news. "About the vase?"

"Well, I was hoping I'd have one about the vase, but no luck. I use the vase to focus my attention when I meditate because it makes me feel calm and centered. Like I'm in the right place, doing the right thing. It gives me hope when I'm worried about something—especially if I'm worried about you or Jeremy. You know, Aristotle said, 'Hope is the dream of the waking man.' It definitely gives me good vibes."

She paused for a second and then rushed on. "Anyway, my dream didn't have anything to do with the vase, but I wanted to share it with you so you'd know that you're not the only person with weird dreams."

Mom paused theatrically and said, "I dreamed I was in a parade, walking next to a mule. Can you believe that?" She chuckled. "There was a band playing and people cheering. I was passing out leaflets about women voting and the mule kept trying to knock off my hat, when he wasn't trying to get friendly with a goat that some little boy had on a lead in front of us. People kept laughing at them and I was having so much fun." Mom laughed again.

My heart stopped when I heard the word "mule," but it started again with her laughter. She sounded so…free and happy. I was about to tell her the Derry dream but stopped before I opened my mouth. To Mom, her dream was funny and the vase was something that helped her meditate and stop worrying about Jeremy and me—worries that, until Jeremy's accident, I hadn't realized she carried. Why clutter things up? Besides, I wanted to get on the road.

"You're right, Mom. It's a pretty funny dream."

Chapter Twenty-eight

A talk with the woman behind the counter

and other curious things

I finally made it out the door and into my car. On the way to Bedlington, I mulled over the information I'd collected about the objects from Astrella's. I now knew I could control whether or not I had a dream by using the quartz to block it. I could still use the "reading" ability GPop helped me develop to find out information about an object without dreaming about it, although reading objects didn't seem to have the same clarity and depth as the dreams.

The objects seemed to bring something positive to each person who had received them—calm and freedom from worry for my mother, safety and peace for Steve's family, peace and closure for Barbara, peace and purpose for Ross—even hope and resolution for me with the ashtray. Perhaps the objects addressed the things people kept hidden from the world.

Why I was having the dreams and what I was supposed to do with them, if anything, was still a mystery. I didn't know if other people also had dreams like mine about the objects from Astrella's. What if I bought something at another curio shop? Would I have dreams then too? And why was this happening now?

The last time I had been down to see Melanie, two weeks earlier, I hadn't stopped by Astrella's. Melanie and I were too busy and, to tell the truth, between the new intensity of our relationship and worry about Steve and Katy, I didn't have a lot of mental room for the dreams. But questions were still swirling around in my brain, and this time, I would get some answers.

I arrived in Bedlington around 11:30. In the January rain, Astrella's looked as dark as ever, but I opened the door without hesitation and strode inside. Mrs. Astrella was in her usual place behind the tall wooden counter but the ever-present red and black turtleneck and maroon shawl had been replaced with a light green turtleneck and a dark green sweater. A Christmas present?

She was reading Carlos Castaneda's *Journey to Ixtlan* and she lowered the book when I walked in. I glanced around to see if anything else had changed. The Moroccan hand drum was gone from the third shelf and there was a huge old-fashioned suitcase on the floor near the lowest shelf.

I strode to the counter. Daria Astrella met my eyes with a direct gaze as if we were opponents in a joust; as if she had been waiting for me and now things could begin.

"I want to know about the dreams," I said abruptly. I had waited too long for small talk. "Why am I dreaming about the objects I buy here? Every time I buy an object from this shop, I have a dream—a vivid, unforgettable dream that happens to be true. Why?"

She put Carlos face down on the counter and focused her eyes on the book as though gathering her thoughts. A minute crawled by and then she looked up, off into space. "Tell me about your dreams."

She said this almost as if it were the next step in a formula, or a response to a secret code. So, standing before her at the counter, I detailed all four of my dreams to Daria Astrella at warp speed. During my rapid recital, she stared off into space. There was no reaction to any of the dreams that I could see; she asked no questions and made no response. I might have thought that she had fallen asleep except that her eyes were open. Despite my speed, it took a long time.

Finally, I was done with my recital. She said nothing for a moment and then she asked, "What have you done with the information from the dreams?"

"What? Nothing. I…," Her question surprised and confused me. Then I thought about it. "I've told four people about my dreams. One of them was worried and thought I should explore what the objects mean to me; one told me to stop buying stuff here if it bothered me and one of them thought I should pay attention to the dreams. The last one thought I should tell my girl-friend about them."

She nodded once. "Good advice."

"Which one?"

"All of them."

I thought about that for a nanosecond. "Look, does anyone else have dreams after they buy something here?"

Daria Astrella shrugged. "Not everyone dreams about the objects, but everyone who buys an object gets the one that is right for them. If they aren't right, the objects come back to the shop. Or, someone passes them to the right person. Some people, like my late husband, have a gift for connecting the right person and the right object."

It was an answer, but not the answer I needed.

She pointed to the suitcase on the floor. "This suitcase came back yesterday. Sometimes I make a mistake. What do you think?"

Was she insane? What did I care about an old suitcase? Was she trying to evade my questions? Her finger kept pointing to the suitcase and finally I looked at the thing. It was enormous, more like a steamer trunk than a suitcase—black cracked leather with tags hanging from the handle and stickers pasted to the front.

"I don't need a suitcase."

"Did you need a marble head or a vase?"

I wasn't willing to concede the point. "Why am I having these dreams? What do they mean?"

The old woman punched buttons on the ancient cash register. The drawer opened. "I can't tell you. Maybe you'll figure it out. Do you still have the objects?"

"I still have two of them." I knew I would not part with the ashtray, but I felt that Barbara Browning might be ready for the painting of her sister one day.

"How do the people who have the other objects feel about them?"

I thought about Mom's call, my own feeling every time I looked at the ashtray, little Brian's belief that Endo Lady was keeping watch over his family, Barbara Browning's new-found peace of mind. "They all seem to have a feeling of peace or safety from the objects."

She looked at me with a blank expression. "That will be five dollars."

For a confusing second, I thought the five-dollar fee was Astrella's price for peace and safety. Then, I realized she expected me to pay for the black monstrosity on the floor.

"What's in it?" I asked, curiosity beginning to betray me.

"Don't know. Could be anything. Still costs five dollars."

I stared at the lamp on the counter, trying to decide whether to walk out the damn door, never to return, or to solve this puzzle. The base of the lamp on the counter wasn't encircled by two intertwined figures as I had thought. Today I could see that it was a human figure of some sort, with draperies flowing behind it as if blown by a wind.

If I left, I might never know any more than I already did. Maybe the suitcase held some answers. At the least, it was one step closer to putting the old woman out of business. The shelves held only the alligator skull, the silver jar and the other skull thing. She wasn't answering my questions; she wasn't friendly and I didn't want a colossal suitcase. But, I was curious. I fished a five out of my jeans pocket.

"If I have a dream about this thing, will you answer my questions?"

As she put the five in the cash register, Daria Astrella said, "I already have. But, maybe by then, you'll have your own answers."

He was almost ready. He had the dreams the way Padgett did and he had found the people the objects belonged to. She could feel the power in him, but whether the boy would be willing to take on the job, she didn't know. Padgett would have known what to do and what to say. All she could do was to let the boy find his own answers. Better to say nothing rather than to risk scaring him off.

Chapter Twenty-nine

Hypothesis and experimentation

The suitcase weighed a ton. I muscled the thing out of the shop, hearing the crash and thud of some heavy objects throwing themselves around inside it. Fortunately, the car was parked on the street, only about fifty feet away from Astrella's. Heaving the suitcase into the trunk of my car made me wonder if I should get serious about working out at the gym.

I locked the car and walked to Betsy's. The place was packed with the Sunday lunch crowd and a group of four was standing outside under the shelter of the awning waiting to get seats. I opened the door and peeked in. Melanie was whirling around the floor and Bridget was behind the counter serving coffee with one hand and picking up empty plates with the other. It wasn't an opportune moment to talk. Melanie caught my eye and smiled. I smiled back and gave a head nod toward the door, letting her know I'd be back later. The foursome glared at me when I got outside, as if they thought I was trying to crowd in front of them.

I had a few hours before Melanie got off work. The siren call of the suitcase in my trunk came to me loud and clear, but I didn't have anywhere to pull the monster out and open it. I did have just enough time to take action to answer the question of whether it was just the objects from Astrella's that gave me dreams. What would happen if I picked up something from another curio store or even a yard sale? I got into the car and drove back toward Eugene, which was only a few miles from Bedlington. There was a town north of Eugene known for its antique malls. I'd look for an object there, something small and inexpensive to use as an experiment.

I drove down South Willamette Street in Coburg, following the signs to the Antique Mall. It was easy to find because the town was small and the building well-marked. Inside, there was a collection of individual antique shops. I walked into the first one on the right, planning to visit each one in turn until I found something that felt right. GPop's method had been to walk the perimeter inside a shop and gradually spiral toward the center, hands behind his back, peering into shelves or gazing at things on walls until something caught his eye. GMa's method was to pick up and touch almost every object in the store. She rarely made a purchase; GPop almost always scored.

I wandered through displays of old magazines and books, ancient souvenirs of long ago vacations, glass cases of spectacles, medals and jewelry, shelves of china and Depression-era glass and small pieces of furniture. That was just the first store.

At the rate I was going, finding something to buy would take forever. I picked up the pace. In the third little store, I greeted the owner standing behind the counter with a nod and started down the perimeter. Along the second wall was a display set up like an old-time kitchen with a wood stove, tins of spices and baking soda, enamelware, a wooden table with matching chairs. A small peach basket on the top of the table with three red apples inside caught my eye. I picked up one of the apples. It was actual size, made of wood and stained red. Except for a faint amount of dust fuzzing the color, it was beautiful in a folk-art kind of way. I tried to buy just one apple but the proprietor said the three went together. He was asking $7.50, but I talked him into a five instead. He threw in the miniature peach basket for free.

I was satisfied with my purchase even though I did have two more apples than I wanted. I tucked the basket of apples into the Saturn's trunk next to the colossal suitcase. I'd do my experimenting on the road after I left Melanie's house.

The next day, while we were driving around the soggy countryside, Melanie said, "I think my Granny Trish is coming up in a few weeks. She wants to meet you."

"You mean she wants to check me out, right? Before she reports back to the rest of the family?" I was teasing, but I knew it was true.

"Not exactly, she's not an enemy infiltrator, she's just …interested," Melanie turned her face towards me with an impish smile. "She's a lot of fun—not stuffy at all. And she really stood behind me when my parents were having fits about me becoming a lawyer."

From the way Melanie had always talked about her, I knew Granny Trish, and her opinions meant the world to my girl. What could I say, but, "I'm looking forward to meeting her."

Chapter Thirty

More than I hoped for, less than I expected.

I left the suitcase and apples out in the car, wanting to set up my second experiment for a time when I could give it my full attention. Melanie was a welcome distraction.

When I left her on Wednesday morning, I drove to Corvallis to touch bases with a new client. That night, in the Corvallis Best Western, I brought in the wooden apples, saving the suitcase, as much as it called to me, for home. It was just too big and bulky to haul in and out of hotel rooms.

The apples were on the nightstand next to the digital clock when I slid between the crisp, cold sheets and made my nightly call to Melanie. After we hung up, I turned on the television and settled in to watch a rerun of *Die Hard 2*.

I wasn't brought up to be rude. But I want to be. It's not so much that I want to call **Mrs.** Louden a prune-faced devil's daughter with the intelligence of a tin of sardines, it's just that I want the freedom to roll it out there if I feel the need to say it. I think it, but just can't get past my upbringing to actually say it aloud. I'm stifled.

I was brought up to be modest and self-deprecating; demure and quiet; a peace-maker, not a warrior. Ladies accept instead of question; they stay put instead of roaming around. I don't know why it's supposed to be that way, but it is, and it's been a mighty wearying forty-two years trying to be what I'm supposed to be instead of who I am.

It's 1928, not 1850, for goodness sake, and I am old enough to where no one needs to warn me that asking questions or stating opinions will prevent me from getting a husband. I already had a husband and the best thing about him was his clothes.

I want to bob my hair and take to wearing trousers all the time—not those silk and satin flowing things in the movies, but comfortable, soft trousers like my husband's old suit pants. I want to trim my own trees and build my own greenhouse. And never wear corsets again.

Thank heavens I bore only boys. Every admonition to sit still, keep knees together and stay clean would have stuck in my craw and choked me before any little girl child would have heard them from me. Neither of us would have survived the upbringing.

How could I have inflicted corsets upon a daughter or made her do embroidery indoors while her brothers were outside tearing up the place?

I played catch and mumblety-peg with my boys until they grew old enough to realize that mothers weren't supposed to do that. It made sense to them that I wore trousers when we played outside. How else could I run to play tag or show them how to climb trees?

When Bill came home from his trips on the road, the boys begged him to build them a tree house, but my husband could no more build a tree house than I could fly. So, I built it while the boys took turns helping or keeping a lookout for nosy old Prune-Face Louden.

Now my boys are grown-up and far away—Farnon traveling with his boss in Singapore and Bentley working on an oil rig in Texas. Bill is six years in his grave and I am supposed to be a lady in waiting—waiting for one of my sons to come home and fix all the things around the house; waiting for a repairman; waiting for some gentleman caller to rescue me while I patiently tat lace or crochet doilies to cover up the worn places on the furniture. Inside my house, where no one can see me, I am building cabinetry and teaching myself to repair the plumbing.

Worrying about what other people think of me has become second nature and I'm sick of it. I don't want to be an old woman sitting inside my house waiting to die and keeping my knees together.

Prune-Face heard me banging away one day and the nosy old thing crept over to see what was up. I was lying partway under the porch, hammering a new joist in place when I heard her clear her throat. I guess she'd been doing it for a few minutes because I was making a lot of noise and her throat clearing had reached the grinding stage before I heard it.

I pulled my head out from under the porch and peered out at her neatly tied sensible black shoes and the bottom of her blue-flowered house dress. Tilting back my head, I took in the rest of her dumpling shaped body and her indignant face as she recognized who belonged to the trouser clad legs sticking out from under the porch.

"Emily Weston, whatever are you doing?"

"As you can see, I'm repairing my porch," I said.

She looked at me, taking in every inch of Farnon's old work boots, Bill's gabardine trousers and flannel shirt and the flowered kerchief wrapped around my head.

"Emily this is not suitable for a woman of your age. You must wait for one of the boys to repair the porch."

"The boys won't be home for another six months and the porch will have fallen to smithereens by then."

"Then hire a carpenter to fix it."

"Can't. Don't have enough money. This porch is a safety hazard—someone has to fix it before a person ringing the doorbell falls right through it. And that someone will have to be me." I slid back under the porch. The sensible shoes eventually clomped away.

I hammered and fumed underneath the porch.

Why can't I do what I want to do? What's the worst that would happen if Prune-Face tells everyone that I do my own carpentry? Maybe the other ladies won't invite me over for coffee and sewing anymore? I'd miss the gossip and Rita Hatchway's lemon cake, but not the sewing—definitely not the sewing.

Instead of sewing sweetly like a lady, I've been working on my indoor projects. I love the tree in the backyard when it's filled with bright red apples. They look like decorations waiting for a party. I'm always sad when the fruit and leaves are gone and the tree is shivering in the snow. So I carved three apples out of some blocks of wood I found in Bill's shop building and sanded them smooth as a baby's butt. The grain of the wood looked so pretty, I couldn't bear to cover them up. Instead, I cooked up the red cake of watercolor from my paint box with some white vinegar and rubbed it on with a piece of sheet. After I got the color I wanted, you could still see the grain right through it. Then I applied linseed oil to protect the wood. They have a powerful smell at the moment, but I have a bowl of pretty red apples to brighten up the winter.

Claire Tepper came by the house after I finished them, knocking on the door softly and giving a quick look down both sides of the street before she scooted through the door. Prune-Face had been talking.

I showed her to the parlor. When I brought in the coffee and some store-bought cookies, Claire was sitting on the sofa with one of my apples in her hand.

"Oh, Emily...there you are. Wherever did you find these pretty apples? They look so cheerful."

"I made them," I said as I set down the coffee tray.

"You painted them?"

I noticed her change in my wording.

"I know people who paint china dishes. They're just beautiful." She sniffed delicately at my combination of vinegar and linseed oil and took the cup of coffee I offered.

"Your house looks so tidy, Emily. I'm envious. That back door of mine is practically shattered, what with Rex charging through it chasing cats and Henry smacking it back when he goes out to play."

Claire's boy, Henry, and his dog had the same way of entering and leaving the house—full speed and without using door knobs. Her back-door was hanging by a hinge and the frame was splintered.

"Fred never has time to fix anything since he got that job in Tulsa. I don't even think he notices how rundown we've got." Claire set the apple back in the bowl with a little pat and took a sip of coffee. "Where did you say you got these apples?"

Later that week, I fixed Claire's back door. While I was painting the trim, Rachel Parson peeked over the fence and asked if I could take a look at her chicken coop. While I was fixing the ramp into the coop, Evelyn Pritchard from across the street came over to visit Rachel and let it slip that her faucet was leaking and her husband wouldn't be home from the Shriner's Convention for three days.

They pay me in meals, mending and silence. If a husband questions the no-longer-leaking faucet or a magically transformed porch step, they feign surprise. Our little block is looking almost spruce.

Claire's got a list as long as an arm of things to be repaired—falling down fences, window sashes, a chipped tile. Together we've cobbled together a tool kit, made from a few real tools, some knitting needles and a meat tenderizer. You can do an awful lot with a knitting needle besides knit.

Yesterday, during sewing circle, Prune-Face said that she almost put a foot through her porch—the wood was so rotted. She slid her eyes in my direction as I blotted blood off my thumb where the needle stuck me.

Today, I showed up on her porch with my tools, my hair tucked up under Bentley's old newsboy cap and wearing Bill's trousers. After I'd worked for almost an hour, Prune-Face brought out a glass of lemonade and then scuttled inside. The lemonade was almost as good as mine and the pair of work gloves she left on the tray made the job a lot less painful.

I woke up laughing, seeing Emily Weston's handyman disguise in my mind. I looked at the red digital numbers on the clock radio—3:22. As always with these dreams, there had been a series of detailed images and I had felt Emily's thoughts—it was like looking through a scrapbook and reminiscing—only they weren't my pictures or my thoughts.

Still feeling as if I were walking through the dream, I reached over and touched one of the apples in the dark, brought it over to my nose. It might have been my imagination, but there was a faint odor of linseed oil.

It wasn't just objects from Astrella's, then. I couldn't decide whether that was good news or not. And why did so many of the dreams seem to be from a woman's point of view? Since the dreams began, I'd already experienced more emotions than in the previous decade. Could they be changing me?

In the next few days, I found myself rushing through client meetings, anxious to be home to explore the suitcase. Still, as excited as I was about the possibilities, I took my time when I arrived home, shelving the sample cases and dumping the contents of my own suitcase into a pile on the bedroom floor before taking a hot shower and pouring myself a beer.

At last, I plopped the suitcase on the living room carpet and parked beside it, anticipation as high as Christmas morning. What would be inside? Why did Daria Astrella want me to buy it? Another gulp of beer and I lay my hands on the cracked black leather. I popped the locks and pulled open the lid, my heart beating with anticipation.

Inside the yawning cavern of the case was a jumble of papers, business cards, metal framed documents sheathed in glass, five big, heavy hard-backed books and a thick charcoal covered official looking paperback book. No jewels, no money, no clothing and no antique comics, stamps or trading cards.

What did I expect for five bucks? Disappointed, but undaunted, I began pulling things out of the case and sorting it into piles.

The framed documents came out first. The biggest one had a diagonal crack in the glass. Inside the frame was a certificate appointing James Harrison to the Selective Service Advisory Board of San Mateo County. Another frame held a certificate claiming that James Harrison had passed his bar exam for the state of California and a third frame held his Notary Public certificate.

The cards I had thought were business cards were florist cards instead, the kind that come with floral arrangements. Most of them said, "In deepest sympathy" or "Thinking of you in your time of grief"—the rest just had names on them. There was a small white printer's box filled with James Harrison's business cards, only a few of which were missing.

Four leather-bound law review books and a pristine copy of a high school geography book copyrighted 1939 from Long Beach High School explained the heavy thumping when I carried the suitcase. The charcoal paperback turned out to be a copy of the water rights of San Mateo County.

There was a mass of what looked to be receipts, bills and a few letters, like someone in a hurry had dumped a bunch of stuff inside, to be gone through later. James Harrison's draft card from 1942 classified him as 4-F, but a draft card from 1943 reclassified him as 4-A. Quite a jump for a forty-one year old man.

A knock sounded at my door. Melanie's voice called cheerily, "Thai food delivery. It's hot! It's fresh!"

I flung open the door. Melanie was balancing a cardboard box with white cartons in it on top of her copper curls and grinning like the Cheshire Cat. She slid the box off her head and handed it to me.

"Forget the Thai. *I'm* hot and *I'm* fresh," she said as she stepped up and kissed me. It was a good kiss and she was right.

I put the box on the kitchen counter so we could concentrate. After we came up for air, Melanie said, "The wiring for Betsy's refrigeration unit went kerblooey and Ross shut us down for a couple of days to get it fixed. So, when I got your voice mail that you would be home tonight, I decided to surprise you. Surprise!"

After we spent some time getting reacquainted, we got around to eating the tepid Thai and talking about everything we'd been doing in the three and a half days since we'd last seen each other.

"What's this stuff?" Melanie asked, indicating the pile of books and papers on the living room floor with a stocking toe.

I told her about the suitcase purchase, still nettled about Daria Astrella's response and mad at myself for buying another object when I hadn't yet resolved what I was going to do about them in the first place.

"You mean you had that thing in your trunk the whole time you were at my house and you didn't bring it in?"

My rationale for not telling her about the objects and my dreams, because I didn't want her to think I was crazy suddenly seemed lame and cowardly.

Her gaze sharpened at the sight of my stricken face and she said, "Dave, what is it? What aren't you telling me?"

Chapter Thirty-one

Melanie has a dream and I come clean

There was a lot I wasn't telling her, but since I had too many questions in my own mind, I wasn't ready to expose Melanie to my inner turmoil. I gave her a smile and said, "I didn't want to spoil our time together with an old suitcase. All there is in it is a bunch of junk, anyway."

Melanie took a breath and looked into my eyes. Then she seemed to pull herself inward as she glanced down at the mess on the floor. "Well, then let's check out this junk," she said lightly as she settled herself on the floor.

As Melanie rummaged through the piles. I sat beside her and pulled out the draft cards, feeling like a jerk.

After a few minutes she said, "Wow, you got this guy's whole life for five dollars. He was a lawyer, he fought in WWII, he was married and he had a heart attack and died on the way to the hospital when he was only forty-six." She shook her head in amazement.

I gaped at her. "How did you get all that?"

Melanie looked at me, eyebrows quirked up in surprise. "From the documents in the frames and the bills."

She held up a white sheet of paper. "This is the bill from the ambulance service and this," here she held up a yellow sheet, "is the bill from the hospital. And they are addressed to Mrs. Bernice Harrison. The other stuff is obvious from his bar certificate and the law books." She sat back on her heels. "Elementary, my dear Watson. I bet you can tell a lot more stuff about him from some of these letters and the florist cards," she said, reaching for a stack.

I reached for her. We could play detectives some other time.

Around two in the morning I woke, on the floor, to the sound of Melanie's muttering. She was curled up against my side, sleeping, but being pretty noisy about it. I touched her shoulder. She opened her eyes and glared at me. I thought I'd been very gentle about waking her. I tried to talk her into going into the bedroom to sleep, but she turned over, away from me, and in less than a minute I heard the sound of regular breathing. I got up and pulled the pillows and blankets off the bed and brought them back into the living room. Melanie groaned a little when I slid a pillow under her head, but she did not wake up.

I fell back to sleep as well.

She'd left her geography book behind in the car. It must have fallen out of her school bag. I meant to mail it back to her, but I kept forgetting.

The first time I opened the book was the day after I put my daughter on the bus back to Long Beach. Patty said she was my daughter and I had no reason not to believe her, but I am a lawyer and we like proof.

Proof might have rested in the brown eyes shaped like mine and the strawberry blonde hair that curled back from a widow's peak on her forehead just like Terri's, her mother, but Terri was dead and couldn't tell me the truth. Patty had a birth certificate with a blank where "Father" was listed and only her grandmother's bitter remarks and a few letters to connect her to me.

My daughter, my first daughter. She'd tracked me down using her few clues, put herself on a bus and traveled five hundred miles on the chance that I might be her father. Her courage and resourcefulness took my breath away.

Patty said she was sixteen and a sophomore at Long Beach High School, living with her grandmother in the same house where Terri had grown up. Her mother had been dead a year, killed in an automobile accident on the way to her job at the Long Beach airport. Patty sounded like Terri when she talked and had the same habit of pressing her thumbs into her palms when she was nervous. She brought her birth certificate, a gesture I appreciated for its forethought and organization. The birth certificate showed Patricia Quinlan's birthday as February 24, 1927—eight months after I graduated from law school and seven months after the last time I had seen Terri climbing out of a plane.

I brought Patty's textbook into my office, thinking to write her a note and enclose it when I mailed the book back to her. Idly, I thumbed through it, looking for some evidence of a high school girl's life—notes written in the margins or hearts drawn around a boy's name. The book was pristine except for "Pat Quinlan" penciled on the pupil assignment sheet pasted on the flyleaf. The pages were stiff and held the faintly vomitus smell of the hydrochloric acid used in the printing process.

I held the book and let it fall open, wondering what country would be revealed. Pages 412 and 413 lay before me, one titled "The Far East" and the other titled "The Japanese Islands Compared with the British Isles."

I snapped the book closed. I don't need reminders of the boys I send to the Far East; boys who are losing their lives and taking the lives of others; boys who might never become lawyers or teachers or family breadwinners. For two years we'd been in the war and I saw no end to the need for boys that I, as a member of the Selective Service Board of San Mateo County, would have to send to those faraway lands.

They made me feel ancient, those boys with their narrow chests and bright eyes. Most are only a couple of years older than Patty. I am forty-one, safely weighed down with the responsibilities of a wife and two children, a law practice, civic duties and my mother who depends on her only son. I do my best as a civilian flight instructor to prepare young men to return safely, but it doesn't feel like it's enough.

For me the sky is a place of joy. It's hard to imagine it as a launch for destruction. Every time I'm up in a plane, I think of Terri—the joy she took in flying, the way her face glowed after a flight, her cheery, "Hey Jim, it's a beautiful day in the air," when she reported to me for lessons. To think of that bright ferocious spirit crushed by something as earthbound as an automobile squeezes my heart.

Every waking moment that I wasn't in classes at St. Vincent's School of Law, I spent at Ed Daughtery's flight school, swapping flight time for mechanic work and working as a flight instructor after Ed learned to trust me. The noise of the biplanes landing and taking off on Long Beach made a soothing background for studying law briefs and torts. There was no airport, just the beach and planes skimming along it like seabirds.

Terri took lessons every Saturday with her father's approval and over her mother's strenuous objections. From the first day it was like meeting a kindred soul: one who liked the same things, saw life the same way and who could barely keep her feet on the ground.

Maybe it was natural for two people so in tune in the air to bring that connection back to the earth, but it wasn't right. I was already engaged to Bernice and Teri was barely eighteen the last day we spent together. She had her whole life ahead of her and mine was already plotted out. It didn't occur to me then that Terri's life might already have been changed.

I have another daughter, Henrietta, and a son, Bernard. My wife gave the children high faluting names with great expectations for their social status. I love my children, but I worry that they might end up caring more about their position in life than their contribution to it. What would Hetty think of having a big sister? I'm pretty sure I know what Bernice would think.

My office is the same as it has been for ten years, but it felt small after Patty left it.

"I want to go to college," Patty said, thumbs into her palms. "Grandma says we don't have the money and we don't, but maybe you do."

"Did your mother ever talk about your father?" I asked, looking down at the glass covering my desktop.

"She told me he was a pilot, but that's all she ever said." A tiny frown appeared between her eyes. She looked up from her hands, straight into my eyes. "Grandma told me that you were alive after Mom was killed, but she wouldn't tell me where you were."

Is she my daughter? During flight training later in the week as I talked to young men eager to fly, I kept seeing a young girl flushed with the triumph of her first perfect landing on a crescent shaped beach.

I take out Patty's world geography book whenever there is an unfilled moment in my day and gently open the pages to peek at the lands within it. Today, the Tarascan fisherman on page four hundred and ninety-seven looked as if flinging out the net in his arms might be the busiest part of his day. Lake Patzcuaro was a glass mirror, shimmering and serene behind him. I could hear the low voices of the fishermen nearby and feel the gentle rocking of the dugout canoe, the warmth of the sun on my back and the roughness of the net in my arms. There were no war planes in the air, no bunkers in the background, just light and warmth and peace.

The day after Jimmy Holdenbeck, our next-door neighbor's son, was reported dead in the Pacific, I made myself look at the "Far East" chapter of the book. The photographs show people who look very industrious. The book describes the Japanese as being "mentally alert, energetic, imitative, courteous and proud, with a loyalty for country and emperor which is almost martyr-like."

They killed Jimmy while he was trying to kill them. Martyrs killing martyrs.

When we got into the war, I was thirty-nine, with an arrhythmia that classified me 4F. But things aren't going well for our side and we are reaching for whoever we can get, no matter what the age. Youth, reckless and inexperienced, is in short supply as this war continues.

On Wednesday, we reclassified a group of firemen, only a few years younger than me. Curtis Wilson, my weekly poker buddy, is thirty-six, and going into the Navy to teach young men to fight fires on the ships.

Men like myself are answering the call for experience and knowledge to help us turn the tide, leaving behind wives and sons and daughters. They are throwing everything they have and everything they are into the fray.

Patty's book falls open to page four hundred and seventy-two automatically as I have opened to that page so many times this week. There is a picture of a group of Kurdish warriors on horseback in Northwestern Persia. The caption says that they are feared because of their raids on the bordering villages of other races and that the Shah is trying to subdue them. They don't look subdued. They don't look young either. It's a little hard to tell because the photograph is taken from far away as though the photographer were nervous about the guns the Kurds are brandishing or maybe he was just trying to fit them all in the picture. But their faces are lined and weathered and many of them have long gray beards below their dark moustaches. These are men with families and responsibilities and a way of life they are fighting to preserve.

I don't know why I keep coming back to this photograph. Maybe because it looks like the warriors are pausing only for a half a second before riding away into the mountains, free and fierce. But I suspect it has more to do with the gray-bearded men looking straight into the camera, as if facing danger head-on.

On the Selection Board, I send young men to war; at the training school I prepare them to fly in it. I go home at night to eat dinner with my family while they eat K-rations in muddy trenches or parachute out of dying planes. I sleep in my own safe bed while young men sleep fitfully in the faraway places I have sent them. At the office, I look at the faces of the Kurdish warriors and wonder if any of them would rather be a Tarascan fisherman, peacefully collecting his catch.

Last night I went before the Selective Service board as a petitioner for reclassification. My new doctor didn't find any evidence of an arrhythmia. Today, my Air Corps friends toasted my enlistment and tonight I have to tell Bernice what I've done. She'll fight me on this, but it's too late.

Tomorrow, I'll set up a trust fund for college for Terri's child, my first daughter. My children need choices. They need to feel safe to live their lives. I'm not sending any more young men to do what must be done.

I rolled over, the blankets wrapped around me and became aware of a warm, but empty space where Melanie should have been. I opened my eyes and looked around for her, the dream still enveloping me with thoughts of flight and war. The early morning sun shone weakly through the window and Melanie was standing there, wrapped in my button-down shirt, staring at me with a puzzled, slightly hostile look on her face, reminiscent of a confused black widow preparing to eat her mate.

"Hey," I said softly. "What's up?"

"I thought you were going to sleep forever," my true love said waspishly. "Don't you have things to do?"

I blinked. Who was this woman? She didn't understand. She'd never understood. I wasn't the one who wanted to be a high-priced attorney on his way to the Senate and high society. All I wanted to do was to help people like old Mrs. McGregor keep her property and make sure my children had a safe place to grow up.

"You can't make something of yourself if you stay in bed all day," she hissed. I looked in confusion at the clock on the DVD player. It was seven a.m.

My mind cleared. I wasn't a lawyer. I didn't have children and I didn't know any Mrs. McGregor. I had been inside James Harrison's head, hearing his thoughts—hell, I was thinking his thoughts. I peered at her again. Yes, it was Melanie, not Harrison's Bernice. But she was clearly upset about something. Had I called her Bernice in my sleep? The dream was clinging to me like a soggy blanket. I ran my hands across my scalp, trying to shake it off.

"I'm going to make some coffee," I said, getting to my feet.

Melanie spoke again. Her voice was hard edged, sounding older than her twenty-four years.

"That's just like you, James—always running away instead of standing and fighting through."

James? Who the hell was James? Jealousy washed like battery acid through me. I took a deep breath. In that breath, I realized that while I was still carrying my dream into the day, Melanie might have had a dream as well.

Approaching her slowly and carefully, I said, "Melanie, hey baby girl, Melanie, are you awake?" I touched her shoulder gently and then ran my hand down her arm to her hand.

She stared at me with hostile eyes, but as I continued to hold her hand and call her name, her brown eyes softened and grew wide.

"Dave, I'm so sorry." Melanie's face was stricken with remorse and she put her free arm around my neck. "Oh, my God, I had this awful dream and...it was so real. I feel like I'm still in it."

I wrapped my arms around her and she clung to me. Then I led her to the couch, leaving her there while I made a pot of coffee in the kitchen. "Tell me about your dream."

"I don't know if I can," she said miserably from the couch. "It was so... mean. It's not like me at all...," she trailed off. I knew just what she meant. I brought her a cup of steaming hot coffee, and wrapped a blanket around her trembling body.

"It's okay. I had a dream too," I told her. "I'll tell you mine, if you tell me yours."

Melanie smiled faintly. The dream was bursting out of her and grasping her coffee cup as if it were her last best hope, she told me about it. It was like listening to a stranger. The words she used and the way she put them together weren't like Melanie at all. And the dream was like mine—vivid and clear, with a grip on her that wouldn't let go.

"There was a woman in my dream—James Harrison's wife. She went to clean out his office and took the suitcase to put his things in. She was angry and sad all at the same time and I knew exactly what she was thinking:

"Bernice Harrison wanted an attorney, but what she got was a lawyer. To be honest, a senator was what she had in mind, but it was a lawyer who had lived in her house, slept in her bed and who had a heart attack and died last month.

She walked into his office carrying their honeymoon suitcase in her hand. It was almost unused since that momentous occasion because she always used the beige marbled one with the matching makeup case. Yesterday she had called the office and asked for Carl, James' partner. The secretary, who had been there a year, hadn't recognized her voice, and she had been forced to identify herself before the bitch would allow her to speak to him. Carl came on the phone immediately and said of course he would leave the office open for her on Saturday so she could come in and clear out Jim's effects. If she wasn't feeling up to it, he could have someone box up Jim's things and deliver them. There was no hurry. She refused his offer with as much politeness as she could muster. He offered to come in and help her himself, but this she refused less politely.

The office was just as she remembered: a small rectangular waiting room with oak floors, gray metal filing cabinets scattered haphazardly like Tinker Toys in the corners and against the walls and a gray metal desk for the secretary. Four straight-backed chairs with green leather seats and two end tables, neatly stacked with *National Geographic* magazines and clean glass ashtrays, completed the furnishings. An expensively bound copy of *War and Peace* lay on the end table farthest from the door, as it had ever since she could remember. She'd asked James about it once, whether it had been left there by a client, and he'd joked about the wheels of justice moving slowly, but not that slowly. It occurred to her now that he'd never answered her question.

Two offices led off the waiting room, one to the right and one to the left. Bernice turned toward the one on the right. The door was closed, but as she had known, it was unlocked. James never locked anything. She opened the door to a maple wood desk, a wide-seated banker's chair, two four-drawer metal filing cabinets, a narrow maple bookshelf, a wooden coat rack, and two chairs identical to the ones from the waiting room.

It was a warm and sunny June morning, but the light from the single window behind the desk was blocked by the branches of a gigantic sycamore tree and the room was dim and cold.

Bernice set the suitcase down next to the desk and looked around. Best to start with the desk, she thought. She snapped open the latches on the suitcase and locked the hinge in place to prop the lid open.

Inside the main desk drawer was a scattering of credit card statements for heating oil, gasoline receipts, phone bills, and three utility bills from two years ago. Numerous receipts for repairs on James's 1947 Packard lay next to airport receipts for the airplane he sometimes rented. She stacked everything neatly and tucked it into the suitcase that already held the sympathy cards that had been attached to the vast numbers of flowers and wreaths sent by mourners. Someone had written a meticulous description of each offering on the outside of the envelopes so that she could write thank you notes. Some of the cards were unopened, but she had put them into the suitcase anyway, along with the bills from the ambulance service and the hospital.

The side drawers were empty except for a box of five hundred of James' business cards with about four hundred cards remaining, his notary's seal, and a few pens. Bernice swept the items into the suitcase.

The bottom drawer held a set of keys to the filing cabinets. No pictures of her or the children, no stash of whiskey, no clues to the man she still didn't know after twenty-one years of marriage.

A postcard under the glass covering the top of the desk showed the dining room and exterior of Paul's Restaurant in New York City. She banged the drawer shut and slid the postcard out from under the glass. The back of the postcard was blank. James had never been to New York City that she knew of; he'd never even gone with her to visit her family in Connecticut.

On the top of the desk was a pen cup with two pens in it and four stacks of legal papers. She would leave those for Carl. Bernice wondered if he would get another partner soon or if he would be able to handle James' clients on his own. She didn't care.

She turned to the filing cabinets. The first key she tried opened the top drawer, revealing a neat march of manila folders labeled in James' tidy printing with the surnames of clients. Each of the four drawers was the same and so was the second filing cabinet. She would leave those to the bitch.

Turning to the sparsely filled bookcase, Bernice plucked the *1945 Penal Code of California* and its companion, *Civil Procedures and Probate Codes of California*, and dropped them into the suitcase with a satisfying thump. She wasn't sure why she was keeping the books—maybe Bernard would go into law and want his father's books, although they would be out of date by the time he was old enough.

She reached for the next two books. Standing sturdily between the *Stanford Law Review of 1948*, and the *Rules of Appeal*, was a high school geography book. Curious, she opened it.

According to the flyleaf, it had been checked out to a Pat Quinlan by Long Beach Public Schools. She'd never heard of Pat Quinlan, and James had gone to high school in San Francisco long before the copyright date of 1939. She closed the book and then let it fall open again. A page featuring a large photograph of mounted Kurdish warriors in Northwestern Persia appeared. Some of the text describing the free and fierce lifestyle of the nomadic tent dwellers had been underlined. Did James underline it, or this Pat person? She closed the book and let it fall open again, this time to a picture of Tarascan fishermen on Lake Patzcuaro in Mexico. The caption describing their peaceful life was also underlined. Her mind worked on this puzzle as she placed the book in the suitcase and emptied the rest of the bookcase. Another path she could not follow. So many damned paths and no clues to any of them. She'd thought the office he'd had for fifteen years might hold some key to her husband's internal life, but it was as sterile as a hospital room.

The coat rack was empty. There remained only the framed certificates on the wall to pack. Snatching the biggest one of the cluster,

James' admission to the bar, she plucked it off the wall and slid it into the suitcase. The Notary Public certification was next and she tossed it in, and then she wrenched off the membership to the California Bar and slammed it on top. She ripped the last frame off the wall and hurled it into the landscape of objects in the suitcase. She heard a splintering sound.

Bernice stopped, her breath caught on that fragment of noise. Reaching down gently, she turned the frame over. A single crack spread diagonally from top right to bottom left corner. James' appointment to the Selective Service Advisory Board. Lightly she traced the crack with her white-gloved finger. He hadn't needed to go; he'd escaped into the war leaving her with the children and her unresolved ambitions, just like he escaped into the air in his rented airplane, and now he'd escaped again—not dying in a blaze of glory over the Pacific, but from a heart attack in his office three years after his return. She snatched her finger from the glass, crashed the suitcase lid down and slammed the locks into position.

Heaving the suitcase from the chair, Bernice half dragged, half carried it to the door and wrestled it out into the waiting room. There she rested a moment before setting her lips firmly to begin again. She tasted salt. She pulled off her glove and touched her lips, finding them wet from tears spilling down her cheeks. Brushing the tears aside roughly, she grasped the handle of the suitcase with one hand and dragged it toward the door, leaving a long scratch on the oak floor. She tried again, this time using both hands, and was able to heft her burden off the floor a few inches. Thank heaven, she'd parked right outside the door.

On the way home with the suitcase finally maneuvered into the trunk, Bernice remembered that she had not closed the door to James' office or locked the street door behind her. She didn't stop the car; she didn't turn around. She was never going back."

As she finished telling her dream, Melanie wouldn't look at me, in spite of the fact that I was sitting next to her on the couch and had pulled her back against my chest during the story. Her cheeks, what I could see of them, were scarlet. Her coffee cup was on the table in front of the couch, full of lukewarm coffee.

My head reeled, trying to process her dream experience and the way our two dreams fit together. What could it mean that Melanie had had one of "my" dreams?

Her obvious embarrassment and dismay wrung my heart, pushing my thoughts into the background. I had to tell her, let her know she wasn't alone or responsible for the dream. I kissed the top of her head and said, "You're right, not a fun dream. Do you want to hear mine?"

She nodded. I got us both another cup of coffee and sat where I could see her face while I told her my dream. I told it just the way it happened, as James saw the events in his life and watched the shock fill her face when she realized our dreams were flip sides of the same coin. She leaned toward me as I told of James' worry over the boys he sent to the Pacific. At the end, her eyes were riveted to my face and I knew my Melanie was back, already analyzing what our dreams might mean, how to prove their veracity.

The minute I finished, she threw herself into my arms and we clung to each other like a pair of accident survivors. Then, she disentangled herself and dived into the suitcase detritus on the floor. She emerged with the geography book in her hand. I slid down next to her and together we turned the pages.

Page four hundred and ninety-seven had a picture of a Tarascan fisherman preparing to throw out his net into a glittering lake; page four hundred seventy-two had a lineup of bearded men on horseback—Kurdish warriors according to the caption. We looked at each other in shock.

Then, at last, I told her the truth. All the things I'd been holding back from her—the dreams, the contacts with Daria Astrella and the experiences from Barbara Browning, my mother and Brian all poured out of me like an unstoppable force.

Somewhere while we were cuddling on the couch with my voice growing hoarse from talking, I stopped worrying about whether Melanie would think me crazy. Part of it was the relief I felt from telling her the truth at last, but part was the way she squeezed my arm from time to time or cuddled closer. Melanie wasn't pulling away; she wasn't throwing her clothes on and looking for her car keys—she was letting me know she was in this for the long haul.

I finished talking, feeling as if I had just run a marathon—tired, but with a sense of accomplishment. There was a short pause and then Melanie's voice filled the gap.

"Why didn't you tell me before?"

Chapter Thirty-two

Melanie and I move into the future

"You told your mom and Steve—you even told Daria Astrella, but you didn't tell me? Why?" Melanie's voice sounded curious, but not detached. That voice said I'd better have a really good reason and I knew I didn't.

I shot a look at her from the corner of my eyes. Her soft brown gaze had sharpened. The support I'd felt was still there, but the future attorney was crowding to the front.

When Melanie found out I'd also told Ross, I was going to be in some deep shit. I'd left that part out.

"I had the first dream before we really knew each other and by the time I had the second dream, we were just starting to get together," I said trying to keep the pleading tone out of my voice. "I was afraid you wouldn't want to have anything to do with me if I started spouting a bunch of stuff about weird dreams and magical objects."

"You thought I would stop seeing you just because you had some strange dreams?" Melanie's brows contracted and a hurt expression filled her face—an expression I never wanted to put there again.

"Mel...We were just starting out and...look, I know I should have told you and I wanted to...but..."

"Why didn't you tell me when we were on Tinker's Ridge? I knew there was something then, but I thought you would get around to talking about it if I gave you time. I believed in you, but you didn't believe in me?"

If I could ever feel worse than that moment, it would be hard to imagine. Ross had been right, Melanie wouldn't let me down, but I hadn't been brave enough to trust her.

"I've had some experience with people thinking that I'm a freak," I managed.

"For having some dreams?" she asked in disbelief.

"No…for other things." Even now, I found it hard to get the words out, despite my conversations with my father and Ross. I took a breath. "When I was a kid I used to be able to touch objects and know things about the people who owned them. It was kind of a game I played with my grandfather."

I looked up from my feet to Melanie's face. She was listening, all her attention fixed on me.

"I was pretty good at it so I decided to show off at school one day when I was in sixth grade, hoping to impress someone."

"A girl?"

"Worse—my teacher. I had a crush on her. At lunch one day, I picked up the keychain off her desk. She had a tiny stuffed dog hanging on it. I held the dog and told her what I saw. She called me a liar and threatened to send me to detention if I said one more word." I made a grimace. "The rest of that school year was pretty uncomfortable. About a year after that my dad told me never to do it again because it made me a freak."

Now that I was allowing myself to finally go to the place I'd long avoided, I realized there was a little bit more to my fear. Shortly after the year from Hell with my teacher and Dad's rejection, I'd been home from school with the flu. Mom packed the couch with blankets and pillows, gave me herbal tea to sip and let me watch television. An old black and white movie, "Village of the Damned" came on. Twelve children with paranormal abilities were born into a village. They were definitely freaks—scary, evil freaks. I watched the whole thing with the hair standing up on my head. When Mom checked on me, she was so worried about my pallor that she took my temperature and called the doctor again.

That was it for me. I stopped doing anything with the objects, terrified I'd turn into one of those evil half-humans. Steve and Jeremy would occasionally ask for a story about an object, but I acted bored with that old game and switched gears to wrestling or mountain biking or video games. After a while they stopped asking. I only felt safe about it when GPop was around and when he died, I buried my "reading" ability with him. It was our private game—one I would play with no one else.

Years later, a date and I went to the movies. She wanted to see the new movie about the kid who saw dead people. As the movie went along and the boy became more involved with the dead, I became more and more uncomfortable. Finally, I muttered something to my date about the restroom and popcorn and slithered out into the lobby where I stared at posters of coming attractions and waited for the movie to be over.

Seeing the kid treated like a freak and watching him isolate himself, brought those memories at school and at home to the surface where I pushed them resolutely back down.

So that was what this long-held fear was based on—an old movie and rejection by a teacher. And by my father. When I really looked at it, the Boogie Man wasn't as big and horrible as I'd thought, but it had been powerful. No wonder Dad was such a mess. A weight, long held on my heart, rolled away and I began to feel a strange elation.

In the minute or so it had taken for me to examine my Boogie Man and release it, Melanie had apparently done some thinking too. Her eyes were blazing fiery enough to match her hair. I was heartened when I realized she was indignant on my behalf.

"What kind of teacher calls a kid a liar?" she spat. "You'll pardon me, but your dad sounds pretty rude too."

"My dad had similar experiences and he didn't want me to grow up the way he did."

"Your dad can read objects too?"

"No, but he knows when things are going to happen."

Melanie stared at me. I couldn't get a read on her face, but I hoped she wasn't thinking she'd become involved with a nest of witches and warlocks.

"You said you could read objects when you were a kid. Can you still do it?" Her voice was calm, but I knew I was in for it now. I fought my instinct to squirm away and hide in the bathroom and made myself look at her.

"Yeah. I know where Ross's knives come from. He handed them to me and I saw the guy who'd owned them. I told Ross and then I told him about the dreams." There, it was out, the final bit of withheld information.

"Ross knows you had these dreams and that you can read objects too?" Her voice was pitched higher than her eyebrows. I'd never seen Melanie mad before, but she was really cooking.

"He told me I should tell you." I was too miserable to look her in the eyes. Instead, I gazed at the floor, memorizing the beige carpet fibers.

After the longest moment in my life, Melanie touched my arm and I looked over at her. "Tell me again why you didn't tell me."

"I love you and I didn't want to lose you."

"The first part of that statement is good, but the second part…," Melanie shook her head and made a disgusted face, "is really stupid."

We went for a long walk near the downtown marina that afternoon, wanting to get out of the condo and into fresh air. I told Melanie about my practice sessions with GPop and everything I had found out about the dreams. Not once did she pull away or falter in her interest and support. When we were walking back to the car after a late lunch, I told her about giving the vase to Mom and how she had hoped to have a dream about it.

"Your mom sounds like a woman after my own heart," said Melanie. "I'm going to take a few of these objects home and try to have a dream too."

I knew I loved her before, but that feeling seemed small now. I stopped, unable to move—every part of my being felt ready to burst with the intensity of my love. Melanie stopped as well and looked up at me in concern. Up ahead there was a bus bench. Without a word, I pulled her closer to my side and we walked to the bench and sat down.

I looked into her worried face, memorizing each tiny freckle, the shape of her eyes, the smoothness of her skin. I saw the worry leave her face at the look in my eyes, replaced by a look I can't ever describe, but what my heart knew was love. The same look I'd been seeing on her face for the past two days.

With both her hands in mine, I said, "Melanie Clark, I love you. I don't know if I'll ever be able to show you how much. Do you love me?" Stupid question—I knew the answer, but I needed to hear it.

Her eyes filled and she nodded. Then she seemed to think that nodding wasn't enough and took a breath, "I love you, Dave. I love your good heart, I love how sweet you are; the way you look out for the people you love; I love your dreaming—I love everything about you."

The world went silent. All I could hear was the beating of my heart. Then, words came out of it.

"I want you in my life forever. Will you marry me?" It wasn't planned; I didn't have a ring and we were sitting on a bus bench in the middle of downtown Portland as traffic drove past, but they were the right words.

"Yes." The answer was swift and definite.

I gathered her to me, trying to absorb her inside me and heard, "but not until I'm finished with law school."

I drew back and stared down at her. She stared back for a beat before we both burst out laughing.

As we were driving back to the condo, Melanie said, "Dave, I'm not afraid of the dreams, even though they might be intense. What I am afraid of is being like that couple we dreamed about. They didn't understand each other at all. They didn't want the same things. I don't even think they loved each other. I don't want to be like that." Her voice sounded small and far away in the darkness of the car.

I'd been through something like that with my parents and I didn't want that kind of relationship either. I stopped the car on the side of the road. Wrapping my arms around her, I promised, "We will not be like those people. We won't live separate lives and I won't hold things back from you."

"You're talking to a lawyer, Dave Peltier," Melanie warned. "Those words might not be used against you in a court of law, but they're going to be remembered."

Chapter Thirty-three

Jeremy acts like a big brother and Maude becomes part of the family

We celebrated our engagement with champagne from the grocery store, giddy plans for our future and hours of discussion about the dreams and my last meeting with Daria Astrella—the one that had led to the acquisition of the suitcase. What did these dreams mean? Were they connected to my ability to read objects? Why did the old woman want me to buy the suitcase? What did it mean that Melanie also had a dream? No answers, just questions.

When Melanie drove home on Tuesday afternoon, she took the apples and the ashtray, determined to do her own dream experimentation. Just before she drove away, her face rosy with kisses, she said, "Granny Trish is coming next week. I'm not telling anyone about getting married until after she meets you."

My heart skipped a beat, but I said, "Okay, no ring shopping until after Granny's report."

She laughed and waved as she drove out of the parking lot.

My cell phone rang. It was Jeremy calling to let me know that he had decided to leave for Greece out of Portland, so we could visit before he left. He'd be arriving in two hours—short notice even for my little brother. Some things just don't change.

At the Portland International Airport baggage claim, I waited for Jeremy. He emerged out of a crowd of new arrivals wearing a soft cast and using a cane, but he looked healthy. He surprised me with an energetic man-hug instead of the typical cuff to the head that I'd learned to duck.

He'd stayed with Mom for a few days before coming to Portland. "I've been smudged, blessed and stuffed full of organic, compassionately grown vegetables," he said. "I'm ready for a bacon burger and a basketful of greasy golden fries."

We headed for the nearest Burgerville on the way to the condo. As we spread enormous burgers and fries out over the coffee table in the condo living room, Jeremy looked around at the décor. He laughed at my large quartz paperweight, knowing exactly where it had come from.

With ESPN streaming scores on the TV we inhaled our food and talked about Jeremy's visit with Dad and Sandra which had gone better than he expected.

"Whoa, dude, what you think about Dad being a dad again?" he asked, with three of my sweet potato fries in his mouth.

"I think it's cool," I said. "He told me he plans on being a better father this time. What do you think about no longer being the youngest?"

Jeremy shrugged. "Might be fun to be the big brother for a change." He looked down at his fries. "He practiced being a good dad when I was there, but he's got some catching up to do."

I knew he was done talking about Dad's parenting, but it was clear from his boisterous energy that they had gotten along well.

"I have some news of my own," I said.

Jeremy quirked an eyebrow. "It wouldn't have anything to do with the person you gave the Nano to would it?"

Maybe Jeremy had some of Dad's ability after all. "Yeah. Her name's Melanie and we're engaged."

Both of his eyebrows shot up this time. "Bro, you've been holding back. Drop your load right now."

I pulled out my copy of the photo of Melanie and me on Tinker's Ridge and gave Jeremy the thumbnail version of my girl and our plans.

"So, if you're waiting until after she finishes law school, I'll have a chance to meet this paragon before you're hitched," my little brother commented with a grin, adding, "I'll be coming home for good at the end of May. I've already sent out some resumés for jobs in Southern California, trying to get a feel for things."

Southern California? Resumés? Either Jeremy had undergone a personality transplant or the accident had shaken some sense into him. I contented myself with, "This wouldn't have something to do with Carol Peneman would it?"

"Look, I have to get a job someday. It's time." He grinned. "But, yeah, I wanted to be close to Carol. We've been calling and emailing every day. She's out of the hospital and back home. She'll be back at school next week. She's a trouper, that one." There was pride in his voice.

Jeremy and I went over to Steve and Katy's later that evening. Katy greeted us at the door with hugs. Brian came on a run, looking for Melanie, just as Steve came out of the master bedroom with what looked like a massive pink burrito in his arms. He proudly introduced us to Baby Rebecca whose bright eyes, tiny nose and flower of a mouth were the only movable parts under her pink striped cap. The rest of her, invisible inside the swaddling, looked very uncomfortable. Katy noted my look and reassured me that babies liked being trussed up. I took her word for it.

While Katy fed Rebecca and put her to bed, Jeremy and I had a chance to catch up with Steve. Brian and Jeremy built fantastical Lego creations as I told my best friend about the engagement. Steve insisted on telling Katy and celebrating with a beer despite my warning that Granny Trish's blessing must be given.

When we finally got up to leave, Steve and Katy walked us to the door. Katy said, "Oh, Dave, remember that statue Brian talked you out of?" I nodded. "You know, my mom is British, right?" I nodded again. Letty Brewster still had a bit of a British accent when she wanted to use it.

"Well, she said her Aunt Ellie and Uncle Jamie had a statue head just like that on their mantel in their house in London. She used to visit them every other summer. They never had any children, but they knew how to play and they were a lot of fun. They actually had a name for their statue that Mom thought was pretty funny when she was a little girl. Maude—that's what they called it. Mom couldn't believe that we had the same statue."

I glanced at Steve. His eyes, wide and still, stared back at me. I raised my eyebrows and he shook his head slightly. He hadn't talked to Katy about the dream, then. I smiled, kissed Katy on the forehead and said, "Someday, I've got a story for you."

"What was all that about?" Jeremy asked as soon as we were in the car. I was still exhausted from spilling my guts to Melanie, but my brother deserved to know. I gave him as short a version as I could get away with, but he had a lot of questions. Not one of them had anything to do with doubting my sanity.

"So are you going to re-up? Start reading objects and telling stories like you used to?" he asked.

Jeremy's questions took me by surprise. I hadn't considered incorporating object reading into my regular life. What would be the purpose?

Instead of answering his question, I asked one of my own. "Jeremy, do you have any ability like this?"

"Like you and Dad, you mean." He laughed at my look of surprise. "He asked me the same question when he told me about his secret life as a psychic during Christmas break. I always figured he had some kind of super power." Then he shook his head. "Nope, I've got no super powers as far as I know. Maybe I'm a late bloomer."

We laughed at that, but I felt he might be right.

"Well, if you believe that everything happens for a reason, it sounds like those dreams and your ability to read objects are connected and might have some sort of purpose," said Jeremy as we prepared his bed on the couch. "I'd go for it, brother. It could be fun."

I saw Jeremy off to Greece the next day, feeling hopeful about my brother's future and my own. Did I believe that everything happens for a reason? I'd never really thought about it, but with Jeremy's words and Katy's inadvertent corroboration of my dream about the statue, I could feel something purposeful at work, even though it wasn't yet clear. It would be fun to see Katy's face when I told her Maude's story. Maybe I would write it down for her, although I was fairly sure I would never forget that dream—or any of the others.

Chapter Thirty-four

Eggcups on the ceiling

After a week, Melanie still hadn't had any dreams about the apples or the ashtray, to her disappointment. Gillian was trying to talk her out of the apples for a folk art exhibition and Bethany was concerned that she had become a secret smoker, she told me during one of our nightly conversations.

"I went into Astrella's after work to see if I could buy something else to test out, but there are only two objects left and that old lady wouldn't let me buy either one," Melanie complained. "I told her I had a dream about the suitcase and it wasn't very nice and she said that's too bad and that it probably wouldn't happen again. So I told her my dream even though she didn't seem very interested in it and she said it sounded like I had a connection to the thing and maybe it was a personal problem."

Her run-in with Daria Astrella made me laugh, but it relieved my mind a little, too. Daria Astrella had been cryptic with me, but she had wanted to know about my dreams and seemed to think they would continue. For some reason she didn't seem to believe this was true for Melanie. Maybe the dreams weren't dangerous, but for our future life together I didn't want Melanie to be plagued by them. One of us was enough.

"Oh Dave," she huffed. "What difference does it make? I can still be a lawyer and have funky dreams. You don't have to choose either the soup or the salad just because the server gives you that choice—you could have both, or nothing at all."

Both. What would both mean to me? A life with a real job like Promise computers and a secret job being a conduit for objects and the people who

needed them? I didn't even know how I got the right objects to the right people—it seemed completely random.

My preparations for Granny Trish's upcoming inspection included finding
something to do with the three boxes of egg cups taking up space in the living
room. After some thought, I decided to install pre-made shelving to run around
the walls of the living room to display them up high enough that you could
see their colorful shapes, but not close enough that I would ever have to think
about dusting them.

   While leveling and drilling, I replayed my discussion with Melanie about
the dreams. I was relieved that she hadn't had any more dream experiences with
the objects, but my relief wasn't so much because the dreams could be frightening. It wasn't even about the emotional impact. Being honest with myself, I
was relieved because their intensity and detail had been unique to me, as far as
I could find out, before Melanie's dream. They'd felt like they were leading me
somewhere, somewhere with a purpose—my own special purpose.

   Standing back to look at my handiwork, it was obvious there was going to
be plenty of room to display other small objects on the shelf. Maybe my sub-
conscious had planned it that way. Melanie's words about not having to choose
kept coming back to me and so did her support and Jeremy's. My mother's
feelings about the vase and Barbara Browning's words about the painting were
things I'd been turning over in my mind too. Wouldn't it be cool to find things
that somehow relieved the pain and worry people carried around, unsuspected
by others. Was that the purpose of the objects? Was it my purpose?

   I pulled the packing tape off the first box and reached inside. Bubble wrap
surrounded each cup, adding a deceptive bulkiness. Carefully, I pulled apart
the tape holding the wrap in place and slid the first cup into my hand. It was
delicate white china with hand-painted violets. GMa found it for me, saying my
collection needed some variety. It was beautiful, but it had never been one of
my favorites—too girly. I held it and concentrated.

   Immediately, I saw the brown-haired man who had used it. He ate soft-
boiled eggs every morning, but he hated eggs and the wife who made them. I
put the cup up on the shelf hastily and reached for another.

   The sleek pewter cup that emerged from the bubble wrap belonged to
a woman with a secret. As a teenager, she had given her first child up for

adoption. Now twenty years later, every morning after her husband and children were off to work and school, she found herself wondering about this child, what he looked like, what he was doing. Then she prayed for forgiveness. I put the cup on the shelf with a little tug on my heart.

I didn't remember receiving impressions from the eggcups when I was a kid. I just liked their colors and the adventure of collecting them with GPop and GMa.

I picked up a red and white striped crockery cup. This had been one of my favorites, bright and showy. As I held it, the eggcup seem to warm in my hand. I could hear the ocean—gentle waves against a beach of sand. I smelled flowers, sweet and powerful. The sun filled my vision and I heard a child's voice calling for Morgan to hurry up, the boat was ready.

The sun and warmth disappeared when I put the cup on the shelf. I looked at the time on the microwave. It had been two hours since I started unpacking the cups; with this kind of progress I'd be unpacking until I could collect Social Security along with eggcups. I started pulling cups out of the boxes and putting them on the shelves as quickly as I could. Moving fast seemed to keep the impressions at bay and I had no more visions as the shelves filled.

I wondered as I scooted the cups around with my fingertips whether I would be able to sleep with twenty-two impression-filled eggcups perched on my living room walls. When they were on a shelf running along a wall in my childhood bedroom, they had been right above my bed. I didn't remember any dreams associated with them. Somehow things had changed. Could it be that growing up had triggered something, or could it be the objects from Astrella's?

Chapter Thirty-five

I meet Granny Trish and Melanie almost spills the beans

Melanie's red Camry swooped into the parking lot as I was on my way back from taking out the trash. Both the driver and passenger doors popped open at the same time.

Melanie's long, jean-covered legs emerged first, followed quickly by the rest of her. She was in my arms a tenth of a second afterward. Her white-haired grandmother emerged from the passenger side more slowly, dressed in a fashionable blue sweater, crisp white shirt and black pants.

She looked over the top of the car at me and said, "May I use your restroom?"

I nodded and started to walk her into my condo when she said, "Just tell me which one, I'll get there myself."

While I pointed out the condo, Melanie whispered, "It's a set-up," in my ear. Her grandmother toiled up the steps into my home and I gave myself up to the pleasure of holding my girl. "She just wants to check things out and see what I'm in for."

"My conscience, and my bathroom, are both clean," I whispered back, nuzzling her hair. "No socks on the floor, no panties hanging in the shower—not even yours."

"We'll work on changing your conscience later," said my devil-goddess fiancée, "but I have to use the bathroom too and I don't want to leave Granny up there too long. Who knows what she'll find?"

We went inside a few minutes later to find Granny Trish standing in the center of my living room, looking up at the display of egg cups. "Nice place," she said as soon as we entered, "Who's the naked girl in the bathroom?"

On her way to the bathroom, Melanie threw me a wicked look over her shoulder and kept walking toward the bathroom.

"I have no idea," I said. I didn't know my future grandmother-in-law well enough to answer, "serial killer." "I bought it because it matched the tile and it was only five bucks. Is she naked?"

Granny Trish looked at me and grinned. She held out her hand. "I'm Patricia Clark, since my granddaughter forgot to introduce us. You can call me Tricia."

I shook her hand, saying, "Dave Peltier. You can call me Mr. Peltier." She laughed and seated herself on the couch. I liked her already, but the intelligence in her eyes and the crispness of her voice gave the impression of someone who could keep you on your toes.

While I stood around and waited for Melanie to rescue me, Tricia picked up the geography book lying on the coffee table and peered at the cover.

"Hey, I had a book like this for my high school geography class," she said, surprise in her voice. "This is one old book."

She flipped through the pages. "I remember this book because I caught holy heck from Mr. Cavitz, my geography teacher, for losing my copy and he made me pay for it." Her face lost a little of its excitement. "I didn't lose it though—I left it."

"Was it that bad a book?" I joked, though the hairs were beginning to stand up on the back of my neck once more.

"It wasn't that," she said slowly as Melanie came back into the room. "I hoped he would mail it back, maybe even bring it himself."

"Who, Granny?" Melanie asked.

Tricia Clark didn't answer. She flipped to the flyleaf and gasped. "Long Beach High School—that was my school. This *is* my book. Look—that's my name!" She pointed at the flyleaf where the name Pat Quinlan had been handwritten. "Where ever did you get this?"

My head felt as if 20,000 volts were running through it. I looked at her warm brown eyes wide with amazement—James Harrison's eyes; Melanie's eyes.

"I bought it in a curio shop," I managed to choke out. I thought of my dream about her father and it was as if all the little broken things in the world were healing. "Would you like to have it back?"

As she clutched the book to her chest with shaking hands, a choked sound brought both of us around to look at Melanie. Her eyes were wide, staring at the book in her grandmother's arms. While we watched, she slumped down to sit on the couch as if her legs wouldn't support her. Both of us moved toward her. She waved off our help and sat up straight, eyes focused on Tricia.

"Oh," she said and then again, "Oh."

In that split second as I watched the two women, it came to me that the information I received in the dreams might not always be wise to share—it might be better for people to have their own reactions to the objects.

"Granny, you never told me you grew up in Long Beach." Before I could stop her, Melanie said urgently, "Was your mother a pilot? Was her name Terri?

Patricia Quinlan Clark stared back into Melanie's eyes, so like her own. I could see the pieces and questions falling into place between them.

I dragged the suitcase from the corner of the office. "There are a few extra things that go with that geography book. Would you like to see them?" Tricia pulled her eyes from Melanie's without answering her questions.

I opened the suitcase, pulled out the box of James Harrison's business cards and laid them on the coffee table in front of Tricia. Still clutching the book to her chest, she pulled out one of the cards and read it. Her eyes filled and, as I laid out the bar certificate, the law books, the Selective Service cards and the bills for James' hospital stay, tears spilled over.

Melanie scooted next to her grandmother in concern and placed a calming hand on her back, but Tricia put down the geography book and began to touch the items on the table. When she slowly picked up the bar certificate, I caught Melanie's eye and motioned her into the bedroom.

She left her grandmother reluctantly. At last she stood next to me, with one foot in the bedroom and one foot in the living room, ready to spring to Tricia's side if needed.

"Mel...baby," I tried to get her to focus on what I had to say. Melanie looked up at me with shock still reflected in her eyes. "Let's not tell Granny Trish all the details of our dreams." Despite her quick frown of protest, I rushed on. "Not at first. I know you want to tell her the truth, but ..."

Deliberately I threw a lawyer-like term into my explanation: "If we told her all the details of our dreams right away, it might prejudice whatever dream or feelings your grandmother could have from these things. And she's the one who needs whatever the suitcase brings. The objects I dream about aren't just things— I think they're like messengers. I don't want to interfere with the message."

"You're not just saying this so Granny won't think you're a fruitcake, are you?" Melanie's words were sharp, but her half-smile softened them. Her eyes searched mine as she crossed her arms over her chest.

"Tell her everything you want to; just give her time to have her own feelings, first. Okay?" I held her gaze and slipped my hands over hers as they cupped her elbows. She gave a tiny nod at last and uncrossed her arms, squeezing my hands gently before turning back to the couch.

Tricia was holding the bills from the ambulance and hospital for the day of James Harrison's death. The few tears that had been tracing their way down her face had become rivulets and streams coursing down into the wrinkled canyons around her mouth and cheeks. Melanie slipped an arm around her grandmother and held her close. My heart melted at the sight. I got a paper towel from the kitchen and offered it.

Melanie smiled and began blotting Tricia's tears. Tricia sat up straighter and took the towel. After she wiped her face and blew her nose, she said, "Thanks for the mop, Dave." To Melanie, she said, "I'll be okay, 'cracker.'"

Cracker? Melanie noticed my quizzical look. "It's short for firecracker. Granny thinks the red hair makes me a little excitable."

I snickered and handed Tricia a glass of water. She took a sip, made a face and said, "Too healthy. Do you have anything with a bite?" At my startled look, Tricia gave a half-smile. "I know it's early, but I could use a little Dutch courage."

A whiskey and Coke drinking buddy had left the remains of a bottle of Jack Daniels when he'd helped me move a year ago. It had been at the back of a shelf ever since and was probably nicely aged. I dug it out, found the three smallest glasses I could and returned to the couch.

Tricia accepted her inch of whiskey in the juice glass I handed her; Melanie shook her head. I don't like whiskey any more than cognac, but I touched my juice glass to Tricia's and took a swallow. She drank half of her glass at one wallop.

She took a deep breath and then picked up Melanie's hand. "James Harrison was my father," she said. "I only met him once. I didn't know anything about him except what my grandmother told me." Tricia leaned against the back of the couch. "I didn't even know he was dead until years after it happened."

Melanie and I exchanged a glance. Her eyes were wide and stunned looking.

"I never told you about him—I didn't tell anyone, not even your father." Tricia's voice dropped. "My parents weren't married. He married someone else." Despite her eighty years, I could see the admission was still painful.

Maybe being illegitimate isn't a big deal in the current times, but I could guess how shameful it might have been in the 1930s and '40s. And to have your father marry someone else instead of your mother must have felt like complete rejection. I sat down on the couch on Tricia's other side and offered to refill her glass. She let the geography book lay on her lap as she swallowed the other half of her drink and shook her head.

"Sorry I'm such a mump," Tricia said.

Melanie and I chorused a protest. Her distress was hard to watch, but I hoped the suitcase and its contents would bring peace or closure the way the other objects had brought them to their recipients. But that might come later, when Tricia was alone. I felt as if I had to get her past this point of pain.

"This is pretty intense, Tricia. What about we give it a little breather and have some lunch?"

With Melanie's enthusiastic agreement, we got Tricia up and moving. At the door, she stopped, still clutching the geography book, and looked back at the suitcase.

"I have a lot of questions…" she began.

"Tricia," I said. "That suitcase and everything in it is yours. I'll put it in Melanie's car when we come back." She nodded and walked out to the car. Melanie held back for a second.

"Dave, she needs to know…she's really hurting."

"Does she need to know that her father had marital problems and his wife was a bitch?" She shook her head. "We can tell her everything we discovered in the suitcase, Mel, but let's have faith that the geography book or the suitcase is what she needs and will help her before we jump the gun and tell her about our dreams."

It surprised me how strongly I felt about this. Belief in the power of the objects had come slowly to me, but it was there.

We drove to Mother's Bistro for lunch. Once we were seated, Tricia looked at the two of us and it was clear the questions were coming.

"Tell me again where you found my book," she began. I told her about buying the suitcase at Astrella's, but not why I bought it. Then she wanted to know everything we could tell her about James Harrison. Melanie explained how each thing inside the suitcase had given us a snapshot of Harrison's life. The more we talked, the more Tricia seemed to relax.

Over dessert, it was Tricia's turn to answer questions. The first thing Melanie asked was how Tricia had come to meet her father, although we both knew.

"Until my mother died when I was fifteen, I only knew that my father was a pilot and he taught my mother to fly. After she died, my grandmother let it slip that he was a money grubbing lawyer who'd gotten my mother pregnant and left her for some woman he was engaged to—only she didn't put it that nicely." Tricia's wry smile tried to hide years of pain.

"When I was sixteen, I tracked him down because I wanted to go to nursing college and Grandma said she couldn't afford it. I went to Ed Daugherty's Flight School where Mama had taught on weekends. Often while I waited for her, I would help in the office. I knew where the instructor records were kept. I pretended I needed a job, which I really did. By the time the secretary came back with the news that they couldn't hire anyone, I had found the 1926 record and my father. It even listed his law school as a contact. It took me a month to get to St. Vincent's Law School and check on alumni, but when I found out where he was, I used all the babysitting money I'd been saving for nursing school to buy a bus ticket to San Mateo."

I could feel her determination and desperation after all these years. I couldn't imagine the courage it must have taken for a young girl to risk everything to meet a man who didn't even know she was alive.

"I ditched school on a Friday, told my grandmother I was spending the weekend at a girlfriend's house and caught the first bus to San Mateo. It was late when I got to San Mateo that night, but the office was still open."

She shook her head as if in amazement at her own naiveté. "I was so scared, but I made myself walk in and tell him who I was. I even showed him my birth certificate. I honestly don't think he knew I existed until then."

Tricia pressed her thumb into the palm of her hand, a gesture I remembered from my dream, and continued. "He took me out to dinner when he found out I had come straight from the bus. We went to a steak house—it was the first time I had ever had steak smothered in mushrooms and wine sauce. It's still my favorite food."

She shrugged. "I didn't know what to call him—I still don't. I couldn't call him Dad; it didn't feel right to call him Jim or James, and Mr. Harrison was ridiculous."

Melanie asked, "What was he like?"

"Very kind, but distant. He smelled like Old Spice and he asked a lot of questions about school and my mother. After dinner, he put me up in a hotel and told me to lock the door. The next morning he picked me up and put me on the bus. I never saw or heard from him again…and I don't know why." It was a cry from the heart, despite her stoic appearance.

"Maybe there was a reason why you didn't hear from him," I offered. "There are two draft cards in the suitcase. In 1942, he was classified 4F, but in 1943 he was reclassified 4A.There's also a reference to his service in one of those papers. If he volunteered in 1943, maybe even right after you met him, and was in until the war was over, he might have been overseas for a couple of years."

"It looked like, from the utility bills, he started up his practice again in 1946," said Melanie, picking up the thread, "and then he died in 1948. Maybe he meant to contact you, but he didn't have time."

Tricia silently shredded her paper napkin. In a slow, sad voice, she said, "There was contact, just once. A lawyer came to the house and told my grandmother and me that an account with $5,000 had been set up for my education, provided I graduate from high school. Grandmother didn't want me to take it, but she couldn't stop me after I turned eighteen.

"I went to work for a hospital in Simi Valley after I finished nursing school and on my first vacation, I took a bus up to San Mateo to see him again. The office was still there, but the receptionist told me that he had died the year before."

There was another silence before Melanie jumped in. "He cared about you, Granny. I know he did. You were his first daughter."

I looked at Melanie. That hadn't been in the suitcase.

"What do you mean, his first daughter?" Granny Trish stared at her granddaughter.

Melanie looked at me. I could see her wheels turning. "We found out that James Harrison had a son and a daughter and they were born after you were."

Maybe Tricia thought we'd gotten the information from the suitcase. In any case, she didn't pursue it and we left the restaurant to check out downtown Portland.

We wandered around downtown for a little while before going over to the McDaniels—friends of Melanie's family who lived in Portland and who had invited Melanie and Tricia to spend the night. Tricia seemed distracted and preoccupied. I didn't know her well enough to know whether that was her normal behavior, but I didn't think so. The geography book peeked out of her voluminous zebra-striped purse. It must have been heavy to haul around, but Tricia kept it by her side.

I left after dinner at the McDaniels' house to give them all time to talk. Melanie walked me to the door. "Sorry, Dave, I almost blew it, but I still think she needs to know."

I kissed her and said, "Please just give her at least one night, Babe."

She nodded and said, "I don't think she can take much more tonight, anyway."

Melanie said she would call me in the morning. I waved goodbye to Tricia and the McDaniels and went out to my car wondering what would happen next.

Chapter Thirty-six

Granny Trish takes her leave and I come to a decision

Tricia's pain stayed with me long after I left her and Melanie at the McDaniels' house. I didn't know any old people—all my grandparents were dead or in Iowa, which was about the same thing. I had thought that people eventually got over things with time, but I could see from my experiences with Barbara Browning, my dad and Tricia, that this wasn't always true. Pain was like a deep current in a river, unseen and unsuspected from the surface. Life moved along and people lived their lives, but down deep, that current of unresolved pain kept undercutting their foundation, whittling away at their soul.

I lay in bed, looking up at the ceiling in the dark and wondering how the suitcase, with its load of anger and regret was going to help Tricia with the early years of shame and rejection she still carried in her heart. I rolled onto my side worrying that maybe the objects weren't always right for people, despite what Daria Astrella said. Flopping to the other side I wondered if some of the objects could actually be bad for people.

Staring up at the ceiling again, thoughts about my ability to read objects wove into the worrisome thoughts about the dreams and caused another fifteen minutes of anxiety and several more flip-flops.

There had to be a purpose for being able to read objects besides being a dubious party trick. There had to be a purpose for the dreams, because, in some fashion, I had been responsible for four people receiving a type of solace from the objects I'd bought. With Melanie's purchase of the ashtray on my behalf, I'd also been a recipient of comfort. I turned on the bedside lamp and picked up the ashtray from the nightstand.

Turning the ashtray, letting the light from the lamp play through it and watching the light reflect off the cut glass surfaces was oddly soothing— maybe the way it had been for Barry in my dream and for Katy with the statue. The bottom of the ashtray was smooth. The ridges cut to hold cigarettes were like tiny mountains. I felt my thoughts slow as I turned it over and over.

The objects helped people with their lives. They filled some deep need inside certain people that, maybe, could not be met any other way. I had to believe that this would be true for Tricia, the way it had been for all the rest of us. Despite lack of proof, I didn't really believe the objects could harm anyone. Gradually, as I played with the ashtray, my thoughts grew foggy and I fell asleep with it in my hand.

Melanie called at eight the next morning. The plan to spend a few hours at Powell's Books had changed. Tricia wanted to return to Eugene as soon as possible to catch the train home to Sacramento. They would stop by the condo on the way home. "…and Dave," said Melanie with a catch in her voice, "wait till you see Granny."

This didn't sound good. All the reservations from my fitful night rushed forward again. Whatever had happened to Tricia was my fault for bringing that damned suitcase home in the first place. I tried to hold on to the certainty that Tricia would be okay. My future with Melanie might depend upon it.

Within half an hour, Melanie's Camry drove into the parking lot. Déja vu as both car doors popped open and Melanie hopped out. While we hugged, I kept a weather eye out for Tricia. She emerged from the car and, at first, the only thing different from the day before was her clothing and that she didn't ask to use the bathroom. Then I noticed her smile.

It wasn't a polite, pleased-to-meet-you smile. It was a real, I-just-can't-help-it smile. She walked over to Melanie and me. Before we stepped apart, Tricia wrapped her arms around us. She was glowing and looked years younger than she had the day before.

"You can call me Granny Trish, Dave—seeing's as you're going to be in the family," she laughed.

I quirked an eyebrow at Melanie who smiled and mouthed, "Later."

I hugged Tricia back, my head whirling with the need to find out what was going on. When we went inside the condo, Granny Trish decided to pay a bathroom visit after all, giving Melanie and me a moment together.

Melanie clutched my arm and started talking the minute Granny left the room. "You know how worried we were about her last night?"

I nodded impatiently.

"Well, after you left we stayed up and talked to Bud and Dot for a while and then went to bed. Granny was sitting up in her bed looking through the geography book when I went to take a shower and when I came out, she was holding the book against her chest and she had this look on her face..." Melanie stopped and tears filled her eyes. "Dave, she looked...uplifted. It was amazing." She shook back her tears and continued, "She looked up and saw me staring at her. Then she told me what happened.

"Granny had opened the geography book and was looking at some of the underlined pages when she felt him next to her—her father. It wasn't like a memory, she said, but like he was really right next to her. She could even smell his aftershave and it was like she could hear what he was thinking—about wanting to help people, how he loved to fly and, best of all, how much he loved her and her mother. That's why Granny wants to go home right now—she wants to go through every piece of the suitcase. She was pretty apologetic, but I told her it was okay—that we could hang out with her some other time." Melanie looked at me with her eyebrows raised inquiringly.

I nodded.

"She's just so excited—you saw her... she's just whacked out!" Melanie was bouncing up and down on her toes in her own excitement. Since I was off the hook and still engaged, it was a pretty good couple of minutes.

Granny Trish came out of the bathroom, hugged me again and said, "See you soon, Dave and welcome to the family."

I brought the suitcase out to Melanie's car and then had an idea. While Granny Trish got back into the car, I asked Melanie to open the Camry's trunk. Behind the shelter of the upraised trunk lid, I popped open the snaps on the suitcase and pulled out the box of James Harrison's business cards. I held on to the box and closed my eyes.

Immediately I saw him, sitting at his office desk, writing a letter—one he wouldn't dictate to his secretary. The greeting at the top of the letter read,

"Dear Daughter," and the text of what he'd written up to that point referred to previous letters, letters he thought she might not have received. "I've been writing for four years, probably more for me than for you, but maybe one day you'll realize how often I think of you."

I opened my eyes. Melanie was watching me, waiting.

"What is it, Dave?" she asked as I placed the box back inside the suitcase and snapped the locks closed. I closed the trunk.

"Tell Granny Trish to look for a place her grandmother might have stashed letters. It's been a long time, but I think they're still around."

I leaned forward and kissed her. Melanie gave me a wide-eyed hug and then jumped into the driver's seat.

We exchanged another kiss at the window and I whispered, "It's okay now to tell Granny Trish about our dreams...and anything else you want to tell her." Melanie's eyes met mine. She gave a nod and a smile that reassured me.

"We've got to hurry so Granny can catch the Coast Starlight back to Sacramento, but I'll call you," she called as she put the car in reverse. I waved as the Camry sped out of the parking lot with arms waving back at me from both sides of the car. The entire visit had taken seven minutes.

I stood for a minute out on the sidewalk, a trifle dazed with the impact and speed of Melanie's visit and my own vision of James Harrison. As I turned around to go back inside, the door to Barbara and Vern Browning's condo opened and Barbara came out.

"Hey, Dave," she said, coming to stand in front of me. "I wanted to let you know that Vern and I are moving this weekend."

While I expressed surprise at her announcement and said conventional things about how I would miss having them as neighbors, I wondered what was different about her. She looked the same as always: dressed by L.L.Bean, her light brown hair in its usual middle-aged lady's chin length cut. But there was something different about my neighbor.

"We're thrilled about it," she said. "Vern got a promotion and a transfer to Sacramento, but this will be our last move. I'm finally ready to put down roots and live in a real house in a real neighborhood. I want to be part of a community." She tilted her head up so that her eyes met mine. "And I want to try to make up for what my sister did."

It was a tall order, being as her sister was a serial killer, but as I looked down into her blue eyes, I recognized the difference in Barbara Browning. Always before, she had seemed diffident and almost apologetic. She spent a lot of time looking down at her shoes. Not today.

Today, Barbara was speaking to me instead of to the ground and her small figure stood arrow-straight, loafers planted firmly a hip's width apart. Her voice was clear and definite. I could feel her determination.

Before I could say anything, she said, "Does your offer of the painting still stand?"

I nodded. "Come on in," I offered. "I'll get it for you."

Barbara followed me into the condo. I ducked into the bathroom and removed the painting, wondering what had caused her change of mind about it.

I handed the picture to her. Barbara gazed into the painting for a moment and then gave a quick nod of her head as if what she'd seen had confirmed something for her.

"Uh, how come you changed your mind?" I asked.

"I just needed some time to think. Knowing what happened to my sister seemed to dissolve some things that were keeping me from moving on." Barbara looked up from the painting to me. "I realized I'd been holding back from making decisions—almost as if I was waiting for something. So when Vern's promotion and transfer came through a few weeks ago, I was ready. I enrolled at Sac State and I start summer school in June."

At my look of surprise, she chuckled and shrugged. "I know—it will be crazy moving to a new place and starting classes at the same time, but I don't want to waste one more minute." Barbara's eyes sparkled and her chin jutted out. If anyone could make up for lost time, it was the woman standing in front of me.

She shifted the painting to one hand and offered the other to me. "Thanks for the painting, Dave, and for listening. One of these days, I'll let you know how it all turns out."

I opened the door for her and wished her luck. When the door to Barbara's condo closed, I was still standing at my own doorway trying to remember to close my mouth.

The next day, Melanie called. We'd talked the night before after she'd seen Granny Trish safely onto the train, but today's call came midway through her shift at Betsy's, a rare breach of Melanie's personal work ethic.

"Dave, I've been thinking…," she began.

"Whatever you're thinking must be important if you're calling me from work," I joked nervously, hoping she hadn't changed her mind about being engaged.

"It is. Whatever this is that you can do with objects, you should do. Granny called me this morning before work. She took apart her grandmother's old desk and found a ton of letters her dad had written to her, stuffed behind a drawer. Most of them hadn't even been opened. She was hysterical, laughing and crying at the same time."

Melanie's voice faded away for a second as the hairs on the back of my neck did their usual number and there was a roaring sound in my ears. When I could hear again, she was saying, "I finally got her calmed down, but I had to call and tell you how important this thing that you do, is. I told Granny everything on the way to the station and she agrees with me."

This was it, then. All the planets were in alignment. The invitation had been issued and I was ready.

"If I really start doing this, I might end up with a lot of junk lying around waiting for the right people," I warned her.

"No problem. We'll get a house with a garage, or rent a storage container, or buy a Tuff-shed. This is important, Dave."

I made a quick decision. "I'm on my way down to Bedlington. I need to see Daria Astrella first and then I'll be with you tonight."

I hung up and threw some clothes in my duffle, grabbed my laptop and was on my way to I-5 in three minutes.

Chapter Thirty-seven

The final visit

It was drizzling outside, but traffic was light and the route to Bedlington was more than familiar. In any case, my mind was too occupied to pay a great deal of attention to the surroundings. I was on the way to my future.

Granny Trish's experience and Barbara Browning's determination had been the final push. The dreams and my ability to read objects were real and connected—as if the ability to read objects had been a door opener, a milder version of the dream stories.

Somehow, in ways I didn't yet understand, I had helped match people with objects that could bring them peace. It was as if I was the pencil that connected the dots in a kid's coloring book: I didn't know what the final result might be or where the dots came from, but I did know that I was a vital part of the process.

And I wanted to do it—not from some dark little shop, waiting for the right person to walk in, but out in the world, collecting objects and moving them along to the people who needed them. Maybe Daria Astrella hadn't been trying to mess with me; maybe I'd been given on-the-job training—things I had to experience and figure out for myself in order to make this journey my own.

Melanie's words about being able to choose both instead of one thing or the other rang in my head. My job with Promise Computers, traveling around the state, meeting new people and having the opportunity to check out antiques stores dovetailed with this…hobby? Purpose? As if it were all pre-destined.

I'd never thought of inanimate objects as having a purpose beyond their original design, but then I also don't know how the Universe works. Winona the dreamologist was right: dreams do hold something in their pockets for us—for me at least—something that I could pass along to the right person. When I thought of Granny Trish, the way that knowing about her father had sloughed away years of longing and shame; the way Barbara Browning's knowledge of her sister had kindled a fire in her life, I was willing to give it a shot.

I wanted to help—that was all—and yet it was everything. This was the way I could do it; a way so unique that just thinking about it was disturbing to me. It would require curiosity, which I had in abundance; it would require courage, of sorts, and the willingness to go where the dreams took me, even if that turned out to be frightening, like Derry's death, or even dangerous. Over and over again I would have to allow them to possess me, even if for just a short while. In addition, as far as I knew, all the objects seemed to be related to my family and friends—kind of a limiting prospect.

I would have to face my fear of being rejected as a freak, but with Melanie's support and my family's acceptance, especially Dad's, it already felt easier.

The old non-committal me receded with every passing mile. With two life commitments in the same week—the choice to be with Melanie forever, and now the choice to do whatever this job was, whatever it entailed—my head was exploding.

Excitement at the idea of finding objects, learning their stories and then passing them along to the people who needed them, built inside me as I drove— like the fluttering of thousands of butterflies taking flight.

When I was seven, GPop introduced me to a friend of his, an internationally known and respected artist. Painting didn't seem like a grown-up activity, so I asked him why he did it.

He sat down beside me and said with all seriousness, "It's where the butterflies take me. When I start a new painting, I feel the butterflies fluttering inside me. When I follow them, good things happen."

It hadn't made a lot of sense to me then, but it did now.

The butterflies carried me through the door of Astrella's. Daria Astrella looked up from her perusal of a cruise ship brochure when I came in. The alligator skull was missing from the shelf behind her, but the other skull and the silver jar were still there, waiting.

There was a feeling of power within me, but I didn't feel powerful. The power wasn't from me or for me—it was coming through me. Suddenly sure, I pointed to the silver jar. She handed it to me without a word.

It was heavier than it looked. The chain connecting the small silver cap to the jar was made of sturdy, but delicate looking links. The cap was smooth and without decoration. The jar itself was wide, with horizontal grooves encircling it from neck to base. There were a few tiny pits in the surface. I turned it over and found a maker's mark carved into the bottom. A bit of black tarnish came off onto my hands.

In that moment, as I held the jar, I saw him, a young man in his twenties, on the deck of a ferryboat heading across the Mediterranean. He was examining the silver Turkish jar he had just pulled out of his backpack, wondering how old it really was and how many places it had been before he bought it from the medina in Dar-Salem.

The ferry was crowded and the cackling of poultry from the crates stacked on deck competed with the conversations of passengers lining the sides of the boat, the shouts of fathers trying to keep children from falling overboard and the rumbling of the diesel engines. He loved this, heading off into a new place, surrounded by all kinds of life.

I could hear his thoughts as if they were my own. As he held the jar, I felt his wish that his father could be here, heading off to Al-Jazeera with him.

Every time he took a photograph—of the water sellers with their bright bells, of the mountains in Morocco, villagers in Spain, caves in Crete—it was for his father who didn't understand that it had been his own stories of the turquoise seas and exotic marine life he'd seen in the Navy that made his son long to see the world.

Dale Kerwin put the jar back in his backpack and pulled out his camera.

I opened my eyes as a rush of exhilaration filled me. It wasn't just family and friends, then. The door to my future opened wider than that.

Daria Astrella was nodding as if she'd seen into my mind. Her tucked-in lips curved into a surprisingly warm and sweet smile. "You are like Padgett. I knew you would be the one."

Our eyes met.

"I know the person who needs this jar and I'll find who needs that." I pointed to the skull on the shelf behind her, the last object in Astrella's Antiques & Curios Shop.

The old woman handed me the skull with both hands. It was very heavy and, in the light of the lamp on the counter, I could see that it was not an actual skull, but a life-sized alabaster carving. I ran my fingers over the rock, marveling at its translucent smoothness and seamless artistry.

I pulled out my wallet and handed Daria Astrella a ten-dollar bill, noticing for the first time still another change of clothing. Her green outfit was now a peach colored sweater set that made an unexpected splash of brightness in the dark shop as she reached into the cash register and handed me back a five.

"The skull is not for sale—it's for you. It was given to my husband many years ago. He used it to keep the energy of the objects at bay."

She gave me what might have been a reassuring look. "Don't worry about your...friend. I don't think she will have any more dreams. I didn't—just the once because I was connected to an object. It wasn't for me, just like the suitcase is not for her."

I smiled at her. "The right person already has the suitcase."

Daria nodded and rested her fingers, wrinkled and slightly crooked, on the base of the lamp on the counter. The figure on it wasn't a woman with flowing draperies after all; it was a phoenix rising from the ashes, its wings spread wide.

Journeys are undertaken

In May, Melanie and I moved to Eugene where we found a little house near the University of Oregon. In June, she started summer classes at the School of Law. Nate moved out of his parents' basement and into my condo, renting it until I decide whether or not to sell it.

I miss the convenience and atmosphere of Portland at times, but I can do my job with Promise Computers anywhere in Oregon. We set the extra bedroom up as a shared office and I put up a lot of shelving inside the single car garage for whatever curios I pick up.

We're on a budget, so I've been limiting my curio purchases to ten dollars or less, but I can already see that it won't last. If it calls to me, I've got to buy it. My negotiating skills are improving, but this job isn't going to be a moneymaker.

I mailed the silver jar to Bob Kerwin, my Barstow hospital acquaintance, and got a nice note in response from Edie and a near incoherent phone call from Bob, thanking me. He didn't say anything about his son, but he told me he knew why I sent him the jar.

Daria Astrella sold her shop to a man in Bedlington who'd been trying to buy it for years and she disappeared about forty-five seconds after the escrow closed. Ross told me she had gone on a cruise.

"Will she be back?" I asked. I was waiting to take Melanie home and polishing off a piece of Betsy's Coca-Cola cake at the counter. Ross was taking a quick break between customers.

"I don't think so," he said. "When she brought me the lamp that sat on her counter, she said something about living on a cruise ship." He shrugged. "I didn't know you could do that."

Melanie came out of the kitchen, ready to leave. I nodded to Ross, put out a tip for Bridget and smiled at my girl.

As I was paying the bill, Ross called over. "Hey, tell your mom that I think we could use a rock shop in Bedlington."

Melanie started to giggle. Mom and Ross had apparently hit it off even better than I thought during her visit in April. Ross grinned and disappeared into the kitchen as Melanie pulled me out the door.

Mom not only liked Bedlington and thought Melanie was perfect, but she'd forgiven me for not telling her about the rest of my dreams. The decision to get the right objects to the right people got her nod of approval. It wasn't all peaches and cream, though—some of her New Age friends were planning a field trip to Oregon with me as their lodestone. I hoped it wouldn't coincide with Dad and Sandra's visit. He was mellowing, but an encounter with soul channelers and dreamologists might set him back.

Back at our little house, Melanie disappeared into the back yard and I headed into the office. The afternoon sun filled the room, playing on the glass ashtray on my desk. As I touched the smooth, comforting glass, I smiled, picturing Daria Astrella lounging at the cruise ship pool swathed in her maroon shawl. She'd waited for me to find my own answers, knowing that I wouldn't have been able to accept hers.

My dreams were all so different: Marla, hoping for resolution in the grotto; Ellie's voice telling Jamie that hope was a fire to keep banked in your heart; the sunlight through the glass ashtray illuminating Barry's wish for a better life; James' determination to help young men live and Derry's belief in Brother Anselm—that, somehow, things could be fixed if he could just get home. These stories, these people, are a part of me now.

I can't foresee the future and I don't know how this will work out, but somewhere there have to be others like Padgett and me—conduits between objects and the people who need them. Maybe, someday I'll meet them and we can compare notes.

For now, I have a job, a garage slowly filling with other people's junk and a fiancée going to law school. I'm not waiting around for the right people to find me—I'll be looking for them.

On the Lido deck of the *Sun Shower*, the steward folded towels and kept an eye on the old woman lying in the shade. He'd settled her with a cushion at her back on a lounge chair, but from time to time her lips moved as though she was talking to someone. He hoped she was all right.

Daria Astrella stared out at the limitless blue in front of her. Her new home. When she sold the shop she'd decided to live on cruise ships for the rest of her life and become a legend. Better than one of those assisted living apartments. The cost was about the same. Handsome waiters brought her food, her room was always clean and fresh and she had the excitement of new surroundings. Best of all, every week or so there was a new crop of folks for her stories.

She snorted to herself. That downtown renovator was probably tearing down the shop right this minute so he could build his new "old-fashioned" ice cream store. He'd be selling five-dollar scoops of hand-churned butter fat to people who'd think that the newly installed distressed wood paneling from China was quaint. Wouldn't Bedlington folks be surprised if they saw an old coot like herself wearing fancy dress on Formal Night and socializing at the captain's table?

It didn't matter about the shop—it had served its purpose. There was someone to carry on Padgett's job and he didn't need a store. It had been a kick in the pants to see the sparks in the boy's hazel eyes on the day he came in for the last objects. So full of fire and purpose; not like that first day.

"I got the right one, Padgett, just like I promised you," she whispered to her long dead husband. "He can draw the objects, like you could and he'll know who needs them. But, he's got something else—he can see without the dreams. And he has a girl. Maybe she'll help him like I helped you."

She thought of the long talks they used to have, about life, about love, about how Padgett's real job—the one that counted—was being a conductor of the right things for the right folks.

Things that made people see things they needed to see; feel things they needed to feel. Objects that gently closed off the wrong doors and opened the right ones.

"Little pieces falling into place for people who need them, will eventually fill all the holes," Padgett told her.

She'd believed him, especially after her own experience, but it always seemed like a losing battle, there being a continual renewal of holes in the universe. Still, she wouldn't have changed anything.

A slim, pretty girl carrying a round black tray stopped next to her. "Can I get you anything to drink?" she asked.

Daria looked at the girl's smooth, unlined skin, her face-splitting smile. The warm breeze smelled of promise; the calm sapphire sea glistened in the sun.

"Not a thing, sweetie. Not a single thing."